MURDER IN PHARAOH'S PALACE

An Ancient Egyptian Mystery

William G. Collins

Other books About Egypt by the Author

Behind the Golden Mask

Prince of the Nile

In A Land of Dreams

Murder by the Gods

To Catch the Wind

Taylor and Seale Publishing
2 Oceans Way #406
Daytona Beach Shores, FL 32118

Murder in Pharaoh's Palace

Copyright 2016 William G. Collins

ISBN# 978-1-943789-35-1

Cover design: whiterabbitgraphix.com

This book is a work of fiction. Except for specific historical references, names, characters, businesses, organizations, places, events, and incidents are the product of the author's imagination or are used fictitiously. Any resemblance to actual persons living or dead or to locales is entirely coincidental.

In ancient times

cats were worshipped as gods;

they have not forgotten this.

Terry Pratchett

Dedication

To our beloved Siamese, King Tut.
May his afterlife be filled with
mice and treats and a sunny
doorway to bask in forever.

Acknowledgments

My appreciation to the Daytona Beach City
Island Fiction Writers under the leadership
of author Veronica H. Hart.
To Dr. Robert Hart, veterinarian, for his many
suggestions concerning feline behavior and
physiology. For the encouragement of Chris Holmes,
Amanda Alexander, Bob Kamholtz, Matthew Hudson,
Lois Gerber and Joan King. Their hours of suffering
through Egyptian names and places deserves
special mention. And above all to my wife,
Evangeline who reads it first.

Preface

On October 25, 2013, National Geographic Magazine published the photo of the ancient tomb of a physician discovered seventeen miles south of Cairo. Archeologists found it among other tombs in the necropolis of Abusir. His name was Shepseskaf-ankh, and all of his surgical instruments were intact with other objects from the fourth dynasty during the period known as the Old Kingdom. He is especially associated with a king named Niuserre, who ruled Egypt for at least a decade, 4,400 years ago.

Upon reading the news, my mind raced to what other objects might lie buried with him as well. For certain, there were many of the things the physician would need in the afterlife, and many of the tombs included mummies of beloved pets and favorite sandals, food, and treasured images of family and friends. Thus was born the idea for this novel. Because of Shep's access to Pharaoh Niuserre and his older brother Neferefre, the setting was ready for a story of murder and intrigue. Who better to help the physician solve the crimes than his faithful cat Miu?

While it is true that "Miu" is the Egyptian word for cat, I chose to use it to honor these magnificent ancestors of our many domestic varieties, the Mau. In speaking with several noted veterinarians, I learned of some of the peculiar tendencies of the species relating to hiding things and their insatiable curiosity—qualities they have passed on to cats of today.

Chapter 1

Discovery

"Hold him still!" Shep shouted. "Put the baton in his mouth and let him bite down." He had already given the young man a jug of wine laced with powder from the red poppy to dull the pain. The patient lay on the table and stopped struggling as his muscles relaxed. Two servants helped keep the patient still.

"It's the small worm intestine," the physician said. "It must come out." He poured a little wine over the man's right side and then washed his hands with more. He took a copper knife and leaned over the young man. "Look away, men, if blood offends you. Lady Amira, bring the cotton to swab the blood. Will you be all right?"

The patient's mother rushed to his side. "Yes, my Lord. I will do as you say."

Shep cut into the man's side, a straight deep cut. He made another incision and used small copper clamps to keep the two layers of skin apart. His patient groaned as the physician probed the opening and cut out the small swollen organ. Placing it in a dish, he took a needle and a thread made of thin papyrus fiber and closed off the intestine with a few stitches inside, and then sewed up the outer wound. He left enough space for when the wound would swell.

"It hadn't burst," he told the woman. "Now we must protect him from fever. I'll stay with him tonight and tomorrow. If the gods will it, he should be fine, my Lady."

"The gods be praised." Then, she helped him clean her son and the table. "We are grateful, my Lord. What would have happened to him if he kept on drinking the medicines the priests gave him?"

"He would have died, I'm sorry to say. Priests have very little medical knowledge and help only by using herbs and potions. In this case, your son would have had a painful death."

The patient's father rushed into the kitchen out of breath. Two of his aides accompanied him. "What is it, Amira? What's happened?"

His wife rinsed her hands in water and dried them on a towel before responding. "Something in our son's side had swollen, Husband. The small organ inside almost ruptured, but the physician cut it out in time. Bless the gods!"

"Let me see," the general demanded.

Shep stepped aside so Akhom could examine his son. The warrior examined the neatly stitched line in his son's side, and then brushed the young man's hair off his forehead.

2

"I am grateful, Lord Shepsekaf. I will not forget this."

"He's not out of danger yet, General. We will have to fight the fever, which as a soldier, you know only too well."

The older man nodded. "Take good care of him. He is the captain of his regiment and will one day take my place if the gods allow it."

"Yes, General, at your orders," Shep said. He saw the hint of a smile from the general with his using a military term.

Akhom said, "You know what I mean. We are grateful we have a physician nearby."

One of the general's aides brought a chair for Lady Amira, and she sat next to her son, holding his hand. "Can we move him to his bed?"

"Not yet...let him regain consciousness first, and then we will see how he is doing. He mustn't walk for a week or more. He must build up his strength. What he eats will be very important."

She smiled. "Very well."

Her husband placed his hand on her shoulder and then motioned for Shep to follow him outside onto the veranda.

"Why have I not seen you before, Physician?" he asked.

"I moved to Memphis only a month ago, General. Before that, I lived in Awen where I learned medicine at the Academy."

"You are married then, and have children?"

"No, my Lord. I have yet to find the right woman."

General Akhom laughed. "I don't believe that for a moment, but let us sit and talk awhile until my son awakens."

3

Shep nodded and sat on one of the benches in the family's garden. "He'll be out for at least a day, my Lord, and will have a lot pain when he awakens."

"I'm surprised you are not living at the palace, young man. I would think Pharaoh would want someone as capable as you nearby."

"That's just it, General. I have no desire to die at this early age."

Akhom chuckled. "I understand. To die if the king dies does not guarantee his physician a long life."

Shep liked this man. The general was a large man, well-muscled with a rugged face. His square jaw and deep-set eyes could be imposing, but Shep had seen him smile and it softened into a pleasant look. "I am grateful Lady Tener sent for me, General. I don't know how your wife knew about me. I've only just opened a surgery in the city."

"I'm certain Lady Hasina, our neighbor, told her. She suffers a large variety of illnesses. I'm sure you must have treated her. Her servants would have searched you out. She's tall and has an ugly red birthmark on her neck."

"Ah, yes, I've treated such a woman. She's a very nervous person who can't stop talking."

Akhom grinned. "That's her."

They continued for a good while until the patient regained consciousness. Lady Amira came for them, and they stayed with the young man. The physician checked the patient's pulse and skin temperature every few hours and gave him more powder in a cup of wine to help him sleep.

Over the next two days, his patient developed a fever, but with servants helping to bathe the young man with cool water mixed with powder from the willow tree, the crisis passed.

Three days later, Shep spoke to Lord Akhom. "I will take my leave, General. Your son is now in the capable hands of Lady Amira. The gods have smiled on your family."

4

"They have indeed. I am Pharaoh Neferefre's commander of the northern army. I promise I will not mention your name to any of the royal family. That way, I pray you will live a long life."

Shep smiled. "Thank you, General. Can you promise your neighbor Lady Hasina will do the same?"

Akhom laughed. "No, for her I can make no promises." He handed the physician a small leather purse and thanked him again.

As he walked home, Shep opened the purse and, to his delight, found ten gold pieces. He slung his medicine box over his shoulder and followed the narrow road along the Nile toward home, a satisfying sense of accomplishment making his step jaunty. Only thirty summers old, he enjoyed living alone. As an orphan, he had grown used to not having anyone to depend upon. Tall, when compared to other men his age, his good looks and auburn hair attracted women easily. His hard life as a boy strengthened not only his body but his mind as well. A physician had taken him under his wing, sent him to school, and let him help in the surgery as payment for room and board. He smiled remembering old Re-hesy and those pleasant days.

"Sir, Sir," a boy of about ten years pulled on his robe. "Let me carry it, Sir."

Several other boys joined in the chorus. None of the children wore clothing, but had enough dirt on themselves to make up for it.

"All right, here." The physician handed him his medicine box.

When the other boys saw they had no chance of receiving anything, they ran off.

Shep walked on ahead with his small shadow close behind. At the river's edge, he stopped and inhaled the wonderful fresh air blowing across the water. The sweet fragrance of lotus flowers and purple water hyacinths always made him happy.

"Oh, Sir," the boy called to him. "Look down there."

Shep walked closer to the river's edge. Floating in the water were several newborn kittens, all dead.

"Come away, boy. Someone's drowned an unwanted litter of kittens."

"But they're not all dead, Sir. See?"

The physician crouched down and could hear the faint mewling of what had to have been the runt of the litter.

"Save him, Sir," the boy pleaded.

"Well, Bastet, the cat goddess might be angry if we don't help one of her creatures." He reached into the water and lifted the kitten by the nape of the neck. Its eyes were not yet open, and it mewed pitifully.

"There, there, little one." The young physician cupped it in his hand and showed it to the boy. "We won't know for a while if it's a boy or a girl."

"Ah," the lad said. "If it's a girl, the goddess will be extra pleased."

The physician stood and looked at the kitten more closely. "She will indeed." Its tawny coat already showed distinctive dark stripes here and there.

"What will you call it, Sir?"

"Me? Oh, I'm not going to keep it. Do you want a kitten?"

"Can't, Sir. If I brought another animal home, my mother would skin me alive."

Addressing the tiny animal, Shep said, "Well, come along, cat. We'll have to find you a home."

When they reached the house, the boy gave him his box of medicines, and the physician handed him a copper coin. "That should pay for lots of honey cakes for you to share with your friends."

"Thank you, Sir. I'll share them with my mother. She only has me to help."

"How are you called, lad?"

"Babu, Sir. I've forgotten what it means."

"Firstborn of Osiris," Shep said, "May He watch over you, Babu."

"And you, Sir." The boy waved and ran off.

Inside, Shep put down his box, took a towel from the kitchen, and made it into a nest in the box for the kitten to lie in.

"You're home," a voice called from the back porch. Merit, an attractive woman in her twenties, came three days a week to do his cleaning.

"Yes, my patient is improving. It's good to be home."

The woman looked around the room and said, "What is making that sound?"

"A kitten I rescued from the river."

Merit picked up the towel with the kitten in it. "There, there, baby."

Shep smiled as Merit held the newborn and rocked her back and forth. "I'll find milk for you, little one, and I have just the perfect little basket for you to sleep in."

"I'm not keeping it," he said.

"All right, but you can't get rid of it until she's older. It wouldn't be right. Besides, what would the goddess say?"

"I don't know, Merit. Gods and goddesses don't speak to me."

"Don't be that way, Shep, Maybe if you listened more, they would. You saved it, now you're responsible."

"You win. Feed it, but I want nothing to do with it. Keep it out of the house."

"Humph," Merit grumbled.

Shep liked having Merit around for company. He felt sorry for her since her husband, a soldier, died in battle. Her two children died from fever two years ago. The rest of her family lived upriver at Edfu but refused to take her back. She lived with two other widows, not far from the physician.

"Go have your bath while I prepare supper."

He nodded and walked to the back porch and removed his clothes. When he first moved in, he'd purchased a copper bathtub for himself to avoid bathing in the muddy river. The sun had warmed its contents and he felt his muscles relax as he sank into the perfumed water. The aroma of the fish Merit roasted over the fire made his mouth water.

To Shep's surprise, she walked over to him and said, "One ear or two?"

"Merit! Could you wait until I'm out of the bath?" He still felt embarrassed by her, and instinctively covered himself under the water.

She laughed. "Grow up, Shep."

Later, as he sat at the table, he invited her to join him. They talked about the days they had been apart. Before leaving for the night, Merit fed the kitten once more. She soaked a narrow strip of linen in some milk, and then let the kitten suck on it.

"Give it more later," she said. "It's starving."

"Good night, Merit. Take the cat with you if you want."

"No, my Lord," she answered. "It now belongs to you."

Over the next weeks, the kitten grew and became attached to the physician. Its eyes opened and Shep took it with him to visit his patients. It loved traveling inside his medicine box and rested on a small cotton cloth. The physician left the cover open a bit, so it could peek out. He still hoped that someone would want to adopt it, but no one did.

"It must have a name," Merit said. "The goddess would insist upon it."

Shep placed the kitten on his lap and stared into her mesmerizing gooseberry-green eyes. The kitten looked up and made a strange sound. He said, "I think our cat is a girl, if it were a boy we would have known by now."

"What did she just say?" Merit asked.

"Don't know. I couldn't hear."

"It sounds like 'Meeuuuu'," Merit said.

"Is that your name little one?" he asked.

The kitten yawned and said, "miou." She sat up as tall as she could and looked at them both like a full-grown cat.

"I'm going to call her Ta-miu," Shep said. "Let's hope she becomes a huntress as well and rids the house of all our night visitors."

"Come on Lady Miu," Merit said. "I'll put more milk in your dish."

After lapping it up, the kitten circled the room and climbed onto Shep's lap again. She purred happily and yawned. He put her down so she could climb into her basket, curl up, and fall asleep.

"Do you feel protected?" Merit asked.

"Yes, I now have two women in my life to protect me." He could tell he'd embarrassed her because she placed her hands over her red cheeks just for an instant.

She hurriedly put away the dishes and prepared to leave. "Good night."

"Good night," he called after her.

In the morning as Shep boiled eggs for himself, someone knocked on the door. He walked and opened it to find several guardsmen in front of his house.

"Lord Shepseskaf?" an officer asked.

9

"Yes? Can I help you?"

"Not us. There is an emergency. His Highness, the king's brother ordered us to bring you to the palace."

Shep's stomach tightened. "Allow me to dress and get my medicines."

"Be quick, Physician. The prince will not be kept waiting."

Shep entered his bedroom, took off his robe, and put on his best attire. It had a blue border, the color of a physician. Not knowing the illness, he chose what medicines he thought he might need. He picked up his box and hung it over his shoulder. In a soft voice he said, "Come Miu, we go to meet a prince." He carefully placed her inside with the medicines, closed the lid almost shut, and walked outside, closing the door.

"We brought you a horse," the officer said.

"Thank you, but I never learned to ride."

"Send for a carrying chair! Hurry!" the officer shouted. A short time later, the covered chair, carried by six Nubian slaves arrived. He stepped inside, and they lifted him to shoulder height and followed the guardsmen on the road to the palace.

When they passed through the royal gates, the bearers stopped.

The physician moved the curtain aside and stepped out.

The Captain of the Royal Guard became impatient. "The prince is waiting, my Lord."

Shep adjusted his robe and followed the guards up the steps. When they reached their destination, the officer opened the door for him and Shep walked inside.

"Wait here," the house steward told him.

Shep sat on one of the plush divans and put down his box on the seat beside him. He opened the lid a bit and little

Miu mewed and looked up at him. He scratched behind her ear and she purred.

"Follow me, my Lord," the steward said.

The physician closed the lid, stood, and followed the man. Upon entering the prince's room, Shep made obeisance by lying on the floor, extending his palms toward Pharaoh's brother.

A noblewoman stood next to the prince. He hadn't seen her at first, but assumed she could be prince Niuserre's wife.

"What is wrong with him, my Lady?" he asked.

"I fear it might be poison, my Lord. But that is why you are here—to help him and tell us." She put her hand on his arm. "Our brother, the Pharaoh, must not find out."

"I understand," Shep said, his heart beginning to beat louder.

He approached the bed and found the prince unconscious, unclothed and sweating profusely. When he took the man's pulse he found it racing at a high speed. He examined the eyes and then placed his right ear on the chest to listen to the heart. When he turned over the man's hands, he saw telltale blue marks in the cuticles and Shep shook his head.

"It *is* poison, my Lady. I must give him something to help empty his stomach. You might want to leave. This will be most unpleasant."

"Very well, but I insist his servants stay to help you."

Shep nodded, and opened his box. Removing a clay jar with an emetic made from charcoal, he put some in a cup of wine and forced the prince to drink it. It took a while, but he swallowed it all.

"Help me carry him to the bathing area," he ordered the servants. They lifted the prince carefully and rushed him outside to the tiled place. Immediately, the prince regurgitated the contents of his stomach. The servants washed it away and bathed the prince.

"Forgive me, Highness," he said, and began slapping the prince on each cheek until he came to. "That's better," Shep said.

The servants brought a clean loincloth and kilt and helped the prince into them.

"Lift me up," the prince ordered.

His servants helped him onto a wooden stool.

"By the gods," he exclaimed. "I have never felt such pain. But now it's much better. What did you do?"

Shep said, "I gave you something to make your stomach reject whatever you had eaten and drunk today, Highness. You might feel the need to bring it up again."

A servant brought a pail to the prince and he evacuated his stomach again. Little by little, color returned to his face and when he allowed the physician to check his pulse, it had slowed considerably.

"Help him to his bed," the physician ordered, and followed them back into the bedchamber. The woman watched as the servants changed the linens on the bed, and then she sat on a chair in the corner until they lifted the prince back into bed again.

"Is it as we suspected?" she asked.

Shep looked at the prince for permission to reply, and his highness nodded.

"Yes, my Lady. If we had not caught it when we did, he would have died."

"Gods," the prince exclaimed. "I owe you my life, Healer."

"It is my honor to serve you, Highness."

"Pharaoh, my brother, must never know," the prince said.

"He will not learn of it from me, Highness. I'm frightened for my life just being here."

"Why is that?" The woman asked. She walked toward him.

To Shep's horror, she held little Miu in her arms.

The prince said, "Forgive me, Physician. My sister, Princess Nebet, always interrupts."

Shep bowed his head to her politely. "I am Shepseskaf, Highness. I do not *wish* to be a royal physician. The lifespan of those chosen is short. I'm very pleased the gods have accepted my choice of treatment for his highness."

"We will honor you privacy, Lord Shepseskaf," the princess said. "We will not give my brother your name."

"Thank you, Highness. My biggest concern now is how you ingested the poison in the first place. What have you eaten today?"

"Only the morning meal which included some fruit juice," he paused. "And...oh yes, some apricot pudding which had spoiled. We threw it out."

"Spoiled?" Shep repeated. "And no wine, Highness?"

"None."

Shep shook his head "I would recommend you arrest whoever prepared the meal and all those who had access to the food and the room. Arrest those who had contact with you today, Highness. Use your most trusted guards to question them, but do not allow them to share what they find with his majesty's household staff. Do any servants work in both residences?"

Princess Nebet said, "No, but we trust them all."

"Someone is not worthy of your trust, Highness."

Just then, Shep's kitten mewed. The princess petted her. "Is this cat one of your medicines too, my Lord?"

"Yes, Highness. This is Ta-miu. She is the guardian of the household. She makes me feel protected and brings comfort to my body and Ka."

The royals chuckled. "She has certainly protected this household," Princess Nebet declared. "Will you make her a gift to us?"

Shep shook his head. He had grown too attached the cat and found himself at odds with the royal princess. "I know I should not offend your Highness, but if you would allow it, I cannot part with her. A month ago, I could have easily done so. But now she has stolen my heart. I am her prisoner."

"I could make it a royal command," Lady Nebet said.

"You could but you won't," her brother said. "The physician has our gratitude. When I am better I will show him my appreciation."

"Thank you, Highness. I'm glad the gods have spared you."

"Especially the goddess Bastet," the princess said. "I will offer a sacrifice in her temple of cats." She handed the kitten to him and sat in the chair next to her brother's bed.

"Eat only bread tonight, Prince, and wine that you yourself have opened from a sealed jar."

"May the gods go with you," the prince said.

"Highness," Shep replied.

He put his kitten back into his box and patted her head. A servant escorted him out to the front of the palace and he walked down the steps to the carrying chair. Four guards prepared to accompany him to his house. It pleased him that the prince would not tell Pharaoh about him, but he felt hesitant about the princess. However, since she liked his cat so much, maybe she could be trusted after all.

"Good work, Miu. I'll never let you go now. Not for anyone."

Chapter 2

Princess Nebet

When they reached the house, Shep unlocked the door and thanked the guardsmen. They saluted and left. He went inside and shut the door. He set his medicines down and let Miu out. She jumped off the table onto a chair, and headed for her bowl of water.

When he stepped onto the veranda, a wonderful aroma of fish stew reminded him that Merit had left his supper simmering over the fire. She liked to leave him a meal on the days she cleaned. He used a tin spoon to remove the lid, and inhaled the glorious scent.

After washing his hands, he took a bowl from the cupboard, filled it with the stew, then opened a jar of beer and sat down to eat.

Loud mewling from Miu drew his attention. "Quiet cat! Let me eat in peace."

He took a few more bites but her caterwauling continued. He stood and followed the cat's cries. "What is it?" he asked. Then he heard something moving.

"Who's there?" He grabbed one of the long knives from the kitchen and walked slowly toward the sound of the cat. "Come out. Who is it?"

"It's me, Babu." The boy stood and walked toward the physician. Miu stopped crying, walked over, and rubbed against Shep's ankles.

"It's all right, Boy. Come out on the porch so I can see you."

The boy walked with his head down as if he'd been caught doing something wrong.

Shep laid the knife aside. "It's late. Why aren't you home with your mother?"

"She's dead, Sir. When I came home from begging, I couldn't find her. A neighbor lady said she died from the fever and congestion. She had trouble breathing all this week."

"I'm so sorry, Babu. What will you do? How will you bury her?" Shep asked.

"There can be no burying. Some men threw her body into the river. She's gone, Sir." Tears rolled down his dirty cheeks.

Shep's heart melted at the sight. "You must be hungry. Come and sit with me and eat something. You can sleep here tonight until we can figure out what to do." He went to the cupboard and brought back another bowl, filled it with stew and put it in front of the boy.

Babu picked up a spoon and while acting reluctant at first, gobbled down the food.

"Eat slowly. Make it last, son."

Babu nodded but couldn't slow down.

Shep reached down and picked up Miu. "Thank you Princess for warning me that someone had entered the house. I thought only dogs did that."

The cat made an odd sound like a growl which ended in a loud purr.

"Go to your bed, Princess, while I get Babu settled." He put more stew in the boy's bowl and the child ate it all, licking up the last drops of gravy.

"Follow me, young man," he said. He stood and walked out to the small tiled area. "We must clean you. Help me with these jars of water." They poured four of the clay containers into the copper bath.

"That's enough. Now get in and scrub off all of that dirt, do you hear?"

"Yes, Sir."

Shep went back and sat at the table while the boy washed himself. He had given Babu a sponge and fragrant soap. The boy appeared to enjoy just sitting in the bath.

"Do you do this every day?" he asked. "It's such a waste of water."

The physician walked over and said, "Keep your head down, I'm going to wash your hair. We don't want any lice in the house." He washed the boy's head over and over and finally gave up. He went into his bedroom and returned with a straight razor.

"I'm sorry, son. Your hair must go."

"I don't mind, Sir. Even Pharaoh doesn't have any hair."

The physician smiled and then carefully shaved the boy's head. "Now we must throw all this water into the river. Help me fill the jars and carry them down to the water."

He gave the boy a towel to dry himself and said, "I don't have a loincloth your size, but Merit comes tomorrow. She can make you one."

"Merit?"

"Yes, my housekeeper. Wrap the towel around yourself for now." They carried the jars down to the river and emptied them. The boy had trouble keeping his eyes open. Shep gave him a couple of blankets and laid them on the floor. The boy curled up and quickly fell asleep.

Shep yawned, stretched his arms, and then turned and walked into his bedchamber. He couldn't find the cat but

17

knew she wouldn't be far. He removed his robe and stretched out on the bed, exhausted from the day's events.

Sounds from the kitchen awakened him the next morning. Shep opened the bedroom door, walked out and found Babu tied to a chair.

"What's going on here?" he demanded.

Merit stood on the veranda and poured fresh water into the bath tub. "I've caught a thief. That's what."

"He's not a thief, Merit. He's my guest. Now untie him at once."

"He could be dangerous," she said. "I had trouble tying him to that chair."

"I can believe that. Good morning, Babu," he said. "Did you sleep well?"

The boy shook his head.

"You didn't? Why not?"

"I kept dreaming about my mother in the river with the crocodiles." Tears ran down his face again.

Merit frowned as she untied the boy's arms. "Now why did you make him cry?"

"It's a story for another time," Shep said. "We're both hungry. Give us your best morning meal."

Babu jumped up and ran for the door. "I hear horses, Sir."

Shep walked to the door with Babu behind him. Together they opened the front door.

"It's Pharaoh, my Lord," the boy shouted.

"No. Go wait in the kitchen with Merit."

The Captain of the Guard dismounted and approached Shep's house. The officer saluted before speaking. "His highness, Prince Niuserre, sends you a gift, my Lord Shepseskaf. He said to tell you he's feeling much better."

"I am honored, Captain. Thank his highness for me."

The officer shouted, "Sergeant," and a guardsman walked forward leading a magnificent black stallion.

"He is yours, Physician. I hope *now* you will learn to ride." He smiled when he said it.

"I promise to learn. I am grateful."

The captain saluted and led his men back to the palace.

"Babu, come here," Shep called.

"Take the horse around back. I must speak with Merit for a moment."

"Yes, my Lord," the boy said. He grinned when he saw that he had pleased the physician.

Merit came into the front room. "Your patients give you horses now? Isn't that an expensive fee for treatment?"

"Not if you are related to Pharaoh, Merit."

"You mean the prince sent it? Oh, you've been to the palace. What is it like? What did they look like?"

"We'll speak about it later. First, I'll have to find a place to stable the horse. I'm afraid if I try to keep him here, someone will steal him." Shep's modest brick house was part of a series of well-built homes far enough from the river to avoid the yearly inundation. His neighbors were merchants, scribes and clerks from the city administration, including the mayor's advisors. Thieves were no respecters of class.

"Of course. I didn't think of thieves," she said. She sat on one of the kitchen chairs and looked at him more closely. "Now tell me about the boy."

"Ah, such a story," he said. When he finished, tears ran down her face.

"I'm sorry for being so hard on him. Don't worry. I'll watch him for you."

19

"Good, because I don't want him begging or stealing ,y more. Teach him all you can. He's smart and will be a ,ig help to me some day as an assistant perhaps."

"I've said all along that you needed to find a place for your surgery," she said. "You shouldn't be treating patients here. This is where you live and rest."

Shep nodded. "Well said, but I already have a plan, O Keeper of the House. The people next door are moving and they've leased me their house for my surgery." He made a fake bow and she laughed.

"That means I'll need a sign to put outside. If I can find some paint at the temple, maybe you'd help me paint it."

"I'll try," she said. "Maybe Babu would like to help."

Babu ran inside. "There's a messenger at the door, my Lord." When he saw the worried look on their faces, he added. "Don't worry. I tied the horse to the big tree in back."

Shep returned to the front door. A man, dressed in clothing worn by royal servants he had seen at the palace, handed him a papyrus scroll.

"I'm to wait for an answer, my Lord," the messenger said.

"Very well. Come in and be seated."

Shep walked back to the table and sat down. Unrolling the scroll, he read the message and shook his head. "I feared this," he said to Merit. "I didn't want any connection to the royal family, and this is from princess Nebet. She wants me for something, and I'm to meet her at the temple of Horus."

"Then you must go."

"Can I come with you?" Babu asked.

"No, I'm sorry, little man. Merit has to sew some clothes for you first. You can't go anywhere without clothes, especially not the palace."

"Ah," Babu said.

20

"I enjoy sewing," Merit said. "It will be a happy time for us both"

"If you say so," the boy said. He went back outside with a sulky face.

Shep said, "I don't feel right meeting the princess at the temple. Why not at the palace like yesterday?"

"I'm sure she has good reasons. Put on your best robe again, although I hope one of these days you'll be able to afford a really good one."

Taking a quill and well of ink from the cupboard, he accepted the princess's invitation to meet and handed it to the messenger. "Give it to no one else—only the princess."

"Yes, my Lord." The man bowed his head and left.

Shep washed his face and hands, and then went into his bedchamber and changed his robe. Before leaving, he handed Merit several coins. "This is for the boy's clothes and I want you to buy a new robe for yourself. You deserve it." Her face lit up and he smiled. Bidding them farewell, he headed for the temple.

Upon his arrival at the temple of Horus, a young woman approached him. "I am Princess Nebet's handmaiden, my Lord. Please follow me." She led him to a private garden at the back of the temple. He found the princess waiting for him in the shade of several date palms.

"Good. You've come," Nebet said. "Sit with me, my Lord."

"But Highness," he said flustered. Commoners and even nobles could not sit in the royal presence on pain of death.

"Sit. It is my royal decree. Sit, sit, sit!"

He seated himself on a limestone bench across from her. He studied her and estimated she had seen twenty summers, not more. The skin of her upper body, caressed by the sun, was the color of pale cedar wood from the mountains beyond Byblos. Her breasts were full and firm. She did not wear a formal wig, but combed her natural hair into a side lock that fell over one breast. Her large eyes, cunningly enhanced on the upper lids by green malachite powder, seemed to penetrate his Ka—his very soul.

"First of all," she began, "my brother is doing very well. We are grateful for that, and I say it not to flatter you, Physician, but to let you know we consider you now a friend who can be trusted."

"Thank you, Highness."

"We understand Merit, your housekeeper, has family in Edfu. Is it true?"

Shep became angry. "Merit?" He didn't use polite language but blurted out, "Is the royal family spying on me?"

The princess stood and he thought he had insulted her.

"Yes, we've been watching you, Physician. As you may not know, there are those at court who would be pleased to see the king and his brother out of the way." She stopped pacing and sat down again. "Hear me out."

"Very well."

"We have learned that the poisoner came from Edfu. We only know he goes by the name of Viper. Now, because Merit's family are from the region, we thought you two could travel south and try to find this man. We'll send one of our officers with you and give you a ship."

Shep couldn't believe her proposal. "I'm only a physician, my Lady, and I'm needed here. There are patients who count on me. I'm opening a small surgery and look forward to practicing my profession. I'm not a soldier."

Princess Nebet nodded. "I understand you also have a street urchin to care for now, or have you forgotten him? Take him along with you. People will assume you are a family and that will serve our purpose. The killer won't know we're looking for him."

22

"But Highness, I don't believe Merit will agree to go with me."

"Convince her. I count on you. Take your cat with you as well. She will complete the image of a happy family."

"You may not believe me, Highness, but I have feelings for all three of them—Merit, the boy *and* the cat." He stood and leaned against the trunk of a palm. "What do we do if we discover Viper has followers?"

The princess clapped her hands and an officer of the royal guard moved quickly from out of the shadows to her side.

"This is Captain Pashet. He is going with you. He knows what to do if you find Viper."

"My Lord," Pashet bowed. "You will do nothing whatsoever. I'll meet with the best guards at Edfu, and we'll capture this Viper and his men—if he has any."

"Hmm," Shep said. "You're from Avaris, aren't you, Captain? I recognize the accent."

"Yes, and I have family at Awen. I've seen you at the Academy, my Lord."

"Well, I don't suppose I have a choice, do I?"

Princess Nebet shook her head. "Viper must be eliminated before he tries again."

"All right, I agree. When do we sail?"

"In the morning," Captain Pashet said. "You'll introduce me to everyone as your cousin, and you're returning to Edfu on a family visit to introduce them to your son."

"You've thought of everything," Shep said. He found it difficult to keep the frustration out of his voice.

"This will have its rewards, my Lord," the princess said. "I'll personally see that you are never named the king's physician." Her smile made him laugh.

"Well then, it's agreed," he said. "I'll take my leave, Highness. What about my horse? I have nowhere to stable your brother's generous gift."

Captain Pashet said, "I'll send a guard today and we'll put him in the prince's stable. He'll be fine."

"Thank you, *Cousin*."

"I'll also send two carrying chairs and bearers for you and your luggage at sunrise. Our ship will be at the regular dock, not at the royal berth. We mustn't show any connection to the king's family. Therefore I will not be in uniform, Cousin."

Shep smiled. "Then, Highness, pray to Horus for us. Pray we find your assassin and that the god will keep us safe."

"Go with our prayers, Physician. My brother thanks you."

Shep bowed his head, and left.

"What? Are you mad?" Merit exclaimed. She walked about the front room and then sat out on the porch.

"I couldn't refuse, Merit," Shep said. "They could have found many ways of forcing me to go. Besides, this might turn out to be quite pleasant. You'll be able to find your family again. We will only pretend to be married, but you have to admit that Babu does look a little like you."

She picked up a large wooden spoon and threw it at him. "Such a boy—*this* boy of all boys! I'll have to sew all night to make sure he has something to wear, and I'm not a good seamstress."

"We can also buy things on the way, remember," Shep reminded her.

"Are you two fighting?" Babu asked. He had just walked around to the back porch. "My Lord, there is a soldier

24

outside to take back the horse. Did you do something bad or make someone angry?"

Shep laughed. "No, he's taking him to the royal stables where he'll be well cared for. But Babu, I want you to sit here and listen to something I have to tell you. It's about going on a great adventure. Would you like that?"

"I think so, unless you're just going to take me somewhere and leave me."

Merit shook her head. "No of course not. We wouldn't do that to you."

Shep said, "You are part of our family now. We couldn't leave you anywhere." He told the boy about sailing on the ship to Edfu, far, far away. He made no mention of the real reason for going.

"Is Miu coming too?" Babu asked.

"Absolutely. She belongs with us. He picked up the cat and she reached out a soft paw and touched Shep's face, making everyone laugh.

"We have a lot to do. There are things I need to buy so I'll be back shortly," Shep said.

When he left, he remembered the excitement on the boy's face. "It *will* be an adventure," he mumbled. He tried to convince himself he hadn't made a mistake by agreeing to do this for the royal family.

He returned home with several items. First, a short sword to protect his family. He had learned to fight at the Academy. He opened another bag and removed the new robe he'd purchased for himself. He thought he should look the part of a physician. Another held a surprise new robe for Merit. He hoped he had guessed her size. The purchase of new sandals for himself and his friends brought him to a shop that also sold children's clothing. Fortunately, the merchant's son wore the same size as Babu.

As soon as he arrived home, everyone wanted to try on the new clothes.

Merit came to the front room and spun around so they could see. "It's perfect!"

"Look at me," Babu said. He pulled the tunic on over his naked body.

The physician and Merit laughed. "We'll have to do something about that loincloth, my boy," Shep said.

"I've finished sewing one." She went out on the porch and returned with it. "Try it on, Babu."

Babu started to pull up his tunic, but Shep stopped him and sent him to the bedchamber. "It is not polite to put it on in front of a lady," he explained.

A few moments later, the boy returned. "Do I have it on right, Father?" Babu asked.

Shep said, "Yes, well done." He swallowed hard, his throat constricted with emotion from hearing Babu call him father.

"I'm going to like this adventure," the boy said. "But best of all, I now have a mother and father."

No one slept much that night, except Babu. He fell asleep on the floor with his blankets around him.

Merit finished her sewing in the middle of the night. Shep had already collapsed on a chair in the front room.

"The lamps are almost out of oil," Merit said,

"Why don't you sleep on my bed, Merit, for what little time of the night there is left?"

"Very well, *husband*," she said. "As long as you sleep out here."

"Don't worry, *wife*. Get what rest you can."

He walked over to check on Babu and found Miu curled up near his head, purring away. He realized she had grown a lot. The stripes on her fur were more visible and in a couple more months, she would almost be an adult.

"Sleep well, Miu," he whispered. "Protect us tonight and on our long journey."

26

The physician lay down on the floor and rolled up one of the blankets for a pillow. He blew out the lamp and closed his eyes. As he drifted off, he felt a soft furry paw on his chin as Miu nestled up close to him and purred even louder.

"Good night, princess," he said.

Chapter 3

The Adventure Begins

Shep stood on the dock beside the boy. Babu straddled a wooden crate and turned to watch the sun peek over the eastern sand dunes. He yawned and stretched his arms above his head. Swells from a passing ship gently caressed the wooden pilings before disappearing into the shadows. Even though Babu had only seen ten summers, Shep believed the boy's eyes reflected an ancient Ka wiser than his years.

"Meow," Miu whined, not happy at being confined in a reed basket. Shep had made sure there were some small openings, but she couldn't see very much and mewled again.

"Quiet, Princess," Shep said. "We'll be on board soon." He turned his head as turquoise kingfisher birds dove into the river and shot up again with silver fish in their beaks. The Gossamer wings of dragonflies reflected the morning's sunlight, sparkling like pieces of rainbows flitting across the water.

Another ship set sail filled with troops. Their families waved to them as they departed.

A voice from behind Shep said, "Good morning, Cousin."

"Pashet," Shep replied. "Why aren't we boarding?"

"Look around," Pashet said. "They haven't finished loading the cargo." Rolls of linen, jars of wine, beer, honey and oil—baskets of beads and coarse pottery, crudely made cosmetic pots and toiletries such as combs, mirrors, tweezers and razors waited on dock for the crew to carry aboard.

Shep said, "This is *our* ship, but not our cargo."

"No, but they had to remove these things in order to load corn for the garrison at Edfu, Cousin."

"Of course, I'm sorry. I'm just anxious for us to be on our way."

Pashet nodded. "I understand. The corn will probably be for that company of soldiers who just sailed." The officer perhaps ten years older than the physician, stood taller and pulled on his tunic, uncomfortable not to be in uniform. His deep brown eyes were always on the alert, but they also put people at ease.

Babu pulled on the physician's hand, trying to get him to move. "Come on, Father."

"Quiet," Shep replied.

Pashet said, "Be patient, young man. It won't be long."

Merit walked over to them. "I'm already tired and we haven't gone aboard yet."

"If you'd gone to sleep when you should have, Merit, you'd be rested," Shep teased.

She hit him on the shoulder, making Babu laugh.

Pashet's eyebrows raised.

"It's all right, Captain," Shep said. "Merit and I have known each other since we first came to Memphis, long before I went to the Academy. I worked for a physician in the poor section of town, and she had just arrived from Edfu."

Merit said, "Before they allowed him to wear the blue border on his robe, we were like brother and sister. In fact I always beat him in kick ball."

Pashet looked at Shep and the physician couldn't tell if the soldier would scowl or smile.

Just then, the ship's captain approached them. "I'm Hakor, my Lord Physician. Welcome to the *Wings of Isis.*" The mariner, a large man, in his middle years, had deep piercing eyes. He scratched the thick black hair on his chest and bowed his head to his passengers.

"Thank you, Captain. This is my cousin Pashet and my wife Merit."

"And who is this fine young warrior?" Hakor asked.

"I'm Babu, my Lord. Can I help steer your ship?"

The captain smiled. "We'll see, young master. First, let's bring you all on board and get you settled."

Shep said, "Women and boys first."

Babu hurried up the gangway with Merit close behind. Shep and Pashet followed.

After their baggage arrived, Shep and Merit helped Babu set up his cot in their cabin. Because the ship belonged to Pharaoh, the luxurious cedar lining of the cabin walls filled the room with a pleasant fragrance.

"Where's Miu?" Shep asked. "Seth's entrails! I've left her!" He rushed out and hurried down the gangway. Picking up the carrying basket, he looked in. "I'm sorry, Princess. I didn't mean to leave you." An angry, yet subdued growling emanated from inside as Shep carried her onboard.

Back in the cabin, he opened the basket and let the cat out. Miu sniffed everything, walking around her new domain and poking her nose into every corner.

Out on deck, Captain Hakor shouted, "Up anchor! Away all lines!"

The family came out on deck as the crew prepared for departure. The sail, yellowed with age, was dappled with lighter patches.

"Unfurl the sail!" Hakor ordered. The large rectangular canvas fell slowly from the top spar and filled with the wind, resembling a giant blowfish from the Great Sea. The crew tied the bottom ropes onto the deck to anchor it.

"We've had to change the sail," the ship's captain told them. "*Our* sail has the image of Isis, our mother goddess, but could be recognized as belonging to Pharaoh. We've even painted over the ship's name. We borrowed this canvas from a merchant."

Captain Pashet nodded. "Well done, Captain. I should have thought of it."

"The sail's so big," Babu said.

"Stay close to me, son," Shep admonished. "We must keep out of the crew's way."

The *Wings of Isis* slowly moved out into the river's main channel. Rowers lowered their oars into the water and began long strokes against the current.

Babu sat on a short stool near the mast, captivated by the drummer beating the cadence for the oarsmen. Forty men worked in perfect unison which the boy found fascinating.

On each side of the ship, the riches of the river's fertile banks lay thick with fields of corn, wheat and rye. Along the shore, papyrus and bulrushes stood watch as scaly crocodiles lay unblinking, hoping a tasty tidbit might fall off the ship. White ibis darted for frogs in and out of the tall grasses, while graceful brown ducks quacked their greeting. The passengers breathed in the wonderful fragrances of lotus flowers, wild jasmine and water lilies.

On a bench outside the cabin, Shep seated himself next to Merit. After a few moments, Pashet joined them.

"How many days to Edfu, Cousin?" Merit asked.

"A week, if the rowers don't tire."

"I need to lie down," Merit said. "Keep an eye on our son, Shep."

"I'll keep him out of your hair, my *dear.*"

When she left, Pashet said, "No one talks like that. You'll never convince anyone you're married."

"And I suppose you are, *Cousin?*"

"Yes, ten years now. Just act natural, that's all."

Shep mumbled, "Understood."

For Babu, it didn't take long for the excitement of sailing past hundreds of hippos and crocodiles to wear off, and he took a nap on the bench outside the cabin so as not to disturb Merit.

By day's end, the ship neared Meydum. The captain anchored for the night some distance from shore to avoid insects. The crew prepared supper and soon the strong scent of braised catfish and scorched onions wafted through the air. They opened clay jars of beer and invited their passengers to join them for the tasty meal. Before long, they shared tall tales of life on the river after which the crew sang songs from their villages about monsters and beautiful enticing goddesses.

Someone brought out a drum and the men began to clap their hands to the beat. Several, who had exceeded their intake of beer, got up to dance. Babu got the biggest laugh when he joined in—and proved the best dancer of them all.

Before turning in, the men scrubbed the deck. Shep brought out his medicine box to treat those with rope burns, or cut fingers. He gave special attention to one of his patients he had seen earlier who had broken his wrist. Miu sat beside him as he worked, and even allowed the men to pet her.

"She's a true princess, you know," Shep said. "She won't let just *anyone* touch her."

"She'll be a beautiful cat when she's older," his patient said.

"Shh, don't hurt her feelings, my friend. She's beautiful *now.*"

That night, as they prepared for sleep, Merit took the bed, while Shep stretched out on the floor with the cat. Babu

32

had already fallen asleep on his cot, and Merit blew out the lamp.

Speaking softly to Miu, Shep said, "Tomorrow, Princess, we'll visit the temple of Bastet—your goddess and guardian."

"Me-ow." She nudged him and touched his face. She patted him with her velvety paw before she rolled over so he could scratch under her chin. She lulled him to sleep with her purring that sounded like the beating of a soft drum roll.

When they docked at Meydum, the crew went ashore to replenish their water and beer. Carrying the large, ungainly clay jars was no easy task—they were easily broken in transit. The troop ship that left Memphis ahead of them was doing the same.

"Where do you suppose those soldiers are headed?" Shep asked Pashet.

"South as well, it appears. I'll try to find out from one of their crew."

Shep nodded. "First, come along with us to Bastet's temple. We want to honor the cat goddess and pray not only for a safe journey, but that the gods will lead us to Viper."

Pashet agreed and walked with them up the hill a short distance to the sacred site. Inside the temple, cats were free to roam everywhere. Shep held Miu in his arms and smiled at her reaction to so many creatures like herself. The acrid odor of them became overpowering and the visitors walked back to be near the doors.

"They're everywhere," Merit said.

Babu pointed. "Mother, the great goddess's head looks just like Miu."

"Yes it does, and we must love her as we love our princess."

A priest approached. The slim older man's hair had faded to white, and wrinkles on his forehead and corners of his eyes and mouth told his age. He raised his hands and recited a special blessing on their cat.

Miu sang out a long, melodious "meir-r-r-ow…"

Shep left a monetary offering with the priest for the care of the cats as they went out.

Pashet said, "I wonder how many cats are snapped up by Sobek's servants. Look how close the temple is to the river and the crocodiles. I would wager many of the goddess's feline servants fall in from time to time."

Babu frowned. "I wouldn't want Miu to fall in the river."

Shep said, "Nor I, Son. We must be careful."

They walked through the town and Babu wanted the honey cakes he saw outside a small shop. Merit bought some but only let him eat one.

When they went back onboard, Pashet signaled for the physician to join him in the cabin he shared with the ship's captain. "We have a thief on board, I'm afraid."

Shep scowled. "What's been stolen?"

"My gold ring. I forgot I left it by the water basin this morning before going ashore."

Hakor entered at that moment and heard the end of Pashet's comment. "It can't be any of the crew. They've been with me for more than two years. I vouch for every one of them."

"I'm only saying, watch your valuables."

"We will, Cousin, thanks to your warning."

When he entered the family's cabin, Shep told Merit what he had learned and they went through their things to make sure nothing was missing.

"It's a good thing you wear a money belt," Merit said. "I don't really mind that it gives you a little paunch."

Shep grinned. "Now why would you notice that?"

34

Merit smiled and walked to the open window. "The oarsmen are getting ready, Babu, if you want to watch."

The boy hurried outside and sat by the mast again.

"Where's Princess?" Shep asked.

A soft "meow" from her basket gave the answer.

The physician knelt down and looked inside. "What are you doing in there, little one?"

The cat answered with another "merwooowlll…"

Something shiny caught Shep's eye. "What are you hiding in there?" He lifted the cat out and felt inside the folds of the towel on which she'd been sleeping.

"By the gods, Merit. Look." He held up Pashet's ring. "How'd it get in there?"

Merit shook her head. "Babu must have hidden it there. I don't want to believe it, but he's gone back to his old ways, I'm afraid." She opened the door and shook her head. "I'll bring him."

When she returned, the boy had a puzzled look on his face. "What's wrong? I want to watch the rudder men steer the ship."

Shep showed the boy the ring. "Did you put this in the cat's basket?"

Babu looked at it and shook his head. "No, Father. I've never seen it before."

Merit said, "You don't need to steal anymore, Babu. We take good care of you, don't we?"

"I'm not a thief, Merit."

Both adults noticed he didn't refer to her as his mother this time.

Shep said, "I believe you, Son. Go back on deck and watch the rudder men like you wanted."

The boy left, but his frown spoke louder than any words.

"I shouldn't have done that," Shep said. "I don't believe he took the ring." He sat on a chair as Merit combed

35

her hair with a small ivory comb. Her raven-black tresses shone in the sunlight streaming through the window.

He knelt down and opened the lid of the cat's basket. He took out the towel and something else fell onto the floor. "Look at that," he said. "It's a copper coin."

"Oh," Merit said. "I dropped a coin in here yesterday, but didn't look for it. I forgot all about it."

"You don't suppose. . .no, Princess couldn't do that, could she?"

Merit smiled. "No, but she might if she were a four-footed raven. I remember as a child in Edfu watching the ravens steal shiny things we'd left outside. They would take pieces of metal, even shiny copper coins. They're little thieves."

"Yes, I've seen them. But a cat?" Shep shook his head in amused bewilderment. "Well, I'm taking Pashet his ring."

He found the officer on deck, leaning on the railing and waving to some children running along the shore.

"We found it, Cousin," Shep said, handing him the ring.

"Where was it?"

"In the cat's basket. I couldn't believe it. At first we thought Babu took it but I believe the boy when he said he didn't do it." He paused a moment. "Was princess in your cabin at all yesterday?"

"I left my ring near the water as I told you. But I don't think she came in…wait a moment…the cat *was* in the room! I remember now. Captain Hakor doesn't always close the cabin door and I saw her wander in. Why?"

"We think she's picking up shiny things and hiding them like ravens do. I can't believe it. What a little bandit."

Outside, loud shouts reached them from the bow of the ship. "Look out! Man overboard!" Shep and everyone ran forward.

"It's Pepe! He can't swim," a crewman exclaimed.

"Hurry! The crocodiles!" Captain Hakor yelled.

An oarsman dove into the water and the crew threw him several lines. He reached Pepe and tied a rope around them both and yelled, "Pull!" The strong current made it difficult. A dozen oarsmen, their muscles rippling and glistening in the glaring sun, braced their feet on the deck and pulled on the ropes.

On shore, several of the large reptiles slithered into the water, hoping for an easy meal. Their hopes vanished when the crew succeeded in pulling the two men onto the deck. The crew cheered until they realized Pepe wasn't moving.

"He's not breathing," someone said.

"He's dead," said another.

The crewmen held up two-fingered horn signs against the evil eye, touching their foreheads before turning their wrists away from their heads to expel the evil.

Shep raced forward. "Out of my way."

"He's dead sir," Captain Hakor told him. "There's nothing you can do."

"Give me room." Shep ordered. He knelt beside the crewman and began pressing on the young man's chest. Up and down several times. Then he struck him hard on the chest before pinching the man's nostrils and breathing into his mouth.

"Come on!" he shouted. Then he pushed once more on the chest, and breathed forcefully into the man's mouth.

The man jerked, and expelled some water.

"That's it," Shep said. Then he helped the man sit up and pounded him on his back. The man coughed up more water and then sucked in a great gulp of air.

"He's breathing!" Hakor shouted. "He's alive."

The crew fell immediately on their faces out of fear—their palms turned toward the physician in awe. To them, healers were agents of the supernatural and guardians of sacred potions and spells.

"He's blessed by the gods," a crewman whispered. The word spread throughout the ship.

"Are you all right now, Pepe?" Shep asked as he helped the man stand.

"Yes, sir. What happened?"

"You fell overboard, crewman. I would advise you to learn how to swim." Addressing the rest of the crew, he said, "The same goes for all of you. I won't always be here if you fall overboard. Learn to swim and how to help your comrades who fall into the river."

The crew murmured among themselves, uncertain of what just happened.

Hakor walked with him back to his cabin. "How did you know what to do, my Lord? Did the god Horus tell you what to do?"

"The gods reveal such truths to our teachers at the Academy, Captain. We learned from them that pushing down on the chest helps expel water from the lungs, and you can breathe in the breath of life."

"It is a miracle," Hakor said.

"Call it what you will, Captain. I call it education."

For the rest of the day, wherever he went, the crew bowed their heads to Shep and kept a respectful distance.

"Well done, Cousin," Pashet said. "The crew will now do whatever you say. The gods have touched you and they hope some of your power will rub off on them."

The colorless sky was bleached white by a merciless sun. The day was hot, the air still. Shep put his foot up on the railing and leaned over to inhale the cool breeze off the water. "Where are we now?"

"We're near Dendera," Pashet said. "After that, it will be Thebes and finally Edfu. We still have about three more days until we are there."

38

"I don't know about you, but I'll be glad to be on land for a while."

Pashet smiled. "I agree. I'm one of those who can't swim."

Shep shook his head and headed back to his cabin.

The next day, they reached the town. Hakor told his passengers, "We'll spend the day and night docked here. There's a nice inn in the center of town where you can enjoy a good meal. And there is a large market for your pleasure."

"I'll love that," Merit said.

"And I want honey cakes," Babu said.

"If you eat too many, my boy, you'll turn into one," Shep said.

The boy laughed, pleasing the physician. It appeared Babu had already forgotten they had accused him of being a thief.

They left an unhappy Miu in her basket this time. Ashore, they found the village pleasant. Famous for the beautiful temple of Hathor, it also boasted a center for the worship of Sobek, the crocodile god.

"I don't like them," Babu said, pointing to one of Sobek's statues. "They almost ate the two crewmen yesterday." He paused and hesitated before adding, "And...they took my mother."

His words made the adults cringe and Shep rubbed his hand over the boys head.

"I agree. They're disgusting creatures," Merit said. "Would you like to come with me to the market? If you do, it is on one condition. You may only have two honey cakes."

"Yes, Mother, please." The boy's eyes lit up with pleasure.

Shep watched them go as he and Captain Pashet walked toward the center of town. They visited a surgery where Shep found several physicians working together in a large building.

"Shepseskaf, is that you?" one of them called to him.

"Menkara, you old jackal," Shep replied.

"It's been five years, if my memory's correct. What are you doing here?" Menkara asked.

"We're on our way to Edfu and our ship put in for supplies."

"Let me show you our surgery. It's very unusual and is the first time I've worked with other physicians this way. Each of us specializes in only one type of illness."

"Let me guess. You specialize in bones—am I right? You were always good with those types of injuries," Shep said. "In Memphis, I work alone and try to treat every malady that walks in the door."

"I don't know if I could do that now," Menkara said.

"He helped restore the life of a man who drowned today," Pashet said.

"Oh? I've never tried," Menkara mumbled.

Shep shook his head in amused disapproval. "The crew thought it some kind of power from the gods—rather embarrassing. It's something we all learned, you remember."

"Yes, but it must take real courage to try," Menkara said. "I admire you for doing so."

"Are there truly enough patients here for more than one physician?" Shep asked.

"Too many, my friend. We put in long days, but the pay is good. My wife and I have a nice villa not far from here, and we have three young boys who take up all our time."

"I envy you, Menkara. Maybe I'll leave Memphis and find a place like this."

"You would always be welcome, Shep."

Pashet excused himself and walked outside. He found a bench near a small pool and waited for Shep.

40

Someone ran to the door of the surgery and interrupted the two friends. "A boy's fallen out of a tree, my Lord Menkara. He's in a great deal of pain."

Shep said, "I'll leave you my friend. Maybe I'll see you when we return. Good luck with your patient."

At mid-day, Pashet and Shep sat in the shade of a tall palm in the center of town, enjoying the river rushing past. The triangular sails of the feluccas seen from such a distance resembled the wings of white butterflies skimming the water.

"Sorry about spending so much time at the surgery. I didn't know I'd find someone I knew."

Pashet said, "You are fortunate to have found a classmate from your Academy days. I'm glad you had some time with him."

When Merit and Babu came by, they decided to find the inn and take supper ashore.

They entered the brick covered inn and found Captain Hakor finishing his meal. He invited his friends to join him. They pulled up another table and put the two together. Servants brought more food and it was as delicious as Hakor said it would be.

Pashet excused himself early, telling them he wanted to find out more about the troop ship they had seen earlier.

The family stayed a long time at the inn, and when they left, the sun had already slipped halfway to the horizon. Captain Hakor and other members of the crew walked with them down to the dock.

"We'll leave first thing in the morning," the captain told them. "We've been loading supplies all day. I trust your visit here has been pleasant."

"Very much so, Captain," Merit said. "But I'm afraid my husband will not approve of how much of his money I've spent at the market."

Hakor laughed. "Now she sounds like *my* wife!" He waited until everyone had walked up the gangway before returning on board himself.

Inside their cabin, Shep let Miu out of her basket. The cat ran over to her little box of sand.

"Remember to give Miu fresh sand, Babu," Merit said.

"Listen," Shep said. "Stay here." He ran toward the loud shouting coming from Hakor's cabin. He pushed his way through the crew who were huddled in front of the open door.

Once inside he said, "What is it, Captain? What's wrong?" And then he saw the body of Pashet lying on the floor with a dagger in his chest. Shep knelt beside him and tried to find a pulse but it was too late. Standing, he said, "He must have died instantaneously."

Captain Hakor pulled out the dagger and found a piece of papyrus attached. He tore it off, looked at it and handed it to the physician.

Shep read:

Death awaits you at Edfu.

Chapter 4

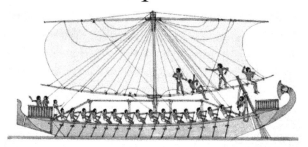

Edfu

"I'll bring the guards," Captain Hakor said.

"Yes, but it is I who will be in charge when they arrive, Captain," Shep insisted. "There is something they need to know about Pashet that can only be told in private."

Hakor frowned. "Surely you can tell me, my Lord."

"No, I'm sorry, Captain. I am under the command of the highest authority."

Hakor became silent for a moment then said, "I understand. I'll bring them to you."

"My friend, after the soldiers have examined the body, see that it receives the best care for burial," Shep said.

Hakor nodded. "We'll take his body to Thebes. They have the largest House of the Dead. I'll see to it personally, my Lord."

"Good. I trust you to make the arrangements. Now I must tell my family."

When Merit saw the worried expression on Shep's face she asked, "What's happened then? Is someone injured?"

"Yes, I'm afraid so. You need to remain calm while I tell you."

Merit sat down and waited. Babu stood beside her.

"Our good friend Pashet has left us for his journey to the blessed afterlife. Someone took his life in Hakor's cabin."

Merit gasped. "How horrible. We just spent a wonderful day with him. I can't believe it."

Babu said. "I liked him."

"We all did," Shep said. "Now the soldiers will come, but I mustn't let them learn too much. His death and his connection to the royal family must be secret. The Dendera guards must not learn of it."

"Babu and I will have nothing to say, Shep. Keep them away from us."

"Agreed."

Merit frowned. "But Shep, won't we still need an officer of the guard with us? Pashet's mission was to kill the assassin. We should turn back."

Shep shook his head. "No. We must do as the prince commanded, Merit. I'll ask for another officer when we reach Thebes. I must do what I was sent to do." Merit's face turned red, but he didn't regret his words.

A short time later, a contingent of guardsmen came aboard.

"Who is in charge here?" a young officer asked.

"I am," Shep said. "To whom am I speaking?"

"I am Captain Ludin, my Lord."

"I am Shepseskaf, Physician, and I am responsible for this ship. Her crew are under my command and we are headed for Thebes with Edfu our ultimate destination."

"Who discovered the body?" Ludin asked.

Hakor walked forward "I did, Officer. We had just returned from town and I found him on the floor of my cabin." He looked at Shep who nodded. They had agreed not to show the soldiers the note.

"Show me the body," Ludin said. Shep and Hakor led him to the cabin.

44

"Why would someone want to kill him?" the officer asked. "Is everything just as it was?"

Hakor said, "Yes, Captain, except I pulled out the dagger."

Ludin called for his aide and gave him the weapon to examine. "Now have the crew carry the body ashore."

"I can't allow it, Captain," Shep said. "It will travel with us to the House of the Dead in Thebes. We will send it back to Memphis after the seventy days of embalming. He had some very important friends in the capital."

"Very well, but do you know why anyone would want to murder him?"

"I cannot say, Captain. I do not have permission to share more than that."

"Oh?" the officer asked. "And why is that?"

"I'm sorry. That is all I can say."

The officer fussed with his menes head cloth, his eyebrows raised in surprise. "If I understand you, Lord Physician, this ship belongs to a higher authority?"

"That is correct. The general would not allow me to mention his name."

At the word 'general,' Captain Ludin's attitude changed immediately.

"I understand, my Lord. How can we assist you?"

"Thank you, Captain, I'll give the general a good report. He knows who has done this criminal act and will pursue it when we arrive in Thebes."

"Very well. You are free to sail. In his majesty's name." He saluted, slapping his fist across his chest.

"In his name," Shep responded.

The guards left and Hakor and Shep remained in the cabin with the body.

"If you would send someone ashore to buy linen sheets, I'll clean and prepare the body. They'll also need to buy a wooden coffin. We'll have to put him in the hold."

Hakor said, "My crew will not be pleased, my Lord. Pashet's Ka may still be on board, but I'll do as you say. We'll sail in the morning as planned."

"Good," Shep said. "I'll send a priest to purify the ship and pray that Pashet's Ka be at peace. That should ease their fears. I also need to send a carrier pigeon to Memphis asking for instructions."

"Yes, I understand."

Shep left the cabin and returned to his own. He told Merit what had been decided.

"It's unsettling to have a dead person on board," she said.

"It'll only be for two days at the most—just until Thebes," Shep said.

"What about his ghost?" Babu asked.

"What? There is no ghost, Babu. Pashet's Ka, that part of us that never dies, is asleep until the embalmers prepare him for his journey."

"Oh, then we must not make too much noise or we'll wake him up."

Shep smiled. "That's right, my boy. We'll sail tomorrow. The sooner we reach Thebes the better. It's a large and wonderful city filled with adventure."

The boy's eyes lit up and he begged Shep to tell him more about the city.

That evening at supper, life on the ship took on a somber mood—no singing or dancing. Nearly everyone turned in early. No one wanted to risk meeting Pashet's Ka in the middle of the night

Babu held Miu in his arms and gazed out the open cabin window. "I can see the city, Father," Babu shouted.

Shep and Merit opened the cabin door and walked out into the bright morning sunlight.

"I'd forgotten how beautiful Thebes can be rising above the river," Merit said.

"I'd forgotten how far south it is," Shep told her. "The magnificent temples are so large and their painted columns resemble our colorful lotus blossoms pushing above the water."

Miu wriggled and twitched in Shep's arms.

"What is it princess?" Shep asked as he placed her on the deck.

The cat led them back inside, sat beside her reed basket and looked up.

"Is something in there you want me to see? Is that it?"

"Rowrrr..."

"All right. Let me look."

He lifted the lid and felt around in the basket. His fingers felt something smooth and round. "Ah, it's another coin. You have been into mischief again, haven't you?" But when he took it out and looked at it, he discovered a round piece of leather from a belt, or scabbard. "It's from Hakor's cabin isn't it? When would you have been in there?"

"I saw her walking along the deck this morning, Father," Babu said. "She must have gone inside."

"By the gods," Shep exclaimed. "This could have come off the killer. If it's part of a scabbard, it's from the murder weapon."

"You must show the guards," Merit said.

"No, what could they do? It means that if Pashet's killer is connected to Viper, we need to find him and prove he killed Pashet. By examining his scabbard we'll find where this missing piece of round leather belongs."

"But you'd have to get close enough to him to see that," Merit said. "If I remember correctly, you're a physician, not a Medjay policeman."

"Medjay? What's that?" Babu asked.

"Pharaoh's private police guards, Babu, soldiers who maintain order in his name."

"Oh, are they good or bad?" the boy asked.

"Usually good. But they are very mysterious. No one knows much about them," Shep said. He picked up Miu and hugged her. "You're a little Medjay aren't you princess? You'll find the killer before we do if we're not careful."

At mid-morning, they docked and the crew secured the ship. Shep went to captain Hakor's cabin and knocked.

"Enter," the older man said.

"I'll leave Merit and the boy onboard, Captain. I must meet with the officer in charge of the local garrison."

"My men will guard them, my Lord, and I'll take the body of your friend to the priests at the House of the Dead."

Shep thanked the captain and disembarked. Instead of hiring a carrying chair, he walked up to the main street and easily found the military garrison. Meeting with the local commander, however, did not prove as easy as he thought.

"He's not here, my Lord," the sergeant on duty informed him.

"When will he be back? This is important."

"I have no way of knowing. The captain has a mind of his own."

"I see. Will you tell him that General Akhom has a message for him? I'll be on board our ship. We just arrived."

At the mention of Akhom's name, the sergeant became nervous. "Yes, my Lord. I'll send my men to find him. He won't be long."

Shep nodded and left the garrison.

48

He headed for the messenger service that specialized in carrier pigeons. Writing on a very small piece of papyrus, he wrote,

"Pashet gone. Send instructions to Edfu."

He paid the man in charge who told him it would only take two days for the message to reach Memphis. He then continued on the road through the market and stopped to buy a few small fish to cut up for his cat. When he passed a seller of honey cakes, he smiled and bought half a dozen.

Back on board, Babu enjoyed the cakes, and when Shep cut up the small fish into little pieces, Miu purred in appreciation. She rubbed against him as he sat and watched her.

"The body's gone," Merit told him. "They took it soon after you left. It is good to hear the crew laughing and singing again. They're gone now except for those guarding our cabin. Hakor left the ship and said he'd be back soon."

"Good. I'm waiting for the officer of the garrison to arrive. There is so much I need to know. What about the crew?"

"I think Hakor told them to be back at sundown. He told me he thought you'd want to sail again in the morning."

"I don't know, Merit. It all depends on the officer. We can't go without guards."

Shep walked to Hakor's cabin and returned with the captain's game of Senet. He decided it might be a good time to teach the boy how to play.

It wasn't until mid-day that a small patrol of soldiers and their officer came on deck. The men stood at the gangway while their officer walked on board. A crewman led him to Shep's cabin.

"My Lord, you have a message for me. I am Captain Pamu. I'm in charge of the garrison."

Merit and Babu took the cat and went out on deck.

"Please be seated, Captain. You have a powerful name. Do you have the strength of the lion as your name implies?"

The man didn't smile. "I like to think so, my Lord. Now what is this about?"

Shep told him everything, except the involvement of the royal family.

"By the gods," Pamu exclaimed. "To kill an officer of the royal guard is a serious crime. His body is here in Thebes, you say?"

"Yes, Captain. I hope to send for it after the days of embalming are complete.

"And you believe you know the assassin?"

"By name only, but it is only a nickname. He goes by Viper, I've been told."

"I see. And this Viper is in Edfu?"

"We think so. I don't want to continue there alone and endanger my family. We need guards to accompany us. Is that possible?"

"I don't know, my Lord. It is highly unusual. I'm certain the garrison at Edfu is prepared to provide the men you need."

"Of course. But if this Viper has men supporting him in the local garrison, it could put us in danger. He has attacked an important official in Memphis, and now has murdered one of the officers sent to capture him. He must have eyes everywhere."

"You mentioned General Akhom, my Lord. You know him well?"

"Yes, I'm his family physician. I recently saved his son, Captain Basa from a serious illness."

"I see. Then I am the one to come with you. I'll choose ten of my best warriors to join us."

Shep smiled and he knew the officer could see the relief on his face. "Bring your men on board, tonight, Captain. We'll sail at first light."

The captain stood. "Shepseskaf is a long name. How may I address you?"

"My friends call me Shep."

The captain saluted and left.

Merit walked back in holding the cat.

"Well," Shep said. "We have an escort. I feel better about the journey now."

"Good," Merit said. "Now go help your son. He's got his foot caught in some rigging and can't get loose."

Shep laughed. "Boys!" he said, heading astern.

It took the *Wings of Isis* two days to reach the small town of Edfu. Shep and Babu enjoyed sitting at the bow of the ship, breathing in the cool air. The physician marveled at the verdant strip on each side of the river stretching out a mile wide—pushed back by the ever encroaching sand. Date palms stood tall, as if guarding the acacia bushes and papyrus at their feet. A quilt work of large green and yellow patches of wheat, barley and lentils covered the fertile land. As they neared shore, the blistering heat from the desert hit them like the sudden opening of an oven door.

Docking proved difficult. A much larger ship occupied several berths, but eventually Hakor eased his ship into place.

"How shall we proceed, Lord Physician?" Captain Pamu asked.

"First we must go to my wife's family, my friend, but the hunt for the assassin is a military matter. We will trust you to begin the search."

"I'll let the garrison know we're escorting a personal friend of General Akhom," Pamu said. "Hopefully, we may learn something about the assassin."

"Very well. We'll meet back on board. Will you need money to feed your men?"

"No, the garrison will feed us, but they are always grateful for a jar of beer."

Shep chuckled. "Of course." When Pamu left to confer with the ship's captain, Shep returned to his room, removed two gold pieces from his money belt and walked to Hakor's cabin.

"We'll meet back here at mid-day tomorrow, my Lord," Pamu said. He saluted and left the ship.

Merit came out and stood at the railing. "The town looks different somehow," she said. "There are so many new buildings, and over there near the market is a temple I've never seen."

"Do you remember where your family lives?"

"Of course. I haven't been gone *that* long."

"Shall we walk there, or do I need to hire carrying chairs?"

Babu exclaimed, "Oh yes, please, please, Father. I've never been in one!"

Merit's lips twisted into an amused smile. Shep asked, "What is it?"

"I was thinking of the impression it would make on my relatives if we arrived in style."

Shep grinned. "Yes, an excellent idea."

Babu placed Miu on his shoulder. "Can Miu come with us?"

"Of course, son," Shep said. "We wouldn't leave a family member behind."

"She needs a collar and leash," Merit said. "She's apt to run off."

"I don't think cats like leashes," Shep said, but by Merit's eyebrows raised in disapproval he added, "You're right. I'll try to find one. Babu will help me."

The boy smiled and ran to the gangway and waited for him. Father and son left the ship a short time later, and headed for the market where scrap pieces of wooden boxes made up the stalls. Everything one might need could be found here.

Babu touched something on every stall they passed—first the bananas, then round barley loaves of bread. The aroma of the freshly baked bread made their stomachs growl. He picked up a small knife from one stall but Shep made him put it down. They found the seller of leather goods and purchased a leash with a collar small enough for the cat. When they returned, the carrying chairs and eight Nubian bearers stood waiting for them.

Inside the cabin, Shep picked up the cat and put the small leather collar, studded with semi-precious stones, around her neck. He attached the leash. She didn't like it. When he put her down she tried to pull away, and then stubbornly refused to move. He picked her up again. "She'll have to get used to it," he said.

Babu scowled. "I don't think so. She's growling a lot."

Merit said, "Let's go down. The bearers are ready, and I'm anxious to see my mother."

Merit appropriated one chair for herself and her small bag while Shep, Babu and the cat rode in the other. The tall Nubian porters lifted them to shoulder height and headed toward the center of the small town. Their skin, black as ebony, took on a bluish tone in the bright sunlight. They followed the road out into the country, and at a crossroad waited for directions. Bits of greenery peeked up through dry and brittle grass, and weeds badly in need of floodwaters lay exhausted in the sun. Brown geese waddled beside the road honking at the porters.

"It's the house with the blue door up ahead," she told the bearer closest to her.

On the path to the door, small children ran out and clapped their hands.

Babu laughed and waved to them, enjoying every moment.

An elderly woman opened the door to see what had caused the commotion. "Who's there?"

Merit waited for them to put her down, then stepped out and approached the woman. "It's me, Merit," she said. "Where is my mother?"

"Your mother? Who's that?"

"Maia," Merit replied.

"There's no one here by that name."

Shep and Babu joined Merit as an old man from a neighboring house walked over. "Maia you said? Are you related?"

"She's my mother," Merit replied.

"My wife told me a couple of weeks ago they had left," the man said. "I don't know where they went. I'm sorry."

Merit turned to Shep. "Surely someone knows."

The neighbor said, "Well, you could ask old lady Sadeh down at the house with the fig tree in front. Her mind tends to wander, but she may remember."

"Thank you, Grandfather," Shep said, using the title of respect for the elderly man.

The visitors stepped back into their chairs and the porters carried them down the hill to the house in question. Babu walked alongside with Miu on his shoulder to the delight of the children. The mud-brick two-room houses stood close together with palm-thatched roofs. Several had whitewash on the front of them, and cloth strung across the entrance. Made from old linen scraps, it looked more like a quilt than a curtain. Common folk could rarely afford wooden doors.

Merit got out and called the woman's name. When no one answered, she tried again.

"Who's there?" a feeble voice asked. A hand slowly moved the cloth aside and a woman looked out.

"Pardon, Grandmother," Merit said. "I'm looking for my mother. Her name is Maia and she used to live in the house with the blue door."

The elderly woman, perhaps in her eighties, studied the young woman's face.

"You look like my granddaughter, Hapu. Where have you been? You haven't come to see me in so long."

Merit glanced at Shep. "No, Mother Sadeh, I'm not your granddaughter. I've traveled all this way from Memphis to see my mother, Maia."

"Maia? Who's that?"

Shep said, "It's hopeless, Merit. The woman's mind is confused. Isn't there anyone else who might remember you or your mother?"

"I don't think so. I've been gone for so long. I can't remember anyone else."

The small delicate woman with shoulder-length dark hair walked down the two steps from her door. She folded her arms across her chest and stood face to face with Merit. "What has happened to you?"

"What do you mean, Grandmother?"

"You've changed. You look so much older now."

"Yes I am."

"Wait. I know you now. You resemble Merit."

"I *am* Merit!"

"Your family is not there anymore, my child." She pointed to the house up the hill. "They were a good family but now they're gone."

55

"Yes, I know, but do you know where they went?"

"Are you sure you're not my granddaughter? Why hasn't she come?"

"No, I'm Merit, not your granddaughter."

"A group of men came and took them all away," the elderly woman said. "All of them. There was a lot of crying and shouting. Their leader was a bad man."

"A bad man? Who was it, old one," Shep asked.

"Did you know him?" Merit asked.

"No," she said. "But his men called him *Hhh-faw*!"

"*Hhh-faw*? Are you sure, grandmother?"

The woman nodded.

Shep mumbled something and turned away.

"What is it?" Merit asked.

"*Hhh-faw* is one of the old words." He paused before adding, "When you pronounce it, it imitates the sound of the viper."

Chapter 5

Abu

Merit cursed, "By the gods! They've taken my whole family."

"We'll find them, Merit, I assure you. Captain Pamu will help us. I promise," Shep said.

Merit got back into her carrying chair and ordered the bearers to return to the ship.

When Shep and Babu returned to theirs, the boy asked, "Why is Mother upset?"

"She's worried about her family, my boy. She doesn't know where the bad men have taken them." Shep tried to hold the cat still but Miu mewled and tried to chew on her leash.

"Stop, princess. You'll break your teeth." He gave in finally, and undid it. She jumped up onto his shoulder and began to purr in his ear which tickled him, making him laugh.

"Look at her, Babu. Miu is trying to cheer us up."

Babu became very serious and stared into the cat's face. "Maybe she knows what we're thinking."

"Hmm, you might be right. I've wondered the same thing. Her eyes can go right through you."

When they reached the ship, Shep paid the owner of the slave bearers, and the family returned to their cabin. They had no sooner settled in, than someone knocked at the door.

Babu opened it and greeted the ship's captain. "*Iiti.* Hello, Captain."

"What is it, friend?" Shep asked. "Come in."

"You've received a message from Memphis, my Lord. It's unopened." He handed it to Shep who broke the wax seal and unrolled the small papyrus. He read the message and rolled it back up.

"What does it say?" Merit asked. It was the first time she spoke since visiting her family's home.

"It's confusing," he said. "It said, 'Falcon target not fledgling. Destroy threat'." He turned to the captain. "Thank you."

Realizing the physician wasn't going to share the meaning of the information, Hakor left the cabin.

Shep stood by the open window and stared across the river.

Merit sat on the edge of her bed waiting for him to explain the news to her.

He said, "It's obvious the falcon is Pharaoh, of course. Apparently, he was the target of the poisoning, not his brother, the fledgling, as the prince and princess thought."

"But anyone could have sent it," Merit said.

"You may be right. I don't know who sent it and there's no royal seal—but there isn't room for one anyway." Shep paced around the cabin and then sat down on the floor near the cat's basket. Miu climbed onto his lap and settled down and began to make her mesmerizing purr.

He said, "Merit, what if Viper knew we were coming? He could've sent the message. Only he would know that someone attacked the king's brother, but why would he have come so far south?"

"It's confusing," Merit said. "My only concern now is what will he do to my family?" She sighed and pulled back the bedcover. "I'm tired; I'm going to lie down."

"Of course, I understand. The soldiers will return tomorrow and maybe they'll know more about the band of assassins. Try to put it out of your mind until then."

Babu interrupted. "Can I walk Miu around deck with her leash, Father?"

"Very good," Shep said. "She needs to become accustomed to it."

Leaving Merit in the cabin, Shep kept an eye on his son as he attached the leash to Miu and walked her slowly along the ship's railing. The cat tried every way to pull on the leash, but eventually forgot about it entirely and began to sniff places along the deck as she always did.

After several times around the ship, Shep and the boy stretched out in the shade of the great sail and closed their eyes. They dozed off until Merit came to call them for supper.

The crew prepared succulent roast chicken with steamed vegetables, and they ate together out in the fresh air. The adults shared jars of beer, while Babu drank fresh pomegranate juice.

It pleased Shep that the boy had gained a little weight. Taking on a pompous voice he said, "As the boy's physician I say he's looking good."

Merit laughed. "I think it's all the honey cakes he's been enjoying."

The next day, Merit went to the market and took Babu with her.

Shep looked for the ship's captain but he wasn't in his cabin. Instead, he found him on deck, sitting near the large rudder oars.

Hakor asked, "What will you do if the soldiers don't know where to find the assassin?"

"I won't know who to turn to," Shep said.

Hakor said, "Many times when I don't know which way to go, I followed my gut."

"And are you ever wrong?"

Hakor laughed. "Many times, I'm afraid."

Merit and Babu came looking for Shep. The boy said, "There are soldiers coming, Father."

"Yes, I know, Babu. We're waiting for them."

The boy shook his head. "No, I don't mean the four soldiers who came with the captain two days ago. This time, there are so many I can't count them."

"What?" Shep exclaimed.

He and Hakor stood and hurried to the gangway. They found an entire company of a hundred soldiers, fully armed, heading for the ship. Captain Pamu and another officer rode in front and dismounted at the gangway.

"Have they come to arrest us?" Hakor asked.

Captain Pamu walked up the gangway and greeted the two men. "There is good news, my Lord," he began. "We've located where the assassin and his men are hiding."

Shep smiled and slapped the officer on the back. "Horus be praised! Great news indeed! But we have more distressing news, Captain. Viper—the cursed son of Seth—has captured my wife's family!"

"Gods!" Pamu exclaimed. He walked to the railing and motioned for the other officer to come aboard. "This is Captain Basa, Lord Physician. He and his men have been waiting for you. General Akhom sent them on ahead to lead in the capture of Viper."

Shep frowned. "Why didn't he tell me you would be here?" Shep said. "I'm relieved but a little angry."

Captain Basa said, "Don't be, my Lord. We only followed the general's orders. He hoped you might find out from your wife's family where these men might be hiding. There are no secrets in a village. He always intended for the army to take over Viper's capture."

"Go on," Shep said.

"We know he's not far from here, believe it or not, my Lord—just a little farther south." The officer turned to the ship's captain. "Captain, we need to bring my soldiers on board."

"Of course," Hakor replied. "They'll have tight quarters, but I'm sure warriors are used to that. We'll manage."

"Babu," Shep called to his son. The boy rushed to him. "Go wake your mother. She'll want to hear our good news."

When the warriors were on board, Shep suggested the crew break open jars of beer and share them with their new passengers. Captains Pamu and Basa and their unit leaders met with Shep in Hakor's cabin. They invited Merit to join them since the rescue of her family was now a primary concern.

Basa brought a crude map and placed it on the table. "We fortunately encountered one of his gang in a tavern. While drunk, he bragged that he was part of a band of the bravest men in Egypt. Their leader had defied even Pharaoh. When asked the leader's name he used the old name *Hhh-faw*. He also told us that they are camped on the Island of Abu. A foolish place to hide in my opinion. It's remote—but is also a trap."

"Is there a dock?" Hakor asked.

"Yes, but I want to propose something. I say we land fifty of my men on the far side of the island, and the other half at the dock, which we know will be under guard. First, you'll bring the ship close enough on the far side so that we can lower dinghies to get the men ashore. There are crocs everywhere so it's too dangerous for them to swim."

"We'll put on extra dinghies," Hakor said. "That won't be a problem. I'm more concerned about the rocks that probably encircle the island."

Shep interrupted. "Isn't it unwise to divide your men? I remember a class at the Academy on leadership which taught 'If you want to go fast, go alone; if you want to go strong, go together.'"

Pamu said, "In this case, my Lord, I think our numbers will give us an advantage. When we attack on the far side first, Viper and his men will try to escape to their ship at anchor. We'll be there to prevent them."

"How do we know that they have a ship anchored at the island?" Hakor asked.

Pamu nodded. "We only have the word of the dead prisoner, I'm afraid."

"We'll have to prevent it from leaving," Hakor said.

Merit had been listening intently. "But won't they kill my family if they see you coming? Or use them as shields?"

"They could," Pamu said, "but we'll move fast and prevent them from doing so."

"I want to be there with you," she said.

The four men looked at each other. Pamu said, "No, I'm sorry. It won't be possible, Merit. You and the boy must remain here in Edfu."

Shep saw the sudden fear in her eyes. "He's right, my dear. It will be no place for you and Babu. Please don't make this more difficult."

Merit looked away, "Very well." She walked over to the window and turned to face them. "I'm going to pray to Mother Isis the whole time you're gone."

The men nodded. "Speed is the key here," Basa said. "But there is also another danger."

"Oh?" Shep said.

"Yes my Lord—the elephants. They give the island its name. *Abu* is the old word for elephant. We know there will be many of them because the river is low. They swim across and eat the bark from the trees. We must avoid disturbing them."

"I've seen drawings, Captain. Surely they're too big to move fast," Shep said.

"Not so," Pamu replied. "I've seen them. The bulls are very aggressive and fast. You know how fast even hippos can be on land. Elephants are faster."

Basa said, "My men will be prepared for them. They know their arrows and spears can't bring the beasts down."

"When do we sail?" Hakor asked.

"Tonight, Captain. There is a new moon and we need the god Khonsu's cover of darkness to land."

"Seth's breath!" Hakor exclaimed. "I can't sail this size ship at night. Also, I've never attempted to go beyond Edfu. I'm told the current is even stronger near the first white water."

Pamu said, "*You* won't have to, Captain. I have engaged a navigator to come aboard. He's sailed to the first rapids many times during day *and* night. He'll guide you."

Hakor smiled. "You've thought of everything. We'll need the oarsmen since there is very little wind at night. Hopefully, they won't make too much noise or they'll alert Viper's men of our approach. They can't ease up or the current will push us back."

"Let's prepare," Shep said. "First, I have to find lodging for my family."

Outside the cabin, Shep took Basa aside. He said in a softer voice, "You need to be aware that there are those

63

higher in power than General Akhom who will be grateful for what you are doing, Captain."

"All we do is for Pharaoh's glory, my Lord."

Shep smiled. "Well spoken."

He and Merit walked to their cabin and he helped put together what she and Babu would need for the next few days ashore.

Shep said, "Hakor has arranged an apartment for you above the Blue Lotus Inn. His wife's cousin runs it, and she'll take good care of you."

Merit nodded but pursed her lips—a sure sign of her reluctance to go.

Shep went with them and stayed awhile. When he bid them farewell, he picked up Miu and rubbed behind her ears. He felt a strong tug at his heart and realized he'd miss her as much as Merit and the boy.

Miu's plaintive mewling continued as Shep left the apartment.

As the radiant ship of the sun-god raced toward the horizon, its golden wake splashed onto the clouds in shades of orange, red and purple. Hakor raised anchor and moved the ship silently into the main channel of the river.

The navigator stood with Hakor beside the rudder men. This far south, the river narrowed, and his instructions were clear and accurate. He used the flickering fires in the villages along shore to stay in the center of the river. It took them until the middle of the night to reach the island of the elephants.

The navigator took them first to the far side. The oarsmen had taken the precaution of greasing the oarlocks before leaving Edfu and were careful lowering their oars into the water.

"Anchors fore and aft," Hakor ordered quietly. "Prepare to lower the dinghies." The small boats slipped quietly into the water. Five soldiers at a time climbed down the side of the ship and rowed ashore. The last warriors pulled the boats up onto the bank. The ship would retrieve them the next day.

Weighing anchor again, the ship sailed around to the west of the island and prepared to wait for the signal from those put ashore.

The only sounds were the chirping of crickets and an occasional chorus of frogs. Suddenly, the cry of a jackal rang out. Captain Basa said, "That's our signal. Move the ship to the dock, Captain."

When they reached the landing, a patrol of warriors jumped down onto the dock and easily eliminated Viper's watchmen. Waving for the rest of Basa's men to join them, the fifty soldiers trotted silently up the road to Viper's camp.

Overhead, the rising sun turned the dawn into a pale milky glow as cries of battle echoed through the morning mist.

Hakor suddenly shouted, "Over there! Those great shadows are moving."

"Gods, it's the elephants!" Shep exclaimed.

The two men climbed onto the roof of the small guard post.

"There are soldiers running on either side of the herd," Shep said. "It looks like our men are leading a crowd of people. Horus save them. They have women and children in front of them. Pray the elephants don't attack."

In the moments it takes to breathe twenty times, three women and a dozen children reached the dock and ran for the ship. The crew helped them up the gangway and took them below.

One of the women fell to her knees in front of Captain Hakor. "Praise the gods you came, my Lord. Thank you, thank you!"

"What is your name, good woman?" Shep asked.

"I am Maia. We are all from Edfu."

Shep couldn't speak for a moment. Finally, with his emotions under control, he said, "Follow me. We'll take care of everyone." Several small children followed her. Shep thought they might be her grandchildren.

Returning to the gangway, he heard Hakor shout, "Pamu and Basa are returning."

He moved to the ship's railing as the rest of the warriors reached the ship. They were pushing dozens of captured men from Viper's band in front of them. The gang, covered in blood, didn't hang their heads in defeat or shame. Instead, they defiantly held them high. Some even spat and cursed Basa's men.

Captains Pamu and Basa walked up the gangway to the cheers of their men and ship's crew. They stopped in front of the physician and saluted.

Pamu said, "We've crushed them, my Lord."

The physician smiled and nodded to the officer. "Well done. What about my wife's family? Are there any more out there?"

"No, they are all here safe and sound," Basa said.

"And Viper. Where is he?"

Pamu smiled. "In Seth's embrace in the underworld, my Lord—trampled to death by one of the big bull elephants."

"I must see for myself. Will you take me to him?"

"We will, my Lord, but allow us to drink something to wash away the taste of blood and dust."

"Forgive me, Captain. I wasn't thinking. Viper's not going anywhere. Break a jar for me."

With the women and children below, the warriors took off their kilts and pulled up pails of river water to wash away the sweat and blood. They sat around in the sun, enjoying their beer and rejoiced in being alive.

Shep spoke privately with Captain Paru. "I need proof this man is actually Viper. There must be something left to identify him."

"Normally I would discourage you from coming with us. As a physician, however, what you find will not be upsetting."

"Not so, Captain. Those whose Ka have departed are never easy to examine. It is not something one looks forward to."

Captain Basa approached them. "We're ready. You can use one of the horses left by the soldiers of the garrison, my Lord."

"Garrison? Do you mean soldiers were stationed on the island?" Shep asked.

Basa nodded. "Yes, that is until Viper's band killed every one of them. My men have found the gruesome evidence on the rocks where their bodies were thrown to the crocodiles." He paused to think how to say the next words. "I'm puzzled why Viper kept your wife's family alive."

"As am I, Captain. In fact, why did he take them in the first place?"

Pamu said, "The reason has gone with him into Seth's underworld."

"Let's go," Basa said. He walked down the gangway and mounted his horse.

"I really can't ride," Shep said, "but I can hold on."

Pamu said, "Don't worry. Your horse will follow mine."

His men gave Shep a hand up and showed him how to hold the reins.

Pamu rode on ahead, while Basa followed. They left the dock and rode out onto the open plain where Viper's men lay fallen.

"He's over there," Basa said. They turned their horses toward a small gulley and reined them in, dismounted and waited for the physician to join them. "It's not a pretty sight," Pamu said.

Shep slid awkwardly down from the horse's back, relieved to be on solid ground, and walked over to the crushed body lying in the dirt. The elephant had smashed the assassin's head, arms and legs. Very little of the torso was left and the insides of the man were strew on the ground around the body. Shep steeled himself and bent over the remains to examine the pieces of clothing. A belt caught his eye and he pulled it off the body. It held a dagger in a scabbard. His heart beat faster as he studied the scabbard closely. A smooth round part of it was missing.

"Thank Horus."

"What is it?" Basa asked.

"It's the dagger used to kill Captain Pashet. My cat discovered the missing piece of its scabbard—it matches perfectly and is our proof."

"Your cat?"

"Yes, I'll explain later."

Shep examined the rest of the body and found Viper's right hand buried deep in the dirt. He lifted it out slowly and discovered a glint of gold. He pulled off a ring from one of the fingers and showed it to Pamu.

"Look closely," he said.

Pamu turned it around and examined it carefully. "By Seth's foul breath, there's a viper and the letters Hhh-faw carved in the center." He handed it back.

Pamu said, "This could demonstrate to the royal family that this attempt on their lives might only be the beginning of an uprising."

68

"I pray you are wrong, my Lord," Basa said.

They helped Shep onto his horse, then remounted and returned to the ship.

Basa said, "I'll leave some of my men here on the island. You'll need the room on the ship for your return to Edfu. You also have Viper's ship. You can send it back for the rest of us and the extra dinghies."

"Of course, Captain, and I assure you I'll make a good report to the general." He made a point of not asking what his men would do with all the dead and captured followers of Viper. He was certain he already knew the answer.

Later that morning, Hakor's ship set sail. The smaller ship used by the assassins sailed alongside with another twenty of Basa's men.

Shep decided he would wait and let Merit explain their unique relationship to the family when they reached Edfu. Fortunately, when he examined them for injuries, he found them all in good physical condition, although her mother suffered from extreme exhaustion. Shep did all he could to make the older woman comfortable and let her rest in his cabin. He went on deck and stayed with the crew.

By mid-afternoon, the ships reached Edfu. Shep walked to the inn and told Merit her mother was safe and she and her family awaited her on the ship.

Merit collapsed in tears onto a chair. "Praise to Isis," she sobbed.

"Why is she crying, Father?" Babu asked.

"She's happy and relieved that everyone is all right, Babu."

The boy walked over and put his arms around her. Merit smiled and rubbed his stubby head.

When they returned to the ship, members of her family shouted her name and clapped their hands. She ran up the gangway and headed to the cabin. Her mother was

69

waiting for her outside. They embraced and wept in each other's arms.

Shep and Babu stayed on deck. They rubbed Miu's ears and she thrummed with pleasure making them smile. Shep was certain his cat didn't like so many strangers in *her* cabin.

"That's all right, Princess," he said. "Tomorrow they'll be going home."

Chapter 6

Memphis

It took two days for Merit's family to move back into their old home. First, Shep had to find another house for the current occupant to move to, and then he paid workers to clean the family home and make it ready, including a new coat of blue paint for the once expensive wooden door. Merit stayed three more days with her mother while Shep and Babu slept on the ship.

Finally, the physician and his family traveled back to Memphis—a week's journey. They arrived at dusk, Shep's favorite part of the day, when the city grew quiet and the aroma of thousands of cooking fires filled the air. Shep and Babu carried Merit's bags to the house she shared with two other widows half a mile from the physician's. Then, back home, father and son settled down for the night.

A neighbor's annoying rooster crowed Shep awake the next morning. He rolled over and opened his eyes. Miu jumped on the bed and curled up next to his face.

"Good morning, Princess. Are you glad to be home?"

"Meorrrl," She put a paw on his nose and cried again. "Miou."

Shep stood, picked her up and walked to the front room where Babu should have been sleeping.

He walked through to the kitchen and out on the porch.

"Good morning, Father," Babu said, scrubbing himself in the copper bath. "Can I still call you Father even though our adventure is over?"

"Of course, my boy. Now hurry and I'll make some toast smothered in honey." He had shown the boy how to rinse his mouth after eating, and then to use a thin strip of bamboo to clean his teeth.

While in the kitchen, he heard a loud, forceful knock at the front door. Shep's stomach tightened as he walked to open it.

"Lord Shepseskaf," a royal guardsman said. "Her highness, Princess Nebet, has summoned you. You will come with us."

Shep had had enough of their highnesses game of cat and mouse. While tempted to say no, he said, "Let me get dressed and I'll come with you. Do I need my medicines?"

"No, my Lord," the guard said.

Shep walked back to the kitchen table. "I must go, Babu. Merit will be over soon, and will prepare supper and leave it for us tonight." The boy smiled and Shep added, "Remember, this is your home now. You have everything you need in my home—*our* home. Do you understand?"

"Yes, Father. Go on, I'll be all right."

The cat brushed against Shep's legs and he picked her up. "Of course you're coming with me, Princess. Her highness will want to see you."

Resting in his arms, the semi-precious stones on Miu's collar sparkled in the sun. A carrying chair awaited and it didn't take the bearers long to deliver him to Pharaoh's palace. In an inside pocket of his robe, he carried the dagger and scabbard as well as Viper's ring.

72

Pharaoh's brother, Prince Niuserre, welcomed him to the royal apartments.

Shep started to make obeisance, but the prince stopped him.

"Join me on the veranda, Lord Physician. We'll have some wine while you tell me more about Captain Paru's report."

"Thank you, Highness. May I put Miu down?"

"Of course. Nebet will be glad to see her again."

"Meourrrr…" She walked around the prince's apartment with her tail held high, poking her nose into everything. She approached the sheer linen curtains blowing in the breeze and patted them with her soft paws. She stepped onto a zebra skin rug, climbed up onto the top of a stuffed lion's head and ran down again, extending her claws as if in battle.

Shep took a chair opposite the prince outside in the shade. He told him everything starting with the journey south and the assassination of Pashet, ending with the attack on the Island of Abu.

"Highness, here is proof that the assassin is dead and his Ka suffers in Seth's underworld." He handed the prince the dagger and scabbard as well as the ring with Viper's insignia.

His sister, Princess Nebet, entered at that moment. "I hope you threw his body to the crocodiles!"

Shep had forgotten her startling beauty She stood taller than her brother. Her figure, firm and well-rounded, stirred in him an emotion he hadn't experienced in a long while. The slant of her eyes enhanced by the silver-green of powdered malachite cunningly dusted the upper lids. Her eyes were the color of emeralds that caught the sunlight. He appreciated the sweet fragrance she wore, giving off the sensuous scent of lotus blossoms. Her light skin reminded everyone of her family's origins near Thinis, in the old Southern Kingdom.

Shep stood and bowed his head. "No, Highness, there was not much of him left. An elephant trampled him to death. But I have since learned all his men, living and dead, were thrown to Seth's scaly servants."

"Good. The balance of Maat is at rest again. Justice has been done."

Shep nodded. Belief in truth, balance, and harmony of all things was something they all held.

"He's brought proof, Nebet," the prince said. He walked over and handed the dagger and ring to her.

"You've seen his body, and you're sure he's dead?" she asked.

Shep nodded and then began to look around the room, concerned now that his cat might have wandered off.

The princess observed his behavior. "What is it? What are you looking for, my Lord?"

"Miu, Highness. My little cat. Where could she have gone?"

Nebet looked toward one of the walls. "Oh, oh. There's a secret passage into Pharaoh's rooms. We are able to enter each other's apartments more easily. Let's pray she didn't go in there."

"May I call her, Highness?"

Nebet nodded.

Shep walked over to the opening the princess showed him and called the cat's name.

A soft "merrrh," whispered back from deep inside the wall.

He called again, and the mewling became louder.

The prince laughed. "Maybe she's found a mouse."

Miu's cries stopped and she suddenly reappeared in the room again. She meowed to the princess and hurried over to her.

Nebet picked her up. "She's beautiful, and look how she's grown. How old is she?"

"Three months, my Lady."

"What's that in her mouth?" the princess asked.

"Give her to me, Highness," Shep replied. He took her. "Open up baby. Come on, put it in my hand."

Miu opened her mouth slowly and something small and shiny fell onto his palm. "What is that?" he asked.

"Let me see," Nebet said, walking over to him.

He extended his open palm to her and she picked it up.

"By the gods, it's one of the king's small gold seals. He uses it only on personal letters."

"She's a clever cat," Prince Niuserre observed.

Princess Nebet placed the seal on the table. She sat down and invited the physician to join them. "My brother and I have talked about what I am about tell you. We haven't revealed to Pharaoh that you are a physician. We told him you are a graduate of the Academy at Awen and have yet to choose your profession. Is that all right?"

"Excellent, Highness, if it will help me live a long life."

Brother and sister laughed.

The prince said, "We were sorry to learn about Merit's family being held prisoner. Captains Basa and Pamu along with their men will receive a reward for their rescue. We think five gold coins for each man and a Gold of Valor for Captains Pamu and Basa. We will also help her family move into a better home.

Shep smiled. The Gold of Valor necklace was a fitting reward. It would carry Pharaoh's name and weigh a deben of gold. "They deserve it, my friends—if I may call you friends."

Prince Niuserre stood and faced the physician. "We *are* your friends, Shep."

The physician liked the shy young man. He carried himself like a Pharaoh. His princely braid hung down on the right side of his shaved head. His large eyes and light skin linked him to his sister.

The prince walked to the railing around the veranda and looked down at the river. "We will now reward you, my Lord. We will build you a villa there, below on the river, but up high enough to avoid the annual flood. It will also have a smaller building next to it for a surgery. We will hire the architect privately and no one at the palace will know about the project."

"I cannot accept such a generous gift in all honesty," Shep said.

The prince raised his voice. "You have no say in the matter. We will speak no more about it."

"Thank you, Highness. I am your servant." Shep looked at the princess and she nodded.

"May I be permitted to ask a question, Lord Prince? There's something that's been troubling me for a long time. If Viper intended to kill your brother, the king, why did he poison *you?*"

"It was my fault," Nebet began. Her eyes darted about the room as if seeking a lost object. Walking over to the door that gave access to the veranda, she opened it and a gentle breeze filled the room. Several strands of her raven-black hair fell across her forehead and she brushed them aside. She took a moment to finger the curtains before she cleared her throat and said, "I know that Pharaoh's servants prepared a special meal for him in his apartment. I entered the secret passageway you and Miu know about, and helped myself to some of the apricot pudding for my brother. Fortunately, I was not hungry. When I saw how sick it made Niuserre, I hurried back and got rid of the rest before the

76

meal began. I told the servants it was spoiled and to throw out all the food and to prepare another meal for his majesty."

"And I will not let her forget that she nearly killed *me*, Physician," the prince said. He grinned and added, "Fortunately you came to my rescue."

Nebet frowned at him. "That is all in the past, Brother. Let us tell our friend about the festival next month."

"Yes, of course. The festival honors Bastet, goddess of cats, and you must come."

Nebet said, "You will be my escort and will bring Princess Miu."

Shep nodded. "It will be an honor, Highness."

Niuserre smiled. "That is, unless that cat of yours plans on stealing any golden baubles from the women during the evening."

Shep laughed. "Please, your Highness. She doesn't think of it as stealing. She's only doing it for me. Cats, like some dogs, retrieve things and bring them to their owners. That's all she's doing. Her only peculiarity is she happens to like shiny things."

"A thief could use a cat like her," Nebet said.

"Never, my Lady. She's not a thief, as I said."

"Very well. Now for your new villa. My brother will send you the plans in the next few days. Don't show them to anyone. Let your neighbors assume you are designing the house yourself."

"As you say, Highness. I'm forever grateful."

"Very good," Niuserre said. He stood and walked Shep to the ornate gold doors of the apartment. "For now, my brother the king does not need to know how close he came to death. He has enough to worry him. You leave us with our gratitude."

The physician picked up the cat, bowed his head respectfully, and left the royal apartment.

Shep opened his surgery in the empty house next door a few weeks later. The rent cost very little, and Merit and Babu helped get it ready. A long curtain divided one of the two rooms into two different examination areas. The other room could seat ten patients. Wood, a rare commodity, made the benches more expensive than two months' rent of the house. He, Merit and Babu whitewashed the walls. Merit painted soothing river scenes on them using dyes made from plants growing along the riverbank.

Babu helped Merit paint a sign on wood that hung above the surgery door. The hieroglyph represented a healer.

When they first returned to Memphis after their journey south, Shep sensed that Merit felt hurt by his indifference. He saw it in her eyes. He thought perhaps she had developed real feelings for him, but wasn't sure. They had never been as close as they had been on the trip, but now he didn't know if she shared his attraction. Rather than look a fool, he hid his feelings and did not encourage her in any way.

The wife of the richest banker in Memphis, a short, heavy-set woman, wearing a wig over her thinning hair, came the first day the surgery opened. Her robe, fashioned from the finest linen, was dyed deep green and embroidered with white jasmine flowers. She had sprained her ankle and would not let anyone else touch her, insisting the handsome young physician treat her personally.

He said, "Put your weight on this crutch, my Lady, and only travel by carrying chair. I have bandaged it tightly and given some powder to your maidservant to help with the pain. Take only a small spoonful with some wine. Keep the wrapping on your ankle until your visit next week."

"Thank you, Lord Shepseskaf. I will do as you say." She fluttered her eyelashes at him, and it was all he could do to keep from laughing.

Her maidservant was a wisp of a creature, so thin one could miss her if she turned sideways. She hurried to her mistress, helped her stand with the crutch and fussed around her like a bothersome gnat. With a great deal of effort, she assisted the woman into the carrying chair waiting outside the door. As the slave-bearers lifted the chair and departed, the poor little woman ran behind, trying to keep up. The dusty cloud caused by four pairs of big feet made her sneeze uncontrollably.

The surgery closed for the mid-day meal, and the three remaining patients waited outside in the shade for Shep's return. He walked next door and found an excited Merit waiting for him.

"Have you been to see it, Shep? They've started on the new surgery."

"No, Merit. I've not had time to walk over there. Does that mean the house is almost finished?"

"I think so, although the foreman didn't say. All the walls are painted, and there are two artists now decorating the front room. The house is beautiful."

Shep smiled. "Are you sure you want to move in with Babu and me? Can you put up with us every day of the week as you did on the ship? You might not like us as much."

Merit laughed. He loved the musical sound she made. He could have picked her out of a crowd of thousands. "Of course I will. I love cooking and caring for my two men."

Shep grinned. "I'll remind you of those words when we've driven you to distraction. Where is Babu, by the way? He isn't in the surgery."

"I sent him to the market to buy herbs for tonight's supper."

"Fine. I missed him. He has become very good at helping me control the patients in the waiting room. Somehow, he knows which one is the most deserving and needs immediate attention. I realize he's only eleven—at least that's how old he thinks he is—but I have to remind myself how young he is from time to time."

"He's growing too fast," Merit said. "He's a good boy and I am proud of what he has become in these few months."

"A scribe will come later today to teach him how to read and write." He paused when her eyes lit up with interest. "You can sit in on the lessons if you'd like."

"May I? Do you think I can learn? None of my family has ever learned to read."

"I'll tell the scribe you will be sitting in with the boy."

"Thank you. Now, come and eat, my once husband but now master," Merit teased.

Shep washed his hands at the basin on the porch, and took his place at the table. Merit had prepared roast chicken, steamed green beans, mashed corn and a small loaf of freshly baked bread. Holding the bread to his nose, he inhaled the wonderful aroma of it, and then smothered it with honey from the small clay jar.

As he was finishing, Babu returned from the market.

"Sit down with your father," Merit told him. "I'll dish up your food."

The boy placed the bag of herbs on the kitchen counter and hurried out to wash his hands. Joining his father, he sat opposite him, and for a moment, the two ate in silence.

With his mouth full of mashed corn, Babu said, "Watch out for old Ibi, Father. He's faking again. When your back is turned, he's able to move his arm easily and without any pain."

Shep laughed. "I know. I feel sorry for the old man. He's just lonely and comes to the waiting room to visit everyone. As long as he doesn't bother us, I don't have the heart to ask him to leave."

Merit overheard and shook her head. "You're too kind. People will take advantage of you if you let them."

When he and Babu returned to the patients, old man Ibi stopped him. "The arm, my Lord. The cast bothers me. My arm is itching something terrible."

"I'll look at it friend," Shep said. "But there are others ahead of you."

"Thank you, my Lord, I can wait."

Shep smiled when the old man sat down next to an elderly widow he had taken a liking to.

A young man stood and said, "I would like to speak to you, my Lord. I have worked in a surgery before and wonder if you need any help."

Shep nodded. "It's true. I could use you, but we can talk later when I've finished with my patients. Just wait here."

"Thank you, my Lord."

Shep called to Babu, "Bring me the next patient."

The boy frowned. "Does that mean you don't want me to help you anymore, Father? I thought you were pleased with me."

"Of course I want you to help. You are very good with my patients, but as more people start coming, we'll both need someone to help manage them."

"Oh," the boy said.

"Now go and call the next patient, please."

The boy walked over to a middle-aged man wearing an expensive-looking dark ochre-red robe. "You are next, Sir."

The tall man stood and entered the examining room. He turned, closed the privacy curtain made of rough linen, and faced the physician.

"Won't you be seated," Shep said.

The man took his place on the wooden stool facing the healer.

"What seems to be the trouble?"

"Snakes," the man replied.

"Snakes? Gods! Has one bitten you? Quick, show me where."

"Not me," the man said. "You."

"Are you feverish? What's wrong?" Shep said.

The man pulled something out of his robe and lunged at the physician.

Shep yelled for help and grabbed the man's arm to stop him. He saw Babu run out of the surgery and knew he'd run to the Medjay post a block away as he'd been told to do with any difficult patient.

"Stop!" Old Ibi shouted as he rushed into the room and hit the attacker with his cast. "Drop it!"

The attacker struck Ibi with something and he let go.

The young man seeking a job rushed in and helped subdue the man. He pulled the arm back the wrong way and the man yelled in pain and dropped something. He and Ibi fell on the man, knocking him to the floor.

Babu returned with a Medjay. The attacker struggled and tried to get up, but the large muscular policeman knocked him out and the man crumpled back onto the floor. The officer of the law was twice the size of the attacker, and he placed his foot on the man's chest to make sure he didn't move.

"Oh," Ibi wheezed and fainted.

"No one move," Shep ordered. He knelt and searched for the object that had fallen from the man's hand. He picked it up carefully. A short needle stuck out from the end of a

82

thick papyrus stalk. Liquid seeped from the tip. Shep sniffed and recognized the odor. They had studied it at the Academy. Snake venom. *"Hhh-faw,"* he said out loud. "A viper's poison."

"Babu," he called to the boy. "Take the patients outside."

"Something's wrong with Ibi, Father. He's not breathing."

"What?" Shep knelt beside the old man, checked his pulse and placed his head close to Ibi's nostrils. "By the gods! He's dead."

With those words, the patients fled from the surgery.

"Babu, go home. Young man, will you take him next door to my house? It is not safe for him here."

"Yes, my Lord."

Shep told the policeman, "Keep him here, soldier. He had a deadly poison in his hand. Stay a safe distance away. He must have used it on Old Ibi, may the god's bless his Ka."

The physician walked out the back with the poisoned instrument and threw it into the red hot coals of Merit's cooking fire.

"Thank the gods," he sighed. He walked back inside and collapsed on one of the benches in the waiting room. He shivered when he thought how close he had come to death once more.

The Medjay called Shep over. "He's not coming to, Physician. What's wrong? I didn't hit him that hard."

Shep shook the attacker, but there was no response. He lifted the closed eyelids, and leaned close to feel his breath and discovered he'd stopped breathing. He felt for the pulse in the neck and found none. Looking up at the policeman he said, "He's dead. Help me get him onto that table." When he examined the man's body closely, he found traces of white powder on his lips. "Poison," Shep said. "He must have deliberately swallowed it during the scuffle with Old Ibi. Death was almost instantaneous."

"Hmm," the policeman said. "Who was he, my Lord?"

"I have no idea. Can you call another policeman to come and help you take him to your fortress for identification?" As an afterthought he said, "Princess Nebet will be grateful." He said it in a whisper and saw the policeman's eyes light up with interest.

The Medjay hurried out to find a colleague.

Babu rushed in. "Are you all right, Father? What happened?"

"Someone didn't like me, Babu. The Medjays will take care of him. Tell the rest of the patients to return tomorrow."

"They're all gone," the boy grumbled.

When the other Medjay arrived, they picked up the body and carried it out. "You must come to the fortress with us, my Lord. Our captain will want to speak with you."

"Of course. Let me wash and I'll follow you. I know where it is."

The physician stood at the police station facing the officer in charge. The mudbrick fortress contained a small barracks for the policemen, a large excavated hole in the ground for the jail, and an interrogation room at the front. An outdoor kitchen filled the room with the rancid smell of burned onions and fried fish. Shep pinched his nose for a moment until he got used to it.

The officer in charge stood as tall as Shep, but broader in chest and shoulders, a sleek leopard in human form. His thigh-length white kilt showed stains of perspiration. A single bronze chain hung around the neck. Though polite, Shep could tell by his stiff posture, he didn't like having a nobleman there. "We can find no information on the dead man, my Lord. Who was he?"

"I have no idea, Captain. I hoped you could tell me."

"We'll try. My men tell me you are a friend of our princess Nebet."

"Yes, that is true."

The man relaxed a little. "We did find a small brand under his left arm. It looks like two lines side by side, curved back around at the ends."

"How could I have missed that?" Shep said. "Show me."

The officer led him out back where they had placed the body. Removing the worn blanket that covered him, Shep examined the brand. "It's from the old writing, I think, from the first dynasty, but it's on its side. "I don't know what it means."

"What are we to do with the body?"

"It is not for me to say, Captain. I never met the man, and he was not a patient. You might ask the priests. At the Academy we learned that many orders of priests use brands for identification."

"A good idea. Thank you my Lord."

"If you need me, Captain, you know where I am."

The officer nodded, and Shep gave the captain a copper coin. "Buy a few jars of beer for your men. I appreciated their help today."

The officer grinned and nodded to him as he left.

At home, Merit and Babu waited for him outside the front door.

"Thank the gods," Merit said. "We were so worried." She embraced him and they went inside.

Taking their places at the table, Merit said, "We thought they might keep you."

Miu jumped up onto Shep's lap and patted his chest to get his attention.

Babu laughed. "We thought it was your fault for fighting with that man."

"What happened to the young man who helped take the attacker down? Where did he go?"

Merit said, "I thanked him and told him to come back in the morning. Is that all right?"

"Yes, of course. I am grateful he was there. I'm so sorry for Ibi. We'll clean his body and take him to the House of the Dead. He tried to save me and it cost him his life."

The cat mewled sadly as if she understood. He caressed her head and ears.

"I'll tell you what happened at the fortress later," Shep said.

Merit nodded, stood and walked to the kitchen. She prepared a large river carp seasoned with leeks and a separate pot of cabbage. She added a special dish of red beans with her spicy sauce Babu loved. The adults shared a jar of wine, while the boy drank freshly squeezed tangerine juice.

Miu purred contentedly on the floor enjoying her plate of fish.

After father and son cleared the table, Shep said, "I'll walk you home. I'd feel better if Babu slept there tonight. That is, if that's all right with you. It may only be for a little while."

Merit stammered a moment. "Why. . .why yes, of course."

The boy nodded, picked up the cat and put her into her basket in the front room.

The sun had slipped behind the hills in the west, and a quarter moon appeared pale and weak. Stars sparkled like bright grains of salt sprinkled across the sky. As the small family made their way along the river, Shep told them what happened.

"But Viper's dead and so are his men," Merit insisted.

"Maybe not all, Merit. The Medjays are trying to find out more about the man, but you must admit an attack with viper's venom is more than a coincidence."

Babu took Shep's hand and stopped him. "I prayed to Mother Isis that these bad men wouldn't hurt us anymore. Didn't she hear my prayer?"

"Of course she did, Babu. You and Merit have nothing to fear. If they're after anyone, it's me, and she protected me today. That's why I wanted to walk with you back to Merit's house. I think it will be best if you stay away from my house for a while. I'll send you any news I receive."

They continued along the path until they reached her house.

"Good evening, Ladies," Shep said, greeting Aria and Rabiah, who shared the dwelling. They were sitting on the grass in front and he joined them. The house wasn't much to look at—a typical two-room house made from dried mud with palm branches for a roof. With so little rain, removing the branches allowed river breezes to pass through.

For a few quiet moments, they enjoyed the smell of the thick vegetation and fishy smell of the water. A chorus of frogs began to chant, joined by the chirping-honk of tall elegant cranes in search of particularly tasty singers.

As darkness enveloped them, Shep stood and bid them goodnight.

Babu led Shep a little distance away from the women. "Father, when you told us about the mark under the attacker's left arm, I think I know what it is."

"Do you?"

"Yes. It is one of the hieroglyphs we learned with the scribe during my first lesson."

"What is it?"

"I think it must be the glyph for the letter 'S.' Our teacher told us it is the first letter of the name of the god Seth. He rules the underworld and the darkness. The crocodiles are his servants so he must be a very bad god."

Shep ran his hand over the boy's fuzzy head. The hair had almost completely grown back. "Thank you, Babu. That is going to help us find who these people are. I knew you were very smart from the first time you carried my medicine box."

"So did I," the boy grinned. "Good night, Father. Take care of Miu."

"I will. Good night."

Walking back with only starlight to guide him, Shep thought over the events of the day, and the strange meaning of the attacker's brand of the letter 'S'. He was so preoccupied he almost stepped on a snake dashing across the path in front of him.

"Gods! I hate snakes."

Back home, he entered the empty house. Miu greeted him from her basket and he let her out. He lit a small oil lamp in the front room.

"We're on our own, princess," he said. "I'm counting on you to protect me.

Chapter 7

Lumeri

Shep dreamt a snake was chasing him. It reached out to bite him on the face. He awoke with a start and found Mui gently patting him on the cheek as she always did when she wanted something. "Ow," he groaned as he sat up; his right arm still sore from yesterday's attack. "What is it, Princess?"

"Meoawl."

He ran both hands through his hair and stretched his shoulder muscles before picking her up. "Ah, it's your water dish. I'll fill it. I'm sorry, your highness."

Miu expressed her appreciation by purring and trilling loudly.

Shep reached for a clean linen towel and walked toward the porch. Someone knocked on the front door. He walked over, but didn't open it.

"Surgery isn't open yet. Come back later," he said.

"I'm not here for treatment, my Lord," a man's voice said on the other side. "I came yesterday to find out if you needed an assistant."

Shep hesitated a moment, and then opened the door.

"Of course. Yes, and I am glad you were there. You helped save my life. Come in, come in."

As they stood facing each other, Shep estimated the young man's age as perhaps twenty summers old. The first thing he noted were the young man's eyes. They were large, their color a dark greenish brown, with specks of green that sparkled like malachite. He was as tall as Shep, had very curly black hair, and a pleasant smile.

"Good morning, my Lord. I hope this is not an imposition."

"Morning," Shep answered. "Come in and wait for me while I wash and get dressed."

"Of course, thank you. My name is Lumeri, by the way."

The physician nodded and headed back to the porch. A short time later, after washing and dressing, he put on his leather sandals and returned to his visitor in the front room. He smiled when he found the cat curled up on the man's lap, her eyes closed, purring away.

"I see Princess likes you," Shep said. "Her name is Miu but she rules like a royal." He sat on the divan opposite his visitor and studied him once more. The young man kept his hair short and his features were well-proportioned, like those of the northern sea peoples.

"Forgive me," Shep said. "Tell me your name again."

"Lumeri, my Lord. My friends call me Lou."

"I don't know how to thank you for what you did. If the assassin had struck you with his weapon, you would have joined the old man in the afterlife. I have to give you a job now as my way of thanking you."

"The gods were watching over you too, my Lord. I was glad I was there."

"Indeed." Shep paused. Miu's purring was so loud he could hear it across the room. "Have you worked for a physician before?"

"Yes. My last master practiced in Avaris, the old capital. A month ago, he died in a boating accident, so I came to Memphis with my sister."

"I see. I'm sorry for the loss of your master, may his name be remembered."

"Let it be so," the young man recited. "Lord Ahmose was a good and wise man. His patients were devastated by the news of his passing."

"Tell me your background in the healing arts," Shep said.

"I was with Lord Ahmose for ten years, my Lord. I knew absolutely nothing and owe everything I learned to him, including reading and writing and how to mix his medicines. I can set bones, sew up wounds, and many less important treatments, giving the physician more time for serious cases."

"You've learned the best way, my friend," Shep said. "Even physicians learn by doing. I'm impressed."

"Does that mean you could use me?"

"Most definitely, but I will know better after you've assisted me today, if that is your wish." Shep was pleased to see the broad smile on Lumeri's face.

The young man followed him out through the back of the house and next door into the waiting room of the surgery. They lifted old Ibi's body and Lou brought pails of water so they could wash and prepare him for burial. Shep went back to the house and returned with a clean sheet to wrap the old man in.

Several patients knocked on the surgery door, but Shep told them he had to take care of the old man first and that they would open when the sun was directly overhead. He sent Lou out to rent a small wagon and donkey. They took Ibi's remains along the riverside to the House of the Dead. It was almost mid-day when they returned.

"We'll have to grab a piece of bread and some beer before we reopen," Shep said.

As Shep and his new assistant entered the waiting room, he said, "I have an extra white tunic you can wear. You can change in that examining room." Shep walked over to his supply closet and took out the tunic and handed it to him. As he walked toward the front door, Lumeri pulled his old tunic up over his head and Shep winced when he saw scars cut deep across the young man's back. He turned, and opened the front door.

Patients entered and took a place on the long benches. Lou walked over and greeted each one, giving them a tin token of differing colors.

Shep missed Babu, but knew the boy and Merit were safer where they were.

A soft mew announced the cat's arrival. She jumped up onto a bench, and then leaped to a window sill where she stretched out in the warm sunlight. She groomed herself and used her paws to smooth out her long whiskers.

The afternoon passed quickly and as there were no more patients, Shep told Lou they would take a short break next door. Lou locked the door, turning the wooden sign on the door to the pictograph that showed a man eating at a table.

Miu followed them, rubbing against her master's ankles as he walked.

Shifting two chairs into the shade on the porch, Shep and his new friend shared some warm beer and watched two large merchant ships sail past. Children on shore jumped up and down, shouting and waving to the sailors. The sky was the light blue color of a cowbird's eggs and a lonely hawk rose in circles on spiraling hot thermals.

"I have to ask you a question if you don't mind. How did it happen?" Shep asked.

"What, my Lord?"

"The scars on your back."

"Oh, you saw." It was as if a dark shadow fell across the young man's face, and he paused before answering. "It happened before I worked for Lord Ahmose. In fact, the physician found me near death and nursed me back. My father did it. He whipped me mercilessly when I tried to stop him from abusing my sister. She's three years younger. We ran away, but my wounds were so deep a kind neighbor gave us a canoe and we escaped. I learned later I nearly died, and if my sister hadn't found Lord Ahmose, I wouldn't be here today."

"A tragic story and I'm sorry. The gods have been unkind to you but it is good to know they sent you Heka, the god of healing in the person of Lord Ahmose."

"Yes, my Lord, and I am grateful the god led me to you this day."

Shep divided a small round loaf of barley bread and they helped themselves to some goat cheese before returning to work.

The rest of the afternoon passed slowly. As Lou closed the door of the surgery a guardsman pushed it back open before he could lock it.

"We're closing," Lou said.

"Step aside. I'm on royal business."

Shep walked over and said, "What is it? What do you want?"

"I have been instructed to bring you with me, Lord Shepseskaf."

"Only if you tell me what this is about—that is, if you know."

The guard scowled. "Of *course* I know. If my Lady summoned you, that's all *you* need to know."

93

"First I must wash and change, Guardsman, and then I'll come with you. I live next door, so I'll meet you at the door."

The soldier nodded and went back outside. Lou locked the door while Shep took the small leather bag with the day's income, and carried it home.

Miu met them, uncurling and sitting up straight on a porch chair.

"We need to discuss wages and work days," Shep told his new assistant. "We can talk more in the morning, if you are willing to work."

Lou said, "Thank you, my Lord. Do you want me to stay and watch Princess while you're gone?"

"That would be kind. Make my home yours while I change." He walked into the front room and let in the guard. "I'll only be a moment," he told the man.

He put on his best robe, and changed sandals before going out the door with the palace guard. When they reached the palace, the guard led him inside but to a different location than before.

"This isn't the way, is it?" Shep asked.

The guardsman didn't respond, but walked straight ahead. He stopped at a beautifully carved cedar door decorated with golden ibis, and waited for the guard inside to open it.

Inside, a servant bowed to the physician. "Wait here, my Lord." He turned and walked into the royal apartment.

Shep looked around at the beautiful paintings on the walls depicting the life of Pharaoh. He felt a breeze and turned toward the veranda, overlooking the city.

A woman's voice spoke behind him. "Lord Shepseskaf? Welcome."

Shep turned and immediately fell to the floor in obeisance to queen Khentkaus. "Your Majesty," he said.

"You have our permission to stand, my Lord."

Shep stood and studied the woman. Pharaoh's wife was a head shorter than he, and her beautiful face needed no makeup. He liked that she didn't cover her eyes with either black kohl or green malachite powder.

"Sit here with us as we talk," she said. She took her place on a cushioned divan and indicated he should do the same on the one facing her. Soft linen curtains blew gently in the breeze and the fragrance of sweet jasmine filled the room, mixing with the scent of the cedar walls.

"I speak to you now, my Lord, without my husband's knowledge." She changed from the royal 'we' and addressed him as an equal. "It concern's the king's health."

Shep's stomach tightened. He would die if, as a physician, he treated the royals. He was too young to die.

The queen continued. "Lord Qar, the royal physician, must never learn of this conversation."

"I understand."

"Something is wrong with my husband, but Lord Qar does not know what it is. He's told me it had to be the influence of magic or demons, maybe even spirits."

"What? Surely not," Shep said. "Our understanding of the healing arts does not hold to such superstitious beliefs, Great Lady. Our Ka, that part of us that never dies, is important—it is part of our being of course, but I think Lord Qar is mistaken. We use the skills the gods have given us to heal—along with prayers and guidance from them."

"Good, I agree. I would like you to examine him. Oh, I can already see the fear in your eyes. I don't want you to think in any way the law requiring the king's physician die when he dies, applies to you. I want you to examine him as a friend of the king's brother. We will invite you here for a meal and you could evaluate his condition and tell me what to do."

"You mean the prince and princess will be there too?"

"Yes, of course. Is that a problem?"

"Oh no, Majesty. It would please me very much."

"I am glad. We will invite you to an informal supper in two days' time."

"Agreed, Great Queen."

She smiled. "We will send a chair for you."

Upon entering the house upon his return, Lou said, "Is everything all right?"

"No, I am invited to take supper with the living gods of Egypt in two days."

"But, it is a great honor, my Lord."

"Yes there will be just the five of us, including the king's brother and sister."

Lou laughed. "You say it as if you were going to a neighbor's house for the evening."

Shep smiled. "You're right. It *is* a great honor. But why do I have a gnawing pain in my stomach?"

Lou laughed. "Well, if anyone should know the symptoms of an ulcer, it should be you, my Lord."

Shep laughed. "Get out of here."

"Goodnight, my Lord. Miu and I became better acquainted. She likes to pick up and hide things doesn't she?"

"Yes, she does. Do you have very far to walk?"

"No, we live near the temple of Horus, so it isn't far."

"Good night, Lou. You may call me Shep. My friends do."

"No my Lord, not yet. For the moment, you are master. That's fine for now."

"Very well, see you in the morning."

The next two days passed without incident. Shep liked his aide and found him extremely capable and good with the patients. To be able to entrust him with those with broken arms or fingers, cuts and abrasions freed Shep to spend more time with the elderly patients, mothers-to-be and more serious illnesses. Lou also proved to be a good cook. While his meals were not as tasty as Merit's, he prepared fish and chicken to perfection.

Shep and his aide decided to walk the next day to Merit's house for a visit. They went during the mid-day break. Babu didn't take to Lou as Shep thought he might. He would have to reassure the boy that Lou was not taking his place and that he needed Babu to help with the patients.

Merit told Shep how much she missed him, which pleased him. She also liked his new assistant.

Late in the afternoon of the second day, the royal carrying chair arrived. Shep wore his new robe purchased for the occasion. It had a deep-blue border only physicians could wear, and was made of the finest linen.

Lou stayed with Miu again, and wished Shep well.

Upon Shep's arrival at the palace, the king's steward escorted him to the dining room. Princess Nebet welcomed him, as did Prince Niuserre, but their faces showed puzzled surprise.

"It is good to see you again," the prince said.

When Pharaoh and the queen entered, Shep started to make obeisance, but the king told him to stand.

"We are just friends this evening, Lord Shepseskaf. Please be at ease."

The family remained standing until his majesty took his place and motioned for them to sit down.

Shep examined the food brought by the servants, and smiled with delight. Aromatic dishes of pheasant, quail, several steamed vegetables, and many varieties of fruit, most Shep had never seen or tasted.

Princess Nebet encouraged Shep to tell their majesties about his cat, and he spoke of her as a parent does a child. Their majesties were amused when he told them the mischief she caused. Never once did Shep mention his profession.

"She reminds me of our old trouble-maker," Pharaoh Neferefre said.

Shep found the resemblance of the two brothers uncanny, although the king had a hint more blue in the irises of his eyes, and a squarer chin. His middle-age paunch was barely noticeable because he held himself in a formal position when seated.

He smiled when he told Shep about Apophis, the royal cat. "He would sit just like me when I was on the throne and turn his head back and forth as I do. It made her majesty laugh every time."

"Old Apophis brought laughter to the palace," Queen Khentkaus said. "Did he not, Nebet?"

The princess grinned. "Do you remember, Majesty, when he hid behind the throne as the Phoenician ambassador entered to present gifts to the king? Apophis jumped up onto brother's shoulder, scaring the ambassador. He thought it was a spirit. The man fell on the floor in a faint."

The king laughed long and hard. "We miss him," he said when he calmed down.

"He awaits us in our tomb, Husband," the queen said. "He is no doubt enjoying himself with Bastet and all the animal gods and goddesses."

"Even so," the king said. He held his gold cup filled with wine, but his hand began to shake and he had to put his other hand on it to steady it. Shep sighed softly. He had seen it before and knew how to treat it if the king passed a simple test, but first the king would have to permit it.

The king addressed him. "Where do you live in Memphis, my Lord?"

98

"Not far, Majesty. It is a modest home on the river. I am building a new villa and it is in fact almost finished. I didn't realize how expensive it would be when I started."

"My wife tells me you studied at Awen. Did you know old Saho? He was a terror when I studied there."

"Yes, Majesty, and he still is a holy terror. His knowledge of mathematics and physics, however, is almost god-like."

"Well spoken," the king replied. "If I had not been a prince, I am sure he would have fed me to the crocodiles."

The family laughed again, and their reaction pleased the king.

For the rest of the meal, the family talked about the prince's hunt that bagged the pheasant for the night's meal. When the king stood, the meal concluded. He walked around the table and spoke directly to his guest. "Will you bring your cat with you one day? I would like to meet her."

"Yes, Majesty. She would love that."

"I bid you all goodnight." Pharaoh smiled, held out his arm for the queen and then, followed by an entourage of servants, they left.

Princess Nebet whispered, "What were you doing here, Shep? This was unexpected."

"It is a private matter, Highness. I cannot say."

"Humph. I see, well goodnight." After she and her brother left, the steward came to lead Shep to the door. As he was about to go out, the queen appeared along with two handmaidens from a side passage and called him back.

After waving the servants away out of earshot she said, "Well? Were you able to see what might be wrong with my beloved?"

"Yes, Majesty. You need not alarm yourself. I can give a simple test to perform with ants and his majesty's water. If successful, I will know the treatment. I believe his hand is shaking, not because something is wrong in his head or brain, but there is an imbalance caused by the sweetness of dates. Does he eat a lot of cakes and pastries sweetened with them?"

"Yes of course. His sweet tooth forces him to sneak them from the kitchen."

"He must stop at once, my Lady. If he does, the organs of his body will return to Ma-at and be in balance. We call this the sweet sickness. It is serious, but it can cause tremors and the hands to shake. I'm surprised Lord Qar didn't recognize it."

The queen sat down abruptly on a chair nearby. "I am so relieved. I have heard of surgeons opening people's skulls because of the shaking, and I did not want that to be the remedy. Praise the gods."

"You are the key, Majesty. You must watch him like a falcon."

Queen Khentkaus stood, and broke the law by taking his hand. "I am grateful."

"Majesty," Shep said. His emotions didn't allow him to say anything more. He bowed his head, turned, and followed the baffled steward out of the apartment.

The next morning, Shep's surgery had a surprise visitor. Lou escorted a distinguished man into the examining room. He wanted to see the physician. Lou told Shep the man was waiting for him in the first room.

When Shep entered, the nobleman scowled at him. The man must have seen sixty summers, and his prominent hooked nose resembled the curved beak of the ibis. Shep had to look away to keep from smiling. The man's wide mouth revealed worn-down yellow teeth, and when his eyebrows drew together, his plump face contracted into a frown.

"Do you know who I am?" the man asked.

"I do not, my Lord," Shep replied.

"I am Lord Qar."

Shep had trouble swallowing and cleared his throat. "Lord Qar. Why has Pharaoh's physician chosen to honor me with a visit?"

Qar put his hands on his hips and raised his voice. "Did you, or did you not visit with their majesties last night?" He waited for an answer, but when Shep didn't give one, he added, "Don't deny it. The servants saw you."

"I don't deny it. Princess Nebet invited me. She and the prince helped me on my journey to Edfu to visit family."

Some of Qar's bluster left him. "I didn't know. Is this true?"

"Yes, my Lord. We journeyed on the *Wings of Isis*, along with the late Captain Pashet of the Guards. But, why are *you* here? If you think I wish to be physician to Pharaoh's household you are mistaken. I have never, nor would I ever desire to be in your position. I love life too much."

Shep's remark made Lord Qar smile. "Well, I loved it too. I had only experienced thirty summers when the royal family made me their physician. The job has aged me."

Shep smiled. "Then there is no misunderstanding between us?"

"Perhaps not. Does his majesty know you are also a physician?"

"No, my Lord, he does not, and I do not want him to know."

"Good," Qar said. "Then he'll not hear it from me. I'll leave you to your patients."

Shep bowed his head politely as the physician left the surgery.

Lord Qar returned to the palace and headed for the chamberlain's office.

Lord Setmena asked, "What did you find out?"

"I do not believe our young physician has any connection to Pharaoh. His sister was simply helping him travel to Edfu on a personal matter."

"I see, and you believed him?"

"Yes, my friend. He's not had enough experience to be the king's physician and he doesn't seek the post."

"Good. We can't let anyone spoil this," the chamberlain said.

"I can assure you this physician will not stand in our way."

Chapter 8

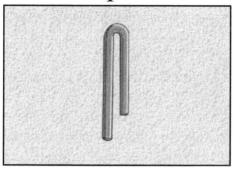

The Brand

Early in the morning two days later, Shep walked along the river to Merit's house. He found Babu lying on his blanket. The small room he shared with Merit smelled of mold and dampness. With no ceiling, the palms fronds making up the roof shifted letting in the sun. He realized how uncomfortable it must be for them.

Babu sat up and when he saw Shep couldn't stop the tears. "When can I come home, Father? I don't like it here and I miss Princess."

"It's not safe, Babu. I can't protect you at my place," Shep said.

The boy hugged him around the waist. His sobs broke the physician's heart.

"Well...maybe you could come home just for tonight, if Merit agrees. One night wouldn't be bad."

Babu smiled and wiped away his tears on his dirty arm.

"I'll come for you after work. Be ready and please wash up. You look like a sand lizard."

"I'll be ready," the boy promised.

When Shep returned home, Lou met him on the porch. He had heated water and prepared a hot herbal drink.

"I'm letting my son sleep here tonight. I think he should be safe. I've missed him."

"He's a good boy, Shep. He needs your steadying hand."

"I know Miu will be glad. She's missed him and is always curling up on the floor where he sometimes sleeps.

"You make him sleep on the floor?"

Shep frowned. "He likes to." He finished his drink, stood and stretched. "It's time to open the surgery."

By mid-morning, the waiting room had filled with patients coughing and clearing their throats. Lou left the waiting-room door open for what little fresh air the hot sun mercifully let sneak past.

Lou opened the examination room curtain and interrupted the physician. "Excuse me, Lord. The high priest of Seth is here asking for treatment."

"Put him in chamber two. I'll come right in when I've finished here."

When Shep entered the examining room, he found the priest sitting on the wooden stool.

"I'm not used to being kept waiting."

Shep scowled. "I'm not apologizing for our procedure, my Lord. All patients are equal here. I've brought you in before the other patients because you make them nervous."

As Shep turned away, the priest said, "I see now it's true what the princess said about you."

Shep turned back and looked at the round, holy man. Like other priests elevated to higher positions, he ate and drank too much and never walked anywhere. His shaved head glistened with sweat and the merciless expression in his eyes made Shep frown. The folds of flesh under his robe moved like waves on the water. He wore gold everywhere— around his neck and on his fingers and toes. "What *did* the princess say, my Lord?"

"That you were a young man who had strong convictions."

Shep smiled. "In that, she's correct. Now please tell me what's troubling you."

"It's my left shoulder. I can't use it. I've thrown it out of joint I think."

"Will you pull down your robe my Lord?"

"Of course." The priest, tried, but Shep had to help him lift his robe over his head and pull it off completely. Exposed, the dislocated bone pushed up from the man's shoulder. The priest's odor was overpowering, his undergarment indescribable. Shep handed him a sheet to wrap around his lower body and steeled himself to examine the shoulder. The man did so with obvious discomfort.

Shep said, "Now let me see." He touched the arm and tried moving it, but when he lifted it a little, the priest cried out in pain.

Shep said, "It's the swivel bone, my Lord. It's come out of the socket. I must put it right. It will be very painful, so cry out as loudly as you need to." He walked to the curtain and called for Lou to join him. The two men took hold of the shoulder.

"At the count of three," Shep said. "Ready? One—two—three!" They twisted the shoulder and arm and the priest screamed as the bone popped back into place.

"Ah, by all the gods!" the priest exclaimed. "That's it! You've done it. I can move it now."

"Not for a while, my Lord. I'll rub in some ointment to relieve the pain and you must wear a sling to keep the bone in place. No quick moves. Favor it and let people wait on you more than usual."

Lou asked, "Do you want me to prepare the ointment?"

"No, I'll do it. Carry on." Shep walked to the medicine cupboard and returned with a small clay jar. Upon opening it, a strong fragrance of cloves and the oil of coriander seeds filled the air. He gently massaged the balm into the man's shoulder. As he did, he recited a prayer. "Come Remedy. Come thou who expellest evil in this man's bones and shoulder."

As Shep massaged the skin, a mark on the man's neck behind the ear, caught his eye. Examining it more closely he discovered a brand in the shape of the letter 'S.' This one slightly resembled a shepherd's crook. A shiver ran down Shep's spine. It was the second time he had seen that symbol on a person. It couldn't be a coincidence. He wiped his hands on a cloth and handed it to Lou. "I don't believe I learned your name, Holy One."

"I am Ru-hak, a servant of Seth and his most faithful follower."

Shep didn't react, but said, "You can dress now, my Lord. I'll help you."

Before the priest left the examining room, he handed the physician a gold coin. "I am grateful, my Lord Physician. I shall recommend you to my brother priests."

Shep nodded and walked him to the door where, outside, a carrying chair awaited. His slaves had been napping but quickly jumped up and helped the priest into the conveyance.

After he had gone, Shep asked Lou to burn some incense to rid the surgery of the disgusting odor. He needed time to think. He left his assistant to handle the three or four patients left in the waiting room. As he walked back to the porch of his house, he decided the brand on the priest's neck didn't necessarily mean anything sinister. Priests of Seth probably accepted the brand when they were novices and his surgery might be the closest to their temple.

Washing his hands, he sat on the porch and waited for Lou to close up. It wasn't long before the young man brought him the leather bag of the day's receipts.

106

"Can you stay for a short time with Miu? I've decided to walk to Merit's house and pick up my son."

Lou nodded, washed his hands, and sat at the table. "This is a peaceful place, my Lord. You were wise to choose it."

"Agreed. I'll be back in no time."

The walk along the sacred river always pleased him. Clumps of papyrus growing close to shore hid all kinds of creatures. He shouted and waved to someone he knew passing in a canoe and the owner waved back. He stopped abruptly. "There it is again," he mumbled, as a black snake slithered across the path. He stomped on the ground, making it race away.

As he neared the house, Merit saw him coming and greeted him warmly.

"Where's the boy?" Shep asked.

"He's off with some of his friends. He'll be back soon enough."

"If he's out stealing and begging, I'll blister his behind."

"No, he wouldn't do that again, but he's missed your guiding hand these days."

Shep sat on the old bench outside her house. It faced the river and he loved the fragrance of Hapi's sacred waters. Lotus flowers and water hyacinth blooms added to the pungent smells he loved. Ibises walked at the water's edge looking for silver minnows and speckled frogs. There was a sudden explosion of water as a gigantic crocodile swallowed three ibises before diving back into the muddied water.

Merit screamed and ran for the house.

"Gods! What a monster," Shep exclaimed.

After they had calmed themselves, he told her about Lord Ru-hak's visit and scratched his head for a moment. "I can't figure out how these two instances involving the sons of Seth are aimed at me. I have never done anything against the temple or their followers."

Merit brought him a piece of bread. He nibbled it and threw a small piece to two brown ducks waddling by.

Babu came running to the house with two of his friends. The others were older and Shep frowned—he'd seen them before. When the two older boys looked back at the path, they ran off without a word. Shep turned his head and saw the reason. A Medjay policeman ran past, stopped, and then ran back and grabbed Babu.

Shep jumped up. "Unhand my son, officer. What has he done?"

The tall Nubian enforcer of the law looked Shep over and released his hold on the boy. "I caught the three boys stealing from one of the market stalls, my Lord. The owner is a widow and they stole her day's income."

Shep grabbed his son by the nape of the neck. "Is this true, Babu?"

The boy didn't answer and he shook him harder until the boy finally said, "Yes, it's true."

"Do you know how much money was taken?" Shep asked the Medjay.

The man shook his head.

"I'll give you all my copper coins. Let me count them." He opened the small leather purse he carried in a pocket and dropped thirty coins into the man's hand.

"That's more than enough, my Lord. Keep your boy away from those two river rats."

"Thank you, officer."

The policeman saluted and headed back to the market.

Merit grabbed one of Babu's ears and pulled him over to the bench. "You are in so much trouble, young man. Your father may not want you anymore."

Her words made the boy hang his head and his eyes filled with tears. He stood, walked over to the small willow tree at the river's edge, broke off a branch and handed it to his father.

"Beat me with it, my Lord. I deserve it."

Shep threw the whip down. "Your punishment is just beginning Babu. First, you will wash the waiting room in the surgery each day for a week. Benches, floors, everything."

The boy nodded. "Yes, Father."

Shep turned to Merit. "We'll be going now." He growled at Babu, "Go on ahead of me."

The boy walked a little way, taking his time and kicking pebbles off the path with a vengeance.

Merit said, "I'm glad you didn't whip him. We both know he had enough of that in his old life."

"I miss you, Merit," Shep said. "Not only for the cooking and the cleaning, but just having you around." He said it with affection. "I want you to know that you are more than just my housekeeper, and more than a sister." He took her by the hand and led her to a spot on the riverbank. Blue wild hyacinth flowers surrounded them. He held her close to him and looked into her eyes. "When we move into the new house, will you be my wife, Merit? I love you and would be very proud to have you join me in marriage." He smiled when her eyes glistened with the beginning of tears.

"You are a nobleman, my Lord. Will people accept me as your wife?"

"The general, the prince and princess do already, Merit. I want us to make it official before the gods and authorities."

"Then I accept, my Lord, and I will try to be the best wife for you and mother to your son."

He embraced her then they kissed with passion. It was something he had wanted to do ever since they sailed together to Edfu. "You have made me very happy, my Lady.

I'm the luckiest man in Memphis because you are also the best cook in town."

"Well, some wise woman once said, 'The way to a man's heart is through. . .'" and she didn't finish.

Shep had already walked a short distance, but he turned and shouted, ". . .through his liver!"

"Oh you!" She turned and walked back to the small bench and sat down. Laughing, she shouted after him…"His liver! Only you would say that!"

Miu was so happy to see Babu she pranced all around him. He picked her up and she thrummed, sounding like a very large bumblebee.

Lou was sitting on the back porch and had promised to show the boy how to play *Maahes,* the game of war. The numbered cards would also help Babu learn his glyphs.

"I have a proposal, Lou, but you may not like it," Shep said. "As you know, I'm moving into my new house soon and I wonder if you and your sister would like to move in here. There would be no rent to pay because I own this house, and you could save some money."

Lou couldn't speak. He put his cards down on the table and paused to control his emotions. "It's too generous, my Lord. We don't deserve it. I'll have to think about it."

"Why not bring your sister with you tomorrow?"

"I don't know. I don't want to be obligated to anyone."

"I understand, but it is only a suggestion," Shep said.

The cat meowed and walked over to her food dish. "Meowrr."

"All right, Princess. We're hungry too," Lou said. He and Babu made preparations to broil some chicken and to roast three ears of corn. The kitchen soon filled with the pleasant aroma, but also with their animated discussion and laughter. Shep was glad to have part of his family back.

Before the sun kissed the western hills, Lou and Babu finished their card game. It was dusk when Lou said good night.

The next morning, when his assistant introduced his sister, Shep smiled at the attractive young woman. She stood as tall as Lou, and her eyes shone brownish-blue like her brother's. Her pleasant face was perfectly proportioned and she kept her raven-black hair tied up with a blue ribbon.

"My Lord, this is Nailah, my sister."

Nailah bowed her head to him. "I am honored to meet my brother's master. He has told me of your generous offer."

"I am pleased to meet someone as beautiful as Isis herself. My home is yours today. I'm glad you could come." He turned to go but then added, "During our mid-day meal break, let's walk over to the new house."

He turned to Babu. "You must go and bring Merit back with you."

"Will I have my own room?" the boy asked.

"We'll see," his father answered. "Only if you behave."

Nailah said, "What a beautiful cat." She sat on one of the chairs in the front room. Miu approached her and jumped up onto her lap.

"That's Princess," the boy said. "Her real name is Ta-Miu."

As Nailah petted the cat, Miu turned and looked up at the young woman's face, then patted her on the cheek.

"Oh," Nailah said. "She patted me with her paw."

"That means she likes you," Lou said.

"Well, Princess. It looks like we're going to get along."

Shep said, "You stay here, Babu, and show Nailah the house. We must open the surgery." His son's countenance fell. "I still need you to come and help me in the surgery after the break, Son."

The boy's face brightened. "Yes, Father."

When the patients entered the waiting room, Shep discovered a man with a swollen jaw. After the physician washed up, he and Lou put on their medical tunics. Shep mumbled to his assistant, "I dislike dental cases. The mouth is too small a part of the human body. I can never get my fingers inside it to be much help."

After examining the man's decayed tooth there was nothing he could do but pull it. He gave the man enough beer to make him drunk, and Lou helped hold the man down while Shep yanked it out.

As the sun reached its highest point, they put the Closed sign on the door and went back home. Merit was helping Nailah in the kitchen. There were freshly baked rolls on the table and Nailah carried in a chicken stew and set it down.

"This smells and looks delicious, Nailah," Shep said. "I can't wait to taste it."

She smiled. "The proof is in the eating, my Lord." And when they tasted it, they bragged on her cooking skills.

"She'll make someone a wonderful wife," Merit said. "Not only beautiful, but a great cook. Come, sit before things get cold."

When they finished, they locked up and walked the short distance to the new house.

Shep smiled when he saw the completed villa. Beautifully designed, he was pleased it had been built at least ten feet above the river level. The architect used white limestone for the foundation and floor. An outside stairway ascended on the side wall, leading to a patio on the flat roof. The wooden scaffolding was gone, enabling Shep and his friends to appreciate the beautiful lines of the building.

"It's amazing," Lou said. "It's fit for a prince."

Nailah said. "They've even carved Ibises and ducks into the borders around the top. Can you see them?"

Shep frowned. "I could never have afforded such an embellishment. Now, let's look inside."

The foreman of the construction crew saw the physician approaching and came out to greet him.

"We've almost finished everything, my Lord. Immutef, the architect, came by this morning and said he would speak with you at your old house."

"Very good. First we'd like to examine the new surgery."

"Yes, my Lord, it is this way." He led them along the walk through a formal garden that would separate Shep's home from his workplace. They climbed three steps to the front door. Inside, a large waiting room displayed pleasant river scenes on the walls. Separate examination rooms were ready, and the tiled pharmacy provided storage and tables for mixing a variety of chemicals and herbs. The rooms smelled of plaster, paint and overall cleanliness, and the ceramic tile floors exuded the essence of coconut oil polish.

Lou said, "This has been well-planned, my Lord."

The two men walked from place to place, pleased with what they found.

The small group returned to the main house where Shep showed them the three bedrooms, one of which was to be Babu's, and then the kitchen and large salon.

"Where's Miu's room?" the boy asked.

"Ha! *Every* room is hers, young man," his father said. "This house will be her kingdom. You know that as well as I." He moved toward the door but when he didn't see Merit, he walked over to her room.

"All this space for me," she said. "I can't believe it, and look at the ceiling. They've painted stars above where my bed will be. It's beautiful. She rubbed her hand along the wooden door and her eyes glistened with emotion. "It's better than the ship."

Shep smiled. "Of course I was hoping you'd share *my* room." It pleased him when she blushed. He took her hand, "We need to head back." He thanked the foreman and said, "We'll let all the workers know when to return for the feast of blessing for our new home."

The foreman grinned. "Remember, lots of beer, Lord Physician."

As they walked back, Babu asked, "When *will* we move, Father?"

"In a week, my Son."

"I can hardly wait. Will Merit come to live with us then?

"Yes. We are going to be married."

"Hurrah!" the boy exclaimed. "Not only a father, but a real new mother."

Shep said, "I'm going to ask the local garrison if I can hire guards to protect us day and night. There's a small building at the back of the villa, behind the garden, where they can lodge."

When they reached the old house, Lord Immutef awaited them on the back porch.

"My Lord architect, the drawings you showed me only a month ago, have become a magnificent villa. We've just been there and marveled at its beauty."

"I'm pleased, my Lord," the nobleman said. "We've begun the decorative wall around the property. It should be finished in five days and will provide the security you wanted."

"That means Princess can run all around and explore, Father," Babu exclaimed.

"Princess?" The architect asked.

"Yes, my friend. Here she is." He picked up Miu and Immutef laughed.

Lou reopened the surgery for the afternoon patients, while Shep took the architect aside and spoke softly. "I don't know how to repay the Prince for my new home. It must have cost a fortune."

"He told me he is glad to do it. As for me, well, I now have a new model to show the people of Memphis what I am capable of doing."

Shep said, "Let us pray Hapi, the river god, will not allow his creation to overflow." The architect didn't know how to take the remark until Shep's grin put him at ease.

"I think people will say my design is too unconventional," Immutef said.

"To each his own," Shep said. "Or, as Merit says, 'There is a lid for every pot.'"

The two men laughed, and the architect took his leave.

When Shep entered the surgery, Lou said, "This was attached to the surgery door." He handed Shep a card, on which the letter 'S' had been written.

"By the gods, not again!" Shep exclaimed.

Chapter 9

Akhom

On a hot clear day a week later, one of the royal guards entered the surgery and motioned for Shep to follow him next door to the back portico.

"Have you seen this, my Lord?" the guard asked. He handed Shep a copy of the card found at the surgery.

"Yes, and I have the mate to it." He handed the guard his card. "What is going on, Captain?"

"This morning, his highness the Prince, found it on his food tray. None of the servants know how it got there." The two men stood silent for a moment. "He wants to meet you, but not at the palace. He commands that you join him on the marsh where he loves to hunt. I'll send someone to collect you at first light in two days. He will come with two horses. Can you ride?

"I think I can manage this time," Shep said.

The officer grinned and left through the front door of the house.

Shep returned to the surgery and told Lou what the guard wanted.

"I didn't know you were a hunter."

"I'm not, but the prince wants to meet with me during his hunt."

"When will you go?"

"The day after tomorrow, at first light."

The next morning, the physician left Lou to handle the morning's patients. "I'm going to the military camp and won't be back until midday."

At army headquarters, he asked to see his friend, General Akhom. An officer went to inquire if the general was available. He returned and motioned to Shep. "Follow me, my Lord."

Shep followed through a maze of corridors until they reached their destination. The officer opened the door and admitted the physician.

"Shep, it's a delight to see you again." Akhom extended his arms in military fashion and Shep grabbed them in the military greeting.

"May we speak privately somewhere, General?"

"Of course, let's go outside."

He led the physician out through the back of the barracks into a private garden. "I like to come here to think," Akhom said. He and his guest sat on short brick benches. "Now tell me why you've come."

"I need information and a few of your men, my Lord."

"Information?"

"Yes." He handed the officer one of the Seth cards.

"It's the letter 'S.'"

"Yes, General. Prince Niuserre and I each received one yesterday. I thought it was the mark of Seth or the preferred religion of Lower Egypt. Their high priest came to me with a dislocated shoulder. When I set it for him, I discovered this same brand on the back of his neck, below his right ear."

"By Seth's entrails!"

Shep said, "I'm meeting his highness on one of his hunts tomorrow morning. Could you invite yourself to come along? The prince trusts you."

"If he'll allow it. In the meantime, I'll have my men find out about this symbol. I'm glad you came to me. This could be a threat to the royal family, but I don't know why you are included. We know that Seth is the god of darkness and confusion. We must keep clear heads."

"Thank you for helping, General."

"Now you also asked about a few of my men?"

"Would it be possible for me to pay four or five soldiers to guard my house day and night? With all these strange messages, and the attempt on my life, I'm afraid for Merit and the boy."

"What do you mean an attempt on your life, Shep? Tell me what happened."

The physician told him about the attack with viper venom.

As Akhom listened, his face grew dark with anger. "And what was done about this?"

"I left it in the hand of the Medjays, General. I knew they would report to the palace if there was anything to fear. It might have just been a crazy person carrying out some kind of vendetta."

"No, these Seth messages are related," Akhom said.

They stood. Akhom walked to the door, turned and spoke again. "I was sorry to learn of the loss of Captain Pashet. He was a good warrior. You and the army did well at Abu. What a horrible experience. The princess told me about it. Such a cruel loss of life. Viper deserved what the elephants did to him—a crushing end was too good for him."

"Agreed. I will tell you more about it tomorrow on the hunt."

"Until tomorrow then.

"In the king's name," Shep added.

118

Akhom saluted and repeated the oath.

Prince Niuserre and the archers of his hunting party crouched down in the marsh grass as still as statues. The morning mist had not yet burned away, and the smell of rotted plants and hippo dung wafted around them.

"Easy…" the prince hissed.

Thirty feet ahead, three gazelles grazed on the wiry grass in the shade of a large scrub palm.

Barely breathing, the prince whispered, "On my signal."

With arrows nocked, and their bowstrings stretched back as far as they could go, the five men waited.

"Now," Prince Niuserre said.

Arrows flew faster than the wind, but the antelopes heard their release. They leapt straight into the air and ran as soon as their hooves struck the wet ground. Only one managed to escape, the other two fell onto the grass, mortally wounded. Two of the archers ran forward and ended the animals' lives with a sweep of their knives.

"Well done, Highness," the men shouted.

"Good shooting, everyone," the prince said. He wiped the sweat from his brow with the back of his hand. He drank long and hard from the water skin one of his men handed him. He wore only his kilt and linen menes head-covering against the rays of the sun, the same as the other archers wore, except gold and silver thread trimmed Niuserre's.

Two men cut staves and tied the antelopes' legs to them for the hike back to the prince's ship.

"Hurry, Highness," one of the archers shouted. "There's a whole flock of wild geese on the water near here."

Niuserre scowled. The gods didn't approve shooting waterfowl when they were resting on the water. They had to be in flight. He hurried after his men and they crept slowly toward a small inlet carved out by the river. A flock of wild black and white geese sat calmly grooming themselves.

"Get ready," Niuserre whispered. He waited until the archers were ready and shouted, "Release!"

The noise sent the geese flying and the prince and his archers loosed arrow after arrow into the dark cloud of feathers rising higher and higher.

"Where's the canoe?" the prince shouted. "Hurry men."

Two warriors jumped into it and headed for the downed geese. They returned with it filled to overflowing. Ravenous crocodiles swallowed the rest still floating on the surface.

"Excellent," the prince told his men. "Back to the ship and let's break open the beer."

His men cheered, and began the walk through the marsh grass to the vessel anchored a half mile away.

"Where's Kebu?" one of the men shouted.

Another said, "He's probably stuck in that mud we had to cross."

The prince sent five of his archers back to find the missing warrior. He and the others continued on to the ship. He pulled off his menes covering and used it to wipe his shaved head. His princely braid hung limply on the right, dripping with sweat. Upon reaching the ship, he removed his kilt and sat on a wooden bench on deck as his servants poured buckets of river water over him.

"Ah!" he exclaimed. "That's more like it." The young man was still in his prime, having lived thirty-two summers. His thin and muscular body was unlike Pharaoh's, his more corpulent brother.

He stood to allow his servants to dry him with towels, and then headed towards the royal cabin.

The party of five returned carrying Kebu on their shoulders. He was dead. "It was an assassin's arrow, Highness. It had none of our markings. He must have gotten in the way."

Prince Niuserre nodded. "Wash him and prepare him in the hold. We will see he receives a proper burial."

Accidents happened and while regretting their comrade's demise, the men did as the prince commanded. Afterward, they carried the geese into the hold, washed the gazelles and left them to dry in the sun. Pharaoh would be pleased to enjoy the game at the royal table.

General Akhom and Shep stood next to each other near the large rudder oars. They had witnessed the prince's successful hunt, but stayed out of Niuserre's way. Each wore a kilt and linen head covering, appropriate attire for the marsh heat and humidity.

Akhom, while in his early fifties, was still fit. With his firm, well-defined chest, his arms were those of a man twenty years younger. Lean, in spite of his age, his warrior eyes remained keen, and didn't miss a thing.

"Are you not going to hunt, physician?" Akhom asked.

"I have a different prey in mind, General. I want to bag the prince so I can talk to him."

Akhom smiled. "Well, first, you need to sit down, my friend. You're sweating a lot. Drink some water." He handed Shep the water skin he carried slung over his shoulder.

The physician lifted it above his head and drank for a good while. "Thank you, friend."

"Go easy, son. It's going to be a long day."

121

"I'm afraid you're right." Then Shep grinned. "Maybe we could tell his men not to find so much game."

Akhom chuckled. "I wouldn't want to try."

The prince exited his cabin and headed in their direction. "Come on, General. You haven't had a chance yet. And what about you, Shep? Don't you like to hunt?"

Shep bowed his head politely. "I'm usually at the other end of the hunt, Highness. I sew up the hunters who have not been treated very kindly by their prey."

His answer made the prince laugh. "I had not thought of that part of it. Well, General, come on, give it a try."

Akhom nodded to his friend and shrugged his shoulders.

When the ship's crew learned that Shep was a physician, they came to him with cut fingers, torn blisters, thorns in the feet and other minor injuries suffered in the marsh.

The air hung hot and still. At the sun's zenith, the prince returned with the general who proudly showed the physician two more antelopes and scores of ducks and geese.

"We nearly got run down by an angry hippo," Akhom said. "I'd forgotten how fast those fat water horses can run."

"Why did you get so close to them to begin with?" Shep asked.

Akhom looked around him and said quietly, "His highness wanted to get closer. He'll know better the next time."

Shep laughed, and offered the general some water.

"You missed a great hunt, Shep," the naked prince shouted, walking along the deck toward him. His servants threw water over him again to cool him off, and to wash away the mud.

"It looks like you bagged a lot more fowl, Highness. The king's table will be eating geese for weeks on end."

The prince said, "No, I am afraid not. My brother will share them with his advisors and friends. They will not last very long. Let me change, and then we can share a light mid-day meal."

"Thank you, Highness," Akhom replied.

When the prince headed for his cabin, Shep said, "He's certainly in a good mood. Is he always this energetic?"

A short time later, the prince called them to his cabin. Dressed now in a fresh kilt and a dry headpiece, Shep marveled at this menes, made of gold threads. It could pay a soldiers wages for a year.

"I like to eat out in the fresh air, if you have no objections, gentlemen," Niuserre said.

"Excellent," Shep said. "That's why we've come, Highness—to enjoy the blessings of the gods in nature."

"Well spoken," Niuserre said. "Although I am sure the general has told you that we came too close to one of Hapi's creatures in the marsh."

"He was probably just protecting his harem, my Lord," Shep said.

The prince guffawed. "His harem—an interesting way to describe them, physician. But I believe you are right."

He clapped his hands, and servants brought grilled fish and goose to their table. Seated in front of the cabin, the diners benefited from the sailcloth awning the crew put up for the prince. Servants held jars of beer until he motioned from them to fill their cups.

The crew ate the same food, savoring every bite. They finished before the prince, and to pass the time began to sing songs of the hunt, and share bawdy stories of their female conquests.

"I am ready to head back to Memphis," the prince said. "But now let us talk about the mysterious marks you have discovered. Tell me about the recent attack."

Shep said, "The most recent attack happened right here, Highness." He showed the prince a small rolled up piece of papyrus. "This was on the arrow that killed Kebu, your archer."

"Gods!" the prince shouted. "It is the sign of Seth!"

"Yes, my Lord," Shep said. "They are connected to Viper, I'm sure of it. A few days ago, a patient entered my surgery and had a concealed needle covered with viper venom. He tried to stab me, but I grabbed him and called for help. My assistant and an old man held him down until a Medjay could subdue him. During the fight, he managed to swallow a poison and died. We found the letter 'S' branded on his armpit."

Akhom asked, "Do all of Seth's priests carry such a brand?"

"I don't know, General, but I have a bad feeling about this. I've seen the hidden mark on the bodies of some of the priests. I fear you've uncovered a long-dead subversive group—followers of my disgraced uncle, Pharaoh Djedefre."

"Djedefre? God's preserve us," Akhom said.

The prince shook his head and his expression changed. "Our ancestors will not be pleased, brothers. They fought for a united Kemet, and unified the Upper and Lower Kingdoms, which has remained to this day."

Niuserre wiped his forehead. "These are men who have sworn a sacred oath to keep alive the memory of Djedefre. I must tell my brother. He must stop them before they destroy the kingdom."

Chapter 10

The Villa

Packing for the move to the new house continued the whole week. Shep, Merit and the boy loaded their belongings into the wagon that would take them the short distance.

Lou and Nailah brought a few things each day to the old house. They were excited to make it their own.

The cat didn't like the upheaval. She mewled a lot.

Shep tried to reassure her. "You'll be all right, Princess, once we're in the new house. It is so much larger, you'll have more places to play and hunt."

"Meowrr." Miu jumped down from his lap and walked over to a small shelf on the wall near the window. Merit had placed a towel there every day and Miu had taken her long naps curled up on it.

"Meowll."

"What is it?" Shep stood, walked over and picked up the small cloth. Little objects fell out of it and he stooped down and picked them up. "What are you hiding? A copper coin, a silver clip from my surgery. What else is in here?" He felt around and pulled out a small gold earring. "This belongs to old mother Kamas. She said she lost it in the waiting room. You're a very bad cat. I'll give it back to her tomorrow."

"Meouff." Miu walked over and jumped up onto the chair.

Shep picked her up and sat her on his lap. She purred and turned around to face him.

"Oh no, tapping on my face won't do. None of your feline charms."

"Mrrrooww?"

"All right, I'll put your shiny things in a small box and take them to the new house. You can have a good time hiding them over there."

Miu pushed her head into his stomach affectionately and lay down.

He really wanted her to pat his cheek, but she ignored him.

That night, he gave Merit his bed so she'd be ready to go with the wagon in the morning. Shep and Babu slept in the salon, and Shep smiled. He had a sense of having done this before.

In the morning, when the wagon didn't arrive, Merit prepared scrambled eggs for everyone. Lou and Nailah arrived pushing a small cart carrying the last of their belongings.

Shep and his family helped them unload everything onto the porch, and then sat down and waited for their wagon. With the surgery closed for the day, Shep used the time to check over the packing of his medicines and substances for the new surgery.

"It's here," Babu shouted. For the rest of the day they made several trips to move everything to the villa.

"We'll each have a bed tonight," Babu said. He clapped his hands with excitement and ran through every room. The next instant, he rushed back. "There are soldiers outside, Father."

Shep walked out on the large porch and found four royal guards below in the garden. He walked down the steps to greet them.

The men stood at attention and the oldest looking guard said, "Where should we set up our post, my Lord? I'm Maya, and these sons of jackals are Pentu, Setka and Yuf."

"Are you their sergeant, Maya?"

"Yes, I regret to say. I'm stuck with this sorry lot."

The other guards shifted uneasily and looked away.

"Well Sergeant, they'd better be able to protect my family, or General Akhom will hear of it."

"Yes, Sir, I understand," Maya said.

"The stone building at the back was meant for a gardener, but could serve you. If not, we'll build a proper guardhouse."

He led the men through the soon to be planted flower garden. The guards went inside the small house and came back out grinning. "This is perfect, my Lord," the sergeant said. "There is even a small place to cook."

"Good. Settle in and come up to the house later. We'll talk about why you're here."

"Very good," Maya said, saluting with his fist to his chest.

Shep and his family spent the rest of the day putting everything in its place.

Miu ran from one room to the next, uncertain where to claim her spot. Her long tail waving above her like an army banner poised to stake a victory.

During a break on the back veranda, Babu said, "I can't find Miu, Father. I've looked everywhere. Would she go back to the old house?"

"Are you sure you've looked everywhere?"

"Yes, Father."

"Not everywhere, Son. She hasn't moved in a long time. Come, I'll show you." He led the boy down the steps and around to the back garden and pointed. "There she is."

Babu laughed and ran over to the garden pool. Miu sat on the low stone border around the water, her back straight, two front paws together, tail unmoving. She looked like a princess on her throne. Only her eyes moved back and forth, following a golden fish swimming first left and then right.

"Miu! What are you doing?" The boy sat down beside the cat and petted her head.

"Meowwww."

"She sounds sad," Babu said.

Shep stood behind his son. "She wants that fish but hasn't learned how to catch it yet."

"I can catch it for her, Father."

"No, no, Son. I think princess has found the perfect place to amuse herself. Let her enjoy it."

That evening, the family ate supper in the new house with Lou and Nailah their first guests. When they finished, they moved up to the rooftop veranda. Comfortable chairs placed to face the river allowed them to enjoy the coolness of dusk. River traffic slowed for the night and canoes flitted in between the feluccas like small water-strider bugs. Songbirds serenaded them as the god of the sun slipped below the sandy hills in the west—his yellow-orange luminescence bathing the river in molten gold.

"I'm going to like this place," Shep said.

Merit smiled. "We'll need another housekeeper. I can't possibly clean a house this size. It's beautiful, but it's going to need servants."

"All in good time, Merit. I've thought about it too. As my future wife, you'll select the housekeeper, and whoever else you may need."

"Me?"

128

"Yes, who better to know what is required? We'll also need a steward who, for example, would meet us up here with lighted lamps and guide us down the stairs."

Lou said, "He must be a man you trust completely, my friend."

"Of course."

Lou and Nailah said goodnight and walked back to their new home.

Merit lit the lamps and placed one in each bed chamber.

Tired from the day's activities, Shep and Merit barely made it into their separate chambers before falling asleep.

The morning sun awakened Shep and he sat up in bed and yawned. Standing, he stretched and heard water splashing. To his surprise, Merit had already placed his copper bathtub on the tiled bathing floor. Decorative tiled walls provided privacy.

"Your bath is ready." She handed him his sponge and small clay jar of scented ash and clay soap.

Miu walked by and rubbed against his shins, her way of saying good morning.

After his ablutions, Shep dressed and ate his morning meal of eggs, fresh bread and melon. He smiled, inhaling the clean air, certain it was cooler than at his former house.

He walked to the door and opened it. As he stepped out, he looked down and gasped. On the polished limestone tile someone had scrawled the letter 'S' in blood.

"Sergeant," Shep yelled at the top of his lungs.

Maya and his men came running up the steps. "My Lord?"

Shep pointed to the floor.

"By the gods!" Maya bent down and put his finger in the blood, touched it to his tongue and frowned. "How'd anyone get in here?"

"My question exactly. You are here to protect my family. I'd say you've failed miserably." He examined the floor once more. "But why write the letter in blood?"

"It's not blood, Sir. It's pomegranate. It just looks like blood."

Shep walked back inside. He was so angry he began to pace back and forth in the front room, clenching his fists. Eventually, he called the sergeant inside.

"I must report this to General Akhom. You've allowed a breach in security. The intruders could have been assassins—and you didn't stop them."

Maya shook his head. "Allow me to speak, my Lord."

Shep nodded.

"I have no defense. The men and I were awake all night. We took turns patrolling the grounds. I don't know how they got in. I'm ashamed and angry. You must send us back."

Shep shook his head. "For the moment, I want you to find how they got in. You're dismissed." He didn't look at the man but heard him slap his fist to his chest before leaving the room.

Merit brought a pail and rag and washed off the writing in front of the door. Miu sniffed around her, interested in whatever the woman was doing.

With the surgery closed for the day, Shep wanted to make sure everything was ready for tomorrow's opening.

"Do you want to come with me, Princess?" Shep said.

She mewed and approached him, rubbing against his ankles, purring her loudest.

He picked her up and headed across the garden to the surgery. Inside, he put her down and greeted his assistant, already hard at work.

"I placed your physician's sign on the wall outside the front gate, Shep," the young man said. "I didn't know where you wanted it."

"Excellent. You picked the perfect spot. By the way, I'm pleased you've started calling me Shep. It almost sounds like we're friends."

"Friends," Lou said.

Shep turned his head when he heard a slight rattling of jars in the medicine room. "What are you getting into, Miu?" Both men walked over and laughed as they found the cat burrowing into a basket of small clay containers. Only her tail stuck out, waving back and forth like a venomous cobra charming its prey.

It took most of the day to arrange everything as Shep wanted, but late in the afternoon, they had a visitor.

General Akhom entered the waiting room. "So, Lord Physician, is everything ready for tomorrow?" He walked around as if inspecting his troops, running his fingers along the counters looking for dust, but then he nodded. The room passed his critical evaluation.

"I believe we are ready, General," Shep said.

Lou bowed his head politely to the commander of Pharaoh's armies.

Shep said, "We were about to leave. Would you like to break open a jar on the veranda?"

"Delighted," Akhom replied.

"I'll see you in the morning," Lou said. He nodded to the general once more and left.

"He seems like a good lad," Akhom said.

"And a fast learner, General. I am fortunate to have him."

The two men followed the stone path through the garden and then climbed the steps to the veranda. The sun had buried its head in the clouds, and the hot humid air cooled a little. They relaxed on chairs facing the river.

Merit arrived with two jars of beer. "I saw you men heading this way."

"When are you going to marry this man, Merit? Some other woman is going to bag him," the general teased.

She smiled. "I may capture him sooner than you think, General. But not until we find someone to help me with this big house." Bowing her head to the old warrior, she went back downstairs.

"Shep, I have just the woman you might need," Akhom said. "She's the daughter of my own housekeeper. Her name is Kema and she has welcomed only twenty summers. She's served with her mother for two years, but wants to learn how to help in a surgery. When she is not working in your house, maybe she could help you. Whatever she might learn would help her find a good husband, my friend."

"It is entirely up to Merit, General. I told her she could choose the woman for the house."

Akhom smiled. "Good, then I'll speak to her when we go down."

"Won't you stay for supper old friend?"

"Thank you, but my wife's mother is visiting and I must be at home. You'll find out about mothers-in-law someday." A guardsman entered the garden and the general asked, "Now tell me about my men. How are they doing?"

"They deserve a severe punishment, General."

"Why? What's happened?"

Shep told him about the writing on the pavement in front of his door.

"By Seth's foul stench! I'll have their heads for this."

132

"That is for you to decide, my Lord. But first I ordered them to find out how it was done in order to make the villa more secure."

"Very well. But I want a full report before I have their heads."

"Promise me you won't do anything until I give it to you, my friend."

"Agreed. But I'm troubled because I failed you." He stood and Shep walked with him down the steps to the front door. Merit came to bid Akhom farewell and he told her about Kema. She asked him to send the young woman in the morning.

Shep said, "Good night, General. Take our greetings to your wife."

"May the gods grant you peace." Akhom opened the door and left.

That evening, after supper, the family relaxed in the back garden by the pool. Miu pranced over and jumped up on Shep's lap. She purred loudly, moving her jaw back and forth.

"What's in your mouth, Princess?" Shep asked.

The cat raised her head toward the sky, then bowed down and spit out something small onto his kilt.

"What is it? A piece of that fish you've been trying to catch?" Shep asked.

"Merrrowll."

"All right, just a moment." He used his kilt to dry off the object. "What have we here?"

Babu walked over and knelt beside his father and picked up the shiny object. "It's a bead, Father. I've seen thousands of them at the market. People string them in their hair. Everyone wears them."

"Where did she find it? It couldn't have been in the garden unless one of the workmen wore it."

Merit said, "She was fussing around me while I cleaned up that pomegranate mess at the front door this morning. She must have found it there."

"Then the person who made the sign dropped it," Shep said. "But it's so common we'll never match it to anyone."

"You're right," Merit said. "Let her put it in her treasure bed."

Shep placed the bead on his knee and Miu sniffed it, picked it up with her mouth, jumped off his lap and hurried up the steps to the main floor.

When Babu went to bed, Shep and Merit sat on the front porch and admired the fireflies along the river, their yellow-green lights outshining the stars.

"These two days have been wonderful," she said. "Work begins again tomorrow."

"Yes, but this time you'll be nearby every day. I'll like that. I'll go to the temple at the end of the week to arrange our marriage."

She reached across and took his hand. "You have made me so happy, Shep. To become your wife and to live in this beautiful home is beyond my dreams."

He walked her to her room and as they said goodnight, he kissed her and felt a strong desire pulling him to stay. After embracing, he closed the door, and walked to his own room. "Good night, my love," he whispered.

The first day in the new surgery went well. Physician and patients adjusted easily to the pleasant environment. Halfway through the morning, a messenger from Pharaoh arrived causing great excitement among the patients.

Lou hurried to Shep's examination room and told him a royal servant was at the door.

Shep washed his hands and went to see what he wanted.

The servant of the king bowed his head. "My Lord, his majesty orders your presence tomorrow for the mid-day meal. You are to bring along the Princess."

Shep smiled. The king meant Miu of course. "Assure his majesty she and I will obey."

The messenger nodded, bowed again and left.

Lou said, "Such an honor, my friend. You are invited by the living god and son of Horus to his palace to share bread with him."

Shep's eyes lit up. "And to think that none of it would be possible without Miu, a little cat I found dying in the river."

For the physician, the rest of the day was a blur. All he could think about was going to the palace. When he told Merit about the invitation, she was excited for him and began to fuss over what robe he would wear and reminded him to shave, and not just his chin.

Shep walked to the small pool and petted the cat on her head. "We're going to the palace, Miu, all thanks to you."

Miu ignored him. She sat still, her eyes moving back and forth as if attempting to hypnotize the gold fish to leap into her mouth.

The next day, when the royal carrying chair arrived, he made it wait while he put the special wide collar on his cat. Its semi-precious stones caught the light. He picked her up and put her in her traveling basket. He knew she didn't like the confinement, but she eventually laid down and closed her eyes.

At the palace, Pharaoh's steward met him and offered to carry the basket, but he refused. He decided to bring the cat in it because he remembered how many long corridors there were for her to get lost in.

"Stop!" a voice ordered the steward.

A finely dressed nobleman approached them. "Who is this?"

The steward said, "This is Lord Shepseskaf, Lord Chamberlain, the king's guest."

The older man walked around the physician with a scowl. He made Shep open the basket and then waved his hand. "Pass on."

As they continued toward the royal apartments, Shep asked, "Who was that?"

"Lord Setmena, the Lord Chamberlain. He's only concerned for the king's safety. We try to stay away from him."

Upon reaching the king's apartment, a guard opened the door and admitted them. Shep put the traveling basket down, took out Miu and held her in his arms.

"Lord Shepseskaf," a female voice said.

It was queen Khentkaus and Shep was so surprised, he dropped the cat and fell to the floor in obeisance.

She motioned for him to stand. "Is this your princess?"

"Majesty, this is Miu."

The cat mewed as the queen petted her gently on the head. Then she picked her up and held her in her arms. Gold embroidery on her long pleated white gown sparkled in the light. Green malachite eye-shadow brought out the beauty of her dark brown eyes, perfect compliments to a pleasant face. Her delicate slender fingers stroked the cat's neck.

Shep panicked, unsure of Miu's reaction, but the cat continued to purr and squeaked out a small "meow."

At that moment, Pharaoh appeared. "Ah, you have arrived."

The king had entered through the narrow passage between apartments, which connected with his brother's.

The physician fell on the floor and held his palms toward the king.

Pharaoh Neferefre said, "Please stand, my friend. This is an informal meeting. Where is—aha! There she is." He walked over to his wife and patted Miu gently on the head.

The cat mewed and Pharaoh took her from the queen's arms. Surprisingly, Miu continued purring. "Come, my Lord. Join us at the table." The king put the cat down and seated himself. The queen sat next to him and invited Shep to sit across from them.

"Will it be all right if Princess walks around, Majesty?"

"I smile when you say that, Shep. I think you are speaking about my sister. Of course, your cat will be fine."

The servants entered and served them a wonderful mid-day meal of baked fish, leeks, bread, goat cheese and fruit. Afterward, the queen excused herself so the men could speak privately.

A shadowy figure moved along the narrow corridor between the royal apartments. It stopped and listened to the king and his guest. A cat moved toward the intruder who kicked it and scared it away. The king and guest were discussing something and the unseen figure waited patiently. A sudden noise startled the shadow, forcing it back into the darkness.

A servant entered and interrupted the king and his guest. "Majesty, forgive me, but the physician's cat has fallen into a small crate in the kitchen and we are unable to get it out. Perhaps if he could come and call it, it might come to him."

"Silence, Sahura. Do not interrupt." Pharaoh turned back to the physician and saw concern on Shep's face. "Oh, very well, go to your princess, my friend. I will drink some wine while you rescue her. We will have plenty of time to continue our discussion."

Shep felt his face turn red. "I was afraid of this, Majesty. I'll return as quickly as I can."

The shadow in the passage heard the servant and guest leave the dining room. It edged closer to the opening and observed the king sip his wine. Something caught the king's attention and he turned his head. "Princess. There you are. How did you get out of the kitchen so fast?"

Pharaoh picked up the cat and the shadow moved forward and plunged a dagger deep into the king's back.

Pharaoh didn't cry out, but fell forward onto the carpet, dropping the cat. It hissed at the intruder and ran into the safety of the dark corridor.

The assassin checked to make sure the dagger had penetrated deep enough to kill the king, and then ran into the passage, disappearing into one of the many corridors of the palace.

Chapter 11

Arrest

When Shep and the servant reached the kitchen, the servant left him and hurried out the back door.

"Where...?" Shep said, but the man had gone. "I've come to find my cat."

The cooks looked at him puzzled and shook their heads. "There's no cat here, my Lord. You are mistaken."

Something was wrong and he ran back to the king's apartment. He heard a woman crying out in anguish, and when he reached the dining room, found the queen on the floor holding the bloodied body of her husband.

"Guards! There he is!" she shouted. "Arrest him! Help!"

Several guards rushed in followed by the chamberlain. "What's happened?" When he discovered Pharaoh on the floor and the queen covered in blood, he shouted, "By the gods! His Majesty! Guards help pick up the king, and call for the physician."

The chamberlain drew one of the men's swords and pointed it at Shep. "Arrest the assassin!"

"No, my Lord. I wasn't here," Shep explained.

139

The Queen stood, her robe covered with her husband's blood. "He *was* here, Lord Chamberlain. I left him alone with the king. There was no one else."

More guards rushed into the room. "Seize him," Setmena ordered. "Take him to his majesty's prison."

"Great Lady," Shep cried out to the queen. "You know I couldn't do this. Please."

The guards grabbed him and tied his hands with leather strips. He couldn't believe what was happening. Several of the men struck him and one blow to the head was so hard he nearly lost consciousness.

When they reached the prison, a guard tore off Shep's tunic and left him in his kilt. They shoved him into a cell with several other prisoners. It was so dark he shuffled his way inside, bumped into a small wooden box and sat down. He rubbed his wounds and felt his right eye begin to swell. Touching his ribs, he was certain several were cracked.

In the darkness, he whispered, "Horus, help me."

Several prisoners overheard and began to laugh. "Horus can't help you in here, friend. This is the last step on the way to the underworld."

Princess Nebet couldn't fall asleep. After the tragedy of the king's murder and with their friend the physician named assassin, she didn't know what to think. Guards now stood watch at her and her brother's apartments. Her brother, Niuserre, was now Pharaoh and everything would change. She put on a sheer linen gown and went to her sitting room. She chose a chair in a cool spot near the veranda where a gentle breeze made the curtains undulate as if in a dance.

The moon god, Lah, provided the only light in her room. In the distance, a dog barked and she thought she heard a cat mewling. They stopped and she turned her head to enjoy the silver moonlight sparkling on the river.

"There it is again," she whispered. "It *is* a cat." She stood and walked toward her door, but the sound wasn't as strong. Walking toward the dining room, the sound grew louder. "It's coming from the passage." Near the entrance, she nearly tripped over Shep's carrying basket. The meowing resumed, and she bent down and looked inside.

"Princess. Poor baby." She picked up the basket and carried it into her front room. Placing it on a small table, she moved her chair closer and opened the lid. After a long spell, Miu jumped out of the basket and raced out of the room.

Shep's first night in prison was worse than he could ever have imagined. The stench from buckets of human waste was sickening. He ran over in his mind the events that brought him to this place and realized he had simply been in the wrong place at the wrong time.

When his three cell mates learned of his crime, they avoided him, talking about him as if he wasn't there.

"He'll be cut to pieces, that's for sure," one said.

"He should have killed himself first, before he was captured. He doesn't stand a chance."

Shep knew there would be no mercy. For someone to have laid a hand on the king meant they had also defamed the gods. He shivered in the cold cell and he needed some water. It was the first such deprivation he ever had to face, but he worried more about his family. The loved ones of murderers faced the same punishment as the accused.

Footsteps approached the cell, and the bright light from a torch made the prisoners cover their eyes.

"Shep," someone called to him.

"I'm here." He had trouble making out who was standing near the bars and moved toward the voice.

"I come from General Akhom. Do not despair. He is working on your behalf." That's all the man said. Shep assumed the man must have been a soldier and that was how he had been able to force the guards to allow him to see the prisoner. His only fear now was that Akhom might be too late.

In the palace, guards surrounded the royal apartments. Their captain had fallen on his own sword upon learning of the king's murder.

Princess Nebet awoke and found Miu sitting at the foot of her bed staring at her.

A familiar voice called, "Are you awake?"

Miu jumped down and disappeared.

It was Nebet's sister-in-law, the queen. "Yes, Majesty. Just a moment. I am not yet dressed." She hurriedly pulled on a short robe and went to open the door. She bowed and admitted Khentkaus. "Come in, Sister. I share your sorrow. You look exhausted."

The queen sat on the edge of Nebet's bed. "I can not believe he's gone, and by the hand of that man." She wore a plain robe and her face bore traces of her tears.

"You mean Shepseskaf?"

"Yes. We should never have invited him here in the first place. It was *your* doing."

Nebet shook her head. "If he had not come, my Lady, Niuserre would have died. Shep is one of the finest physicians in Egypt. He could not have done this horrible thing."

"A physician? You never said. He never told us."

"No, because he did not want to become the royal physician and die when Pharaoh dies."

"But he was the only one in the room with my husband, Nebet."

"I understand, Sister, but there has to be another explanation."

"I do not want to think about it anymore. May I sleep in here? Our bed holds too many memories. Besides, Niuserre is Pharaoh now and must choose a new queen."

"Rest here, Majesty. I will come in and check on you." She walked over and pulled the curtains, darkening the room. She quickly glanced around and wondered where the cat had gone. "Probably in the secret passage," she mumbled to herself.

Merit was beside herself when Shep didn't come home. She sensed something was wrong and mentioned it to Lou when he arrived early for work.

"They may have wanted him to stay overnight," he said. "Supper may have ended late. He probably didn't want to disturb you when he came in."

"I pray you are right." She went into the kitchen and prepared Babu's morning meal.

Merit knew Lou would be anxious when he opened the surgery. It would be only the second time on his own. A short time later, he walked back through the garden to the house.

"What should I do, Merit? The patients are becoming anxious."

"Have you treated any of them?"

"Yes, of course. Most of them."

"Well, tell those who must see Shep that he will be in later. I pray the gods it will be so."

143

At mid-morning, she became alarmed when a group of soldiers arrived with general Akhom.

"What is it?" Merit asked. "What's happened? Is it Shep?"

The general nodded. "Let's go inside and I'll share what I know."

Merit called Babu and told him to go help Lou in the surgery.

Inside she said, "Oh gods. Has he been killed?"

"No, not yet."

"What? Not yet? I don't understand, General."

"Pharaoh has been murdered, Merit—may his name be remembered. Shep is in prison accused of killing him."

"Horus! No. It can't be." Tears filled her eyes and she wept into her hands.

The general stood quietly and waited for her to calm down. "He's not dead yet, Merit, and won't be if I can help it."

"What can you do, my Lord?"

"Well, Niuserre is now Pharaoh, and he knows Shep saved his life, remember?"

"Yes, of course."

"I may be able to convince him to intercede on Shep's behalf."

"Intercede with whom? What are you not telling me?"

"It's the chamberlain, Lord Setmena. He's the one we need to worry about. His name alone tells us he belongs to the followers of Seth. Why Neferefre chose to make him chamberlain is hard to understand."

"What can be done?"

"Plenty. I'll insist on an audience with Pharaoh. It's the widowed queen now who is against Shep. She swears he alone was in the dining room with Pharaoh when he was killed."

"Oh no."

"I've also brought two brigades of men with me. They will surround the house for your protection. When word spreads that Pharaoh is dead and that Shep is the killer, crowds could attack the villa. You must leave. They'll go with you to the ship that will take you to Avaris in the north. Lou grew up there and he'll know where to hide you."

"Thank you, General," she whispered between sobs. She stood and walked around the front room. Tears filled her eyes again but she wiped them away with her apron. "I'm sorry. It's that we just moved into this beautiful place and were going to be married."

"Have courage, Merit. We pray this won't be for long. Gather what you and the boy will need. I'll go tell Lou to close the surgery and to bring his sister. There is a wagon here to carry you to the ship."

Shortly after, Babu climbed onto the wagon. "Where's Miu? We can't leave her."

"We don't have time, son," Akhom said. "She must be lost in the palace. I'm sorry."

The boy pouted but sat next to the soldier who would drive the wagon.

Lou and Nailah climbed in with only a leather bag between them, followed by Merit.

Akhom said, "I'll send a detail of archers with you, Lou." He gave the young man a small leather purse filled with coins. "My men are good hunters, so you'll eat well."

The wagon left the villa and Merit waved to the general as it followed the road down to the port. "Horus, protect Shep and our house," she whispered.

Shep fell asleep exhausted. When someone threw cold water on him and the other prisoners, he awoke with a start.

The gate to their cell was unlocked and a guard entered. He pushed the other three men out and into another cell. Alone, Shep felt even more vulnerable.

"Water," he asked.

"Water? I just gave you water," the guard said, cackling with laughter. "You have a visitor. Stand up."

The cell-door opened and an army officer came inside. He stood near the physician and waited for the jailor to leave. Leaning closer, he spoke in a whisper.

"Listen carefully, my Lord. Your family and friends are on a ship headed for Avaris. Lord Akhom sent a brigade of soldiers with them. There are also two companies around your house to protect it."

Shep knew the man probably couldn't see the relief on his face.

"We're breaking you out tonight, so keep up your strength. You're going to Akhom's villa and will be safe there."

"Praise the gods," Shep whispered. Tears filled his eyes, but he wiped them away. "Tell the general I will never forget this. I will be ready."

"Take courage, my friend. We'll come for you in the middle of the night." The officer tapped on the gate, and the jailer let him out.

The palace was in mourning. The family withdrew from the court to await the dreaded seventy day embalming period of their loved one. Everyone spoke in quiet tones. Custom required the silencing of laughter and singing. The dead Pharaoh's servants shaved their heads and went about collecting Neferefre's personal things for his tomb.

Princess Nebet sent her servants to find Shep's cat. They returned several hours later with Miu in her basket.

"Meow," Miu wailed. Her purr had vanished.

"You miss him, do you not, Miu? I'm sorry, but your master is not coming back."

The cat yowled and tried to get out of what was now her prison.

"No, no. You have to stay in there, Little One. We cannot have you wandering around. We will leave here and go to our river villa where you will be happy."

"Meorrrr."

At that moment, the new Pharaoh entered the living room.

Nebet bowed to him. "Majesty, my sorrow for our brother is unbearable. We loved him—may his name be remembered."

"Even so," Niuserre recited. "I did not want to become Pharaoh this way, Nebet. No one would. His tomb is not finished because neither of us thought it would be needed so soon."

"The sadness in the palace is too much for me, Brother. I want to go to our summer house by the river with your permission."

"Granted. You need not ask."

Miu meowed and scratched at her basket.

"Ah, Shep's cat. What will you do with it?"

"She is a princess, remember, Brother. She should stay with us royals."

"I cannot believe Shep killed our brother. He was kind to me. I will not accept it. Lord Setmena has become obsessed with the man's execution."

"I have never trusted that evil man, Serry," she said, using his nickname. "He is rude and unkind. I hope you do not keep him on as chamberlain."

Pharaoh leaned over and kissed his sister on the cheek. "Leave him to me. And Sister, there will be guards around us now at all times. I am sorry, but I gave the order for our protection."

"Thank you, Majesty." She bowed her head courteously as he left her room.

After she told her servants to pack what she would need for her move to the river house, she walked out into the palace garden and set the basket down next to the small reflecting pool.

Below, in Pharaoh's prison, rats skittered through Shep's cell. They had to be coming in from somewhere, but without light, it was impossible to tell. Dug into the ground below the palace, ground water seeped through the bricks making them slimy and mold covered, He groaned when he tried to turn—his sore ribs painful reminders that he needed medical attention. His right eye had swollen shut and he hoped his legs could still carry him. He had lost all sense of time, but it had to be the early hours of the morning.

The lock on the gate creaked as a key turned. "My Lord," a voice whispered. "Hurry."

"I need your hand," Shep whispered back. "I can't see."

A man took his arm and led him out. "There are steps ahead, be careful."

Shep groaned again with pain and stumbled. It was lighter up ahead, the steps just visible. He and his rescuer stepped over the unconscious guards. Once outside, he inhaled great gulps of clean cool air.

"It's a shame the guards found that cache of drugged beer," the man said. "Here's your horse, my Lord."

"I am unable to get up," Shep said. "I fear my ribs are broken."

"Put your foot in my hands and I'll push you up."

Shep managed to sit in the saddle and hung onto the horse's mane as it followed the soldiers up ahead.

The animals galloped off and Shep held on for dear life. He had never been to Akhom's house, but hoped that's where they were going. The road ascended a long hill until it reached a group of houses at the summit. A gate opened, admitting them into a garden.

"Praise the gods you're alive," Akhom's deep voice greeted them.

The soldier who rescued Shep helped him dismount, and the general embraced the physician.

Shep cried out in pain. "I'm sorry, General. Setmena gave me something to remember him by. I was certain he was going to kill me."

"Seth's buttocks! I'll give him something." Akhom gestured rudely with his fist. "Now, shall I send for the healer, my son?"

"Yes. Unfortunately, this physician is unable to heal himself."

"Come inside and rest."

"Yes, but permit me to bathe first and wash away the smell and filth of my cell."

"Of course, I wasn't thinking. Follow me."

After Shep's luxurious warm bath, Akhom brought him a clean tunic. "I've sent a servant to bring old Benipe. He's still our family healer."

"Thank you, my Lord. If he's able to put me back together again, I'd like to sleep for a week. I've learned you've saved my family. May Horus add fifty summers to your life."

Akhom laughed. "And may the gods keep your loved ones safe until you can join them. Right now, however, we must deal with Setmena. I wouldn't be surprised if he was behind our beloved Neferefre's death—may his name be remembered.

"Let it be so," Shep recited.

In a room reserved for the king's chamberlain, Lord Setmena was throwing a tantrum. "How is it possible? I want every jailer thrown into the river. Seth will be pleased to embrace them in his jaws."

The aide said, "We now believe it was the army who broke him out, my Lord."

"Do we have proof?"

"No, but one of the guards recognized the soldier who came to visit the prisoner yesterday. He was First Army."

"Listen to me, Tebu. I have no doubt Akhom helped the physician escape. I need proof that I can take to Pharaoh."

"Yes, my Lord."

Setmena finally sat down. His shaved head enhanced his sinister profile. Eyes narrowed like a cobra's completed his threatening, reptilian persona. "I don't understand," he said. "Why did the assassin kill the king without consulting me? And who is he? Where did he come from? I fear we have a renegade assassin using Seth's name. It's a sacrilege."

He put his fingertips together. "A servant told me the king's sister has left the palace. Find out why."

Chapter 12

The Pyramid

Darkness shrouded Shep's new villa as if it too was in mourning. Several days had passed since Pharaoh's murder when the royal princess entered the beautiful home. Princess Nebet carried Miu with her in hopes of calming her down. The cat gave her no peace at Pharaoh's summer house, and so they journeyed to the new villa that afternoon. She put the basket down and opened the lid. Miu jumped out and walked defiantly around *her* house.

Sitting in the front room with only a small lamp, Nebet's eyes followed a few small canoes passing by with flickering oil lamps onboard. Abruptly, a door opened, causing her to jump up with fear.

"Shep! By the gods, and General Akhom."

"Good evening, Highness," Shep said, bowing his head. "Please forgive me for a moment."

Because of the cumbersome bandage binding his ribs, Akhom helped Shep sit on a chair. Miu ran to him mewling and nudging him to death. Her happy cries even made General Akhom smile.

Shep picked up the cat and with great effort stood facing Nebet. He measured his words carefully. He couldn't be sure if she would turn him in.

"I'm grateful you've brought Miu, Highness."

"She would have died I think, my friend. She would not eat or sleep, so one of my servants said I should take her home."

Shep nodded. "A wise servant, and I'm in your debt, again." He noticed the worried expression on her face. "Please believe me, Princess. I did *not* kill your brother. I was in the kitchen at the other end of the palace. A servant deliberately took me away from his majesty so the unknown assassin could kill him."

"Pharaoh and I know you could not have done it, Shep. You are a healer, not a murderer." She paused before asking a question. "Who helped you escape from prison?"

"I'm not at liberty to say, Highness. It was a good friend."

"I see. And you do not think I know this good friend who helped you is in command of thousands of soldiers?" She grinned looking directly at Akhom.

"I admit to nothing, Highness," Akhom said. "It is for the chamberlain to make such an accusation."

"Beware, my friends," she said. "Setmena has become very powerful, but you are not in danger from my brother or me, General. We are in fact grateful to know the First Army supports us."

"We do, my Lady. We swear the same allegiance to your brother we gave Neferefre—may his name be remembered."

"Let it be so," Shep and the princess recited.

Nebet turned to Akhom. "General, my brother and I wish to visit the necropolis at Abusir and supervise the completion of Neferefre's pyramid. The architect cannot give us an exact time the work will end. Will you come with us, for our protection?"

Shep interrupted. "General, they must not go. The assassin could strike again."

Akhom nodded. "He's right, my Lady. Allow me to make a suggestion and you can present it to his majesty. I will go first to make sure it is safe for you and Pharaoh to follow."

Nebet stood and walked around the room. She stopped and said, "I will so advise my brother."

"The Army can protect you best, my friends," Akhom said. "We have garrisons everywhere. The Guards do not. At the tombs of Abusir, there is a garrison already in place to serve your Highness."

"I will remind him," Nebet said. "Not that he ever listens to me."

Shep smiled.

She returned his smile. "You must leave Memphis. The chamberlain's men are everywhere. They may even know you are here."

"I doubt that, Highness," Akhom said. "We came in the dark and will leave under its cover. Shep's life is now in your hands, Princess. We beg you not to turn him in."

"Friends, please. I have only returned to this house to bring a cat home. That is all." She stopped and looked around. "Where is she, by the way?"

Shep laughed. "I know, follow me."

Sitting at her favorite spot under the full moon, Miu meowed at the solitary gold fish swimming back and forth in the garden pool.

"She loves this spot," Shep said. "I would think it would depress her, not being able to catch that fish, but she sits there for the longest time." He turned toward Nebet. "I am relieved that you believe I didn't kill your brother."

"I never will believe it." She bent down and spoke to the cat. "Goodbye, little sister. We princesses must take care of each other. Farewell for now."

She stood. "I wish you well Physician, and pray the gods go with you."

"And with you, my Lady."

She reached out and put her hand on his arm.

Receiving a kind of shock at her touch, he rubbed his arm after she left. He couldn't understand the strange attraction he felt. He sat down. When he lifted Miu onto his lap she meowed and growled at the same time.

Akhom said he would walk with Nebet to make sure her bearers were ready.

A short time later, when Akhom joined him at the pool, he asked, "Will you go with us to Abusir? You were with the soldiers who found and killed those Seth followers at Abu. If they are there, you can help me find them."

"I'm worried about Merit and Babu, General. I would go with you if you could assure my family's safety."

"A brigade of my best warriors is with them and I received a message by pigeon that they are safe and have found a place to stay."

Shep said, "I am grateful, now what about my cat?"

"Seth's foul stench, Shep! You'd think she's your child."

"I know, and it's unreasonable, but I feel responsible for her. I'll take the carrying basket. She'll not be in our way."

"It will be light soon. We need to board the ship before Ra brightens the sky."

"Good. Let's pray that Shu, god of the air, will give our sails the blessing of a steady wind."

The *Breath of Horus* sailed majestically around a bend in the river. Her large rectangular canvas filled with the breeze. Long colorful banners trailed behind like the decorative feathers of a pheasant. The pyramids of Abusir rose from the desert plain—stone mountain reminders of the reigns of many past Pharaohs.

"They're so much smaller than those of the Giza plateau," Shep said. "I've never been here before, but some of the crew told me that King Neferirkare's of the fourth dynasty is the tallest."

Akhom nodded. "Yes, it is. The smaller ones began as step pyramids, and later more blocks were added to make them true pyramids."

Rows of soldiers lined up on the dock to meet the ship. As Akhom stepped off the gangway, they snapped to attention, fists across their chests.

A young officer walked forward and saluted. "We are ready for your inspection, General."

Akhom saluted. "Your name, Captain?"

"I am Rimes, General."

"Captain Rimes, take us to the new tomb. I will inspect your men later. We'll sleep on the ship, but will take our meals with you."

"Very good, Sir."

"This is Sinuhe," Akhom added, introducing Shep. "A good friend."

"My Lord Sinuhe," Rimes said. "We are pleased you are here."

Shep nodded and Miu nestled on his arm. Her eyes shone like yellow sapphires in the bright sunlight, giving her a mysterious look that often frightened people.

"The tomb isn't far, General. Would you care to walk or do you prefer a horse?"

"We will walk, Captain. You may tell us about the tomb on the way." He turned and ordered his own company of warriors to disembark and form up behind him.

Rimes did an about face and ordered his men to divide into ranks of four behind the general's men.

"Is the tomb completed, Captain?" Akhom asked.

"Almost. There are only fifty days left until Pharaoh's body leaves the House of the Dead and his sarcophagus arrives. But I am not certain the workers will finish on time."

Shep had served in the House of the Dead at Awen. It was the most horrible experience of his life. While he learned a great deal about anatomy, it took him months to rid his skin of the smell of death.

Shep asked, "Why haven't they finished?"

Captain Rimes fidgeted. "There aren't enough workers, my Lord. Even if you could find more, there is too much left to do."

Shep ran his hand over his hair. "General, can Pharaoh's body be kept in Memphis until the tomb is finished?"

"Yes, it's been done before, many times. But there is a great risk that thieves will get into his gathered treasure. Most of it is already here."

"I see," Shep said. "Is the architect on site?"

The captain nodded. "Pharaoh built a house for him in the village next to the causeway."

The general walked beside the officer while Shep followed behind. He couldn't keep his eyes off the new pyramid rising in the distance. The design placed it at a lower angle than the great stone monuments of Giza. King Neferefre's tomb stood perhaps half a mile from the other two pyramids. It was impressive in size and beauty. Its smooth limestone blocks reflected the sun and one had to look away from the reflected brightness. As they came

156

closer, the temple to honor Horus stood completed, its columns beautifully painted in the colors of papyrus stalks greeting the sun.

"Ah," Rimes said. "Here's the architect now, my Lord General."

A nobleman in a dark red robe stood on the stone steps leading to the causeway. The long stone structure led directly from the river to the tomb. A slave held a canopy umbrella over the man's head.

Rimes said, "General, this is Lord Binra, Chief Architect."

The man bowed politely. "We are honored, General. Would you care to rest before visiting the tomb?"

"Thank you, my Lord, but we have been charged to see how your work is progressing. Lead on."

The architect bowed to Akhom, turned, and walked a few paces ahead of the visitors.

They stopped at the entrance. The size of the pyramid overwhelmed Shep. He strained his neck to find the pyramidion topping it off. The architect led them through the entrance soon to be sealed forever. The slave with the umbrella waited outside.

"Merrow." Miu's eyes grew big as she examined everything. Shep smiled as she sniffed and tucked herself in closer to her master's body.

"It'll take a moment for your lungs to become accustomed to the pressure inside, General," Binra said. "When you think of how much stone is above us, you can begin to sense it."

Shep reached out and touched the smooth wall of the passage. "Such precision." He smelled the limestone mixed with paint and the dust made him sneeze. They continued on a good distance before entering one of the inner chambers.

Miu stuck her neck out and sniffed at the freshly painted images. "Meow."

157

Shep laughed because she was sniffing the image of the cat goddess Bastet. "How could you know that is a cat, you little monkey?"

They entered a treasure chamber protected by a metal gate. Shep and the general followed Captain Rimes inside.

"There's so much gold," Shep said.

Binra smiled. "These sacred objects are for another life, my Lord, and there are more treasures yet to be brought inside. Most of the *ushabtis*—you know, the statues of servants for the afterlife—are not yet in place. The canopic vessels with Pharaoh's vital organs will be brought with his sarcophagus."

"I'm having trouble making sense of the texts on the walls," Shep said.

"That's because the artists have taken the words from the scrolls of the Book of the Dead," Lord Binra explained.

"Ah, now I understand. They are magic spells. We studied them at the Academy."

"Meoowrl." The cat's voice sounded sad.

Shep petted her to reassure her.

"Here we are," Binra said. "We are entering the queen and king's chambers. Only the decorations have been finished. No one could have known the king would die so soon—may his name be remembered."

"Let it be so," the men responded.

Akhom growled at them. "He didn't die, my Lord. He was murdered in cold blood."

"Of course, General. I meant no disrespect."

"None was given, I'm sure," Shep said.

"Thank you," Binra mumbled. "You know that these chambers must be purified by the priests of Horus. It is they who decide where every object is placed."

Akhom said, "Certainly. It is a beautiful ceremony to watch as they prepare the way for the king's Ka to fly to the heavens. I was honored to take part in great Khufu's ceremony."

Magnificent bas reliefs adorned the walls of the king's chamber. They included depictions of him with members of his family, and others placed him on the hunt or in battle. Vivid hues of red and blue appeared to leap from the surface, while the greens and blues of the sacred river made one want to reach out and touch the cool water.

As the visitors walked around the chamber, Binra asked Shep, "What is your profession my Lord?"

"I am a teacher," Shep said. "I've studied the sciences at the Academy at Awen, and enjoy sharing my knowledge with others."

"A worthy life," the architect said. "I admire those who can teach."

Akhom interrupted. "I'm ready for you to lead us out now. I find tombs a bit overwhelming."

"This way, Gentlemen. Follow the paintings."

Miu's meow made Shep smile. She actually sounded happy.

Later, when they reached the architect's home, Lord Binra offered refreshment and an invitation to return for the evening meal. A servant brought them beer and wine. His guests chose beer.

"You can let your beautiful cat down, Lord Sinuhe. I don't have a dog and all the snakes have been frightened away by our construction."

Shep put Miu down. She purred as she sniffed around the rooms.

"I must warn you, my Lord. If you've left any shiny things on the floor, she loves to collect them."

Lord Bina laughed. "She won't find anything, my Lord. Don't worry."

When they finished their drinks, Akhom suggested he and Shep return to the ship.

Shep made kissing noises to call Miu and she came running.

"Yeowl." She stood against his legs and allowed him to pick her up.

Before Shep and Akhom left, they assured the architect they would return that evening.

At the barracks, Rimes told them the villagers were preparing food for the general's company of warriors. "They're always pleased to meet travelers from Memphis. They'll have plenty of broiled fish and beer and will eat well."

"My men will be pleased, Captain. We are grateful," Akhom said.

Shep knew Miu was happy on the warm wooden floor, because she curled up and fell asleep.

"We will be sharing bread with Lord Binra," Shep told him.

The captain frowned. "You'll eat well, Lord Sinuhe. He buys only the finest meat and vegetables—of course he can afford them."

"What's wrong," Shep asked. "I sense there is something you're not telling us."

"I don't want any trouble. I'd better not say."

"What is it, Soldier? Out with it," Akhom ordered.

"Well, Sir, Binra's mysterious. Strange people hang around his place. He always says they're priests, but if so, they're unlike any priests I've ever met."

"Strange in what way, Captain?" Shep asked.

"They meet only at night and the workmen say they have been sneaking into the unfinished tomb to conduct religious ceremonies inside. I've confronted him about it, but he denies it. He says the workers were probably drunk."

Shep looked at Akhom and they both nodded.

Akhom said, "I must return to the ship and make sure everything's ready for tomorrow. First thing in the morning I will inspect your men, Captain."

"Thank you, General. The men will be pleased. I wish you both a good evening."

Shep stooped down, picked up his sleepy cat and he and the general returned to the ship. He put Miu in the cabin and sat on deck next to the general.

"It sounds like a cult of Seth to me," Akhom said. "Horus curse them."

"I hope we're mistaken my friend. What can we do about it?"

"Nothing, until we know for sure. We will keep our eyes and ears open tonight at the architect's house. Maybe they'll let something slip and reveal themselves."

After washing with pails of water on deck, they changed into clean kilts and Shep added a thin tunic over his. "Come along, Princess." He didn't want to leave her alone on board and she was familiar with the architect's house.

A soldier carried a lighted torch ahead of them. Screeching bats overhead serenaded them with their high-pitched cries. A chorus of deep bass frogs sang from the papyrus along the river.

The architect met them at the front door. "Welcome, friends."

"Ah," Shep said. "We are in for a treat. That aroma of broiled fish and leeks makes my mouth water."

"You are welcome to my table, my Lords."

Shep put his cat down and she lay on the soft cotton rug. She purred as he placed a few morsels of fish on a tin saucer.

The beautiful melodies of a harp emanated from a corner of the room. The musician, a young girl, probably from the village, transported them to quieter times and places.

Shep became alarmed when he looked around for Miu but couldn't find her. He stood and said, "Excuse me, my Lord. It seems my cat has wandered off. I'll go look for her."

Outside, he circled the house with one of Binra's men carrying a torch.

"Can you see her?" Shep asked.

"No, my Lord. It may have followed the ramp up into the tomb."

"I don't think so. She doesn't like dark places, even if she is a cat."

"Wait. Listen," the soldier whispered.

"I can't hear anything." Shep tried, but only made out the chirping of crickets and other insects.

"There it is again, Sir."

This time Shep could hear the faint mewling of a cat. "It's her. Come on."

The soldier rushed up the ramp with the torch and waited for Shep to catch up. "I can hear it, my Lord."

"The cat's a she, young man, not an 'it.' Now lead on."

The inside of the tomb was as black as ebony and the flame of the torch could only illuminate a small section of it.

"The sound is up ahead, Sir. I can hear her."

"Go on. She sounds frightened." Miu wouldn't have come this far into the tomb on her own. Someone must have carried her.

"Over here, my Lord," the soldier said.

The thud of the torch falling to the limestone floor echoed throughout the tomb, and when Shep bent down to pick it up, found the soldier gone.

"Hey," Shep shouted.

The sharp claws of his cat climbed his legs, then up onto his shoulder. She hissed and wailed, and he turned to leave the tomb.

"Gods," he cried out, as severe pain struck his back and made him drop the torch. Everything went black as he fell forward onto the limestone floor.

Chapter 13

Avaris

General Akhom carried Shep out of the pyramid in his arms. Out of breath, he shouted, "I need help."

His men came running and he ordered, "Carry him carefully, men. Get him back to the ship."

"Rimes, send your fastest rider to the village and bring the army's physician. Hurry."

The general felt helpless. Moments before, he'd gone looking for his friend and saw a faint light in the long corridor of the tomb and ran inside. He'd picked up his friend and carried him outside. Shep's cat was wailing and wouldn't let him touch her.

After making certain his men carried his friend to the ship, Akhom went back inside and knelt down near the terrified animal. He held out his hand for a few moments. She sniffed him and let him pick her up. She trembled so violently he had to put both hands over her to calm her. Using a wet cloth, he wiped Shep's blood from her paws.

Upon reaching the ship, Akhom said, "Lay him on the table in his cabin." He lifted the lid on the cat's basket and put her inside.

"Where's that healer?" he yelled, the frustration in his voice clearly evident.

Approaching hoof beats brought Akhom back out on deck. Captain Rimes, reined in his horse. A middle-aged man sat behind him. Both men jumped down, raced up the gangway, and followed the general into the cabin.

Rimes said, "The army's physician is here, Sir. He's a good healer and has saved many of my men."

The healer made them turn Shep over onto his stomach and examined and pulled his clothing down in order to examine the wound.

"What are these bandages?" he asked.

"He is healing from previous injuries," Akhom said, not wanting to explain further.

"We need to cut these away. The gods were kind to him. Because of these the wound could have been fatal." With Rimes' help they cut away the old bandages and then he used wine to rinse off the wound.

"It's still deep enough to have affected his vital organs. Where's my bag?" he asked.

Rimes handed it to him.

Opening it quickly, he took out a small clay jar and sutures made from the sisal plant. He applied honey to the stab wound and closed it with loose stitches because the wound would swell. The bleeding stopped. He placed a square of cotton over the stitches, took narrow strips of linen and tied them tightly around his back and chest to keep the ribs from moving. The two soldiers helped lift and turn him until he finished.

Akhom's face was drawn. "Will he be all right?"

"We'll have to wait, my Lord. If the knife cut only muscle and didn't pierce a kidney or other organ, he might live. I'll stay here with him to make sure."

"I'm grateful, healer. You may sleep in my friend's bed. I'll be on deck."

Captain Rimes asked, "Why isn't he awake?"

The army physician shook his head. "His body received a shock. He'll come to in the morning, if the gods are willing."

During all this time, Miu huddled in the safety of her basket.

"I'll let you out, Princess, but you must stay in the cabin," Akhom said. He watched as she meowed and jumped up onto the table and scrunched up against Shep's legs. She mewed softly and lay against him. She sniffed the strange white cloth wrapped around Shep's body. Exhausted, she closed her eyes and fell asleep near his head.

Akhom smiled. "That's right, Miu. Let the goddess Bastet send her healing powers through you."

Shep slowly opened his eyes and moaned as pain reminded him what happened. He raised his head and felt the constrictions of white linen wrapped around his chest and back. He turned his head a little and discovered his friend Akhom sleeping in a chair near him. Something warm was nestled against his right thigh and he knew it was Miu. He groaned again and wanted to sit up, but couldn't.

"Ah, you're still with us, my son," Akhom said.

"Water..." was all Shep could say.

The general filled a cup and brought it to him. He placed his hand behind Shep's shoulders and lifted him so he could sip the water.

"Who?" Shep asked.

"We don't know. The architect and the other damned sons of Seth have fled Abusir. What I don't know is how they knew who *you* were. They couldn't have known we were coming. But there must be a connection to Abu. I have lots of questions, but they can wait. We must make sure your body is healing."

166

"Where is the wound?" Shep asked, grateful for the water replenishing the moisture of his mouth.

"In the middle of your lower back. The army surgeon cleaned the wound and sewed you up. He doesn't know you are a physician, but he looked like he knew what he was doing."

"I am grateful to him."

"The assassin missed your major organs, he thinks. He said he didn't know if your kidneys were injured."

"I pray the gods no. But we'll see now because I must pass water, my Lord, but I can't get up."

Akhom went to the door and awakened the healer who had been sleeping on deck outside the cabin. Akhom told him what his friend needed and the man went aft and returned with a bucket.

When Shep finished, the physician said, "There's no blood, thank the gods."

"I am grateful, my friend," Shep said.

"I am Khati, my Lord."

"Well, Khati, I have rarely been a patient, but the gods are good to have provided such a qualified healer as yourself."

"Thank you, my Lord. As you know, these three days are critical when the fever strikes."

"Yes, I know, and I am in your hands."

"Meow," Miu mewled softly.

"Ah, my princess," Shep said. "Can you put her on my shoulder, friend Khati?"

The healer carefully laid the cat on the pillow beside Shep's head. Miu purred loudly. She nuzzled her head against his, and licked his face. She touched his cheek with her paw.

Akhom stood admiring them.

"Where did you find her?" Shep asked.

"In the pyramid lying beside you. She was trembling so hard, but wouldn't leave. When we returned to the ship, I put her in the basket so she'd calm down."

"I've never seen a cat so attached to someone," Shep said.

"Nor I."

Khati interrupted. "I need to give you some of the red poppy powder, my Lord. It will help you rest. As you know, your body heals better during sleep."

"Go with Akhom, Princess," Shep said. "You need your sleep too."

The general petted her before putting her back in her basket.

Shep slept through the day and night with Khati at his side. A fever developed the next day and crewmen helped carry the physician out on deck where they bathed him constantly with cool river water. The fever lasted for two days, but on the morning of the third, Shep told his friends he was hungry. A good sign.

The day after, Khati allowed him to sit up and try to stand.

Akhom paid the army physician a generous fee of one gold piece. "We are grateful and will remember what you have done."

Khati bowed his head respectfully and returned to the army barracks.

Akhom asked Shep, "Are you well enough to sail on to Avaris, my friend?"

"Yes, but we must inform the royal family about the disappearance of the architect and the unfinished work on the pyramid."

"It's done. I've sent a cryptic message by carrier pigeon. Only Nebet will be able to decipher what has happened here. I've made no mention of you, but that it would take another month to finish the tomb."

Shep nodded. "Excellent, even though I'm not convinced the workmen can do it in that time."

The *Breath of Horus* sailed the next day. Crew and soldiers were happy to be on the move again.

Shep stood next to the railing. The pain in his back muscles diminished with the help of the tight bandages and powder of the poppy. He held Miu in his arms and she meowed as the city grew smaller behind them.

General Akhom joined them. "I think she's saying she's glad to leave the town and I agree with her. We nearly lost you back there. When I discovered you in the tomb, my heart stood still."

Touched by the general's words, Shep said, "I'm glad you were there, General. You took over quickly and I will not forget it."

"Humph!" Akhom cleared his throat. "I don't remember being as angry with an enemy as I was that night. These motherless, illegitimate scum need to be found and destroyed—every last one of them. After I've reunited you with Merit and Babu, my duty is to return and help our new Pharaoh seek them out and destroy them as you did on the island of elephants."

Shep leaned over and inhaled the smell of the river. "How long must we hide in Avaris?"

"There is no way of knowing. I would, however, keep the name of Sinuhe. If the sons of Seth knew you were at Abusir even with the wrong name, how safe will you be anywhere?"

Shep walked back inside the cabin and put Miu down. She jumped up onto the window sill and sat in the sun, washed her face with her paws and then fastidiously licked her coat all over. When she was done, she laid down and napped.

169

It took them two days to reach the former capital, ruled by the Pharaohs of the early dynasties. Shep had been to the city once when he was very young, before the Academy.

At mid-day, the ship approached the city, and because there were so many Phoenician merchant ships, it took some time for the harbormaster to find them a berth. Akhom and his men disembarked and headed for the army barracks. Shep couldn't walk as fast as the general, so the older man slowed his pace.

"I don't know where to begin searching for Merit and Lou," Shep said.

"The officer in command will know. Lou told me he would give the garrison his address."

"That's a relief."

Rank did offer certain privileges. When the soldiers discovered it was a general making the inquiry, it didn't take long for someone to come forward with the information. By mid-afternoon, the weary travelers stood in front of a small stone house by the river. Akhom knocked on the door and a young woman answered.

"Yes?" she asked. "Can I help?"

"I am looking for Lumeri. We were told he lives here."

She turned and called out, "Cousin. You have a visitor."

Lou walked to the door and shouted with surprise. "Merit! Come here. Hurry." He laughed and invited them in. "General, my Lord Physician. Welcome to our house."

With Shep settled in the front room with his family, Lou stepped outside looked around and came back in. "Just making sure our guards are there," he said. "I thought I saw someone in the shadows, but it was just the wind blowing sand."

Merit ran toward Shep and embraced him. He winced causing her to step back. "What is it? You're hurt."

"We'll talk later. I need to sit down."

"Come into the garden so we can sit in the shade."

Nailah and Lou joined them on wooden benches below a tall date palm.

Shep asked, "Where's Babu?"

"Playing kickball with his friends down the road," Merit said. "They love to play all day. He'll be so glad you're home. He worries about you."

Nailah served tangerine juice and Merit insisted Shep tell them everything.

"Let the general tell you about Abusir," Shep said.

In short, precise sentences, Akhom told them what they found at the city of tombs, ending with the attack on Shep.

Lou said, "Gods! You could have died."

The others were so stunned they couldn't speak.

Merit asked, "How is the wound?"

"Healing slowly, but my back muscles tire easily. I'm trying to build up my strength."

Akhom excused himself. "I'll bring Miu. We left her at the barracks until we knew where you were living."

He had no sooner gone than Babu's voice shouted from the front room. "Mother…"

"Out here," Merit called.

"We won, we won!" He ran into the garden, saw Shep and cried with joy, "Father!"

"My boy has become a great ballplayer. Come here, monkey."

Babu ran toward him with his arms outspread.

Merit pulled him back. "Shep has been injured so be careful. Don't squeeze him."

Shep laughed. "Come here, Babu. Let me hug *you* instead."

Babu laughed as they embraced. "Where's Miu? Didn't you bring her?"

"Yes, the general has gone to get her."

"*Nefer*...hurrah! We'll all be together again."

As everyone refilled their cups with juice, Nailah suggested Shep invite the general for supper.

When Akhom returned with the fiber carrying basket, he let the cat out.

Delighted to see her again, Babu held her and petted her. Miu purred and mewled at him happily, tapping his nose playfully with her paw.

That evening, after sharing supper with Shep's family, Akhom returned to the barracks. Shep, Lou and Babu shared Merit's room and she slept in the room with Nailah.

Early the next morning, General Akhom came by. "I've found a house big enough for everyone. There's also a building next door that might serve as a surgery when you feel like working again."

Lou said, "I've made inquiries, my Lord. We can find the medicines you need here in Avaris."

"I hadn't thought of working here," Shep said. "I assumed we'd return to Memphis when the assassin is found." He paused as a thought occurred to him. "I can't be a physician any longer. I'll open an apothecary shop and sell medicines. I can still treat people, but Pharaoh's men will be looking for a physician."

Akhom nodded. "Good, and its best you remain here for now. I'll sail to Memphis and send you messages about what's happening. Keep the name Sinuhe for now. Who knows how many people up and down the river know your real name? Pharaoh's chamberlain will have his spies everywhere just as he had in Abusir."

Babu laughed. "We're going to call you Sinuhe? I like it."

Shep's lips tightened. "Babu, this is not a game, but is very serious. There are bad men who want to take me away from you and Merit. Do you understand?"

172

The boy lowered his eyebrows. "I'm not a baby, Father. I know how to keep a secret."

"Good, now what is my name?"

"You are Lord Sinuhe, noble Apothecary."

Shep grinned. "But you're still Babu, the monkey!"

Their friends laughed with the boy and then General Akhom stood to leave. "Now remember the code words, 'Miu has run away'." You'll know to flee to safety. And 'The Princess prays for you,' will mean you can return. I pray for the gods to watch over all of you."

Merit embraced him and Shep took his forearms in the military salute. As Akhom walked down the street toward the barracks, Shep said to her, "I would have died without him."

Chapter 14

Sinuhe

Two months passed, but still no word from Akhom. Shep and his friends had settled into the house with three bedrooms the general had found for them. Its walls were made of baked mud bricks covered with a clay plaster painted white. It had a veranda facing the river, but Babu complained because he said the frogs kept him awake at night. However, the most important family member, Princess Miu, liked the house and sat for hours on the patio grooming herself. The soldiers left by Akhom helped build a small guardhouse at the back of the garden. They patrolled around the house day and night.

The family also enjoyed the different climate. In the delta, so close to the Great Sea, lush green vegetation surrounded them. They were miles from any sandy desert and the cool breezes from the northern mountains brought refreshing rain—something rarely seen in Memphis.

Shep's apothecary shop proved adequate, but was not anything like the surgery he left in Memphis. Only a few customers came at first, but as the only apothecary on this part of the river, word of mouth soon filled his shop every day.

Lou and Babu were good with the customers. If it were not for the memory of what they left behind, they would consider themselves happy. The name of Sinuhe became known and respected. Their rented house was also close to one of the temples of Horus. Priests often came for medicine and treatment. During their visits, Shep learned what was happening along the river as well as in the city.

At the end of one long day, a young priest came to him with a broken finger. He impressed the apothecary because he told Shep he could have set the finger himself but wanted it done right. Shep estimated that the tall and very thin priest had probably seen sixteen summers. With his head shaved, only his reddish eyebrows revealed a distant ancestor from the far north.

He asked Shep, "Did you study religion at the Academy, my Lord?"

Shep nodded. As he finished wrapping linen strips around the splint he said, "Well, I studied more medicine than religion, but remember, Awen is the center for the worship of Ra and the sun."

"Yes, that's what I've heard. Could those who worship Ra be called sons of light?"

Shep furrowed his brow becoming wary of the conversation. "Yes, I suppose they could. Why do you ask?"

"Well, our leader, Brother Alim, is not pleased. You know that we worship Horus-Ra, so we believe the light of the gods comes to us from them. But now, a different yet old religion has come to Avaris. They worship the god of the underworld."

"And what do they call themselves," Shep asked.

As soon as the young priest began to say it, Shep said it along with him, "Sons of Seth."

"Yes, how did you know, my Lord?"

"They are known in Memphis, holy one. I'm surprised to hear about them this far north."

175

"Our Brother told us to avoid them. He said they are evil and will move against us."

"Brother Alim is right, my friend. Now, how does that finger feel?"

"Much better, thank you." The priest started to hand Shep a copper coin, but he put up his hand.

"For the sons of light, there is no charge. May Horus bless you this day." He handed the priest a small papyrus with a prayer to Horus for healing. "Recite it each morning."

"Thank you, I know the prayer." He bowed his head politely and left the shop.

At supper that evening, Shep shared what the priest told him.

"Say it isn't so," Merit said. "Is no place safe from them?"

"Apparently not," Shep said.

A knock at the door caused Babu to get up. "Maybe it's my friend Tekem," he said, running to answer. He hurried back immediately. "It's a soldier."

Shep went to the door and received a small rolled up piece of papyrus. He handed the soldier a copper coin for him to treat himself to a jar of beer on the way back.

"I'm afraid to read it," Shep said, sitting down and unrolling the paper. It was so small it had obviously flown in on the leg of a pigeon.

"It says, 'Princess prays for you.'"

Merit shouted, "Praise the gods. We can go home."

Everyone became excited except Shep. "I wonder if it's true. If the Seth followers are everywhere, where can we possibly go that will be safe?"

Lou said, "That may be true, Master, but the general must believe there is no danger."

"Think about it a moment, friends. If we return, we can't go back to our beautiful villa. I'm certain they now call it the house of Shepseskaf, the assassin. You are also guilty because you helped me."

A visible gloom fell over the family.

Babu said, "I'm happy *here*, Father. I have so many friends. They respect me because my father is Sinuhe the Apothecary. Everyone knows you."

Shep said, "I think we should remain in Avaris for now. I'll send a message to Akhom saying that Miu is staying. Perhaps he'll come for us when he travels to Pharaoh's entombment ceremony. May his name be remembered."

"Nefer-efray lives," the family recited.

In the end, Shep told Lou and his sister they could return with his blessing, but they assured him they would stay with him. They understood the danger if they went home.

The next day, Shep walked to the military garrison and sent the message to Akhom. He paid the soldier in charge a copper coin. On his way home, a man followed him and made no effort to disguise the fact.

Shep stopped and turned around to face the stranger. "Did you wish to speak with me?"

"Yes, my Lord. You're Sinuhe the apothecary, aren't you?"

"I am."

"I wanted to invite you to a meeting of concerned members of the community."

"Concerned members?"

"Yes, my Lord. Merchants and professional people like yourself."

"I see. When and where is this meeting?"

"At the temple of Seth, where the river bends east. We'll gather at sunset tonight, if you're interested,"

"I'll consider the invitation. Thank you," Shep said.

"Very well. Don't take too long, physician. The worship of Seth the all-powerful is spreading everywhere."

After the man nodded and walked on, Shep mumbled, "That's what I'm afraid of."

Several weeks later when Shep and Lou visited her in her bedchamber, Merit said, "Shave it off. I don't like it."

Lou laughed. "I think it makes him look wiser."

Shep turned and put down Merit's copper mirror. "I *need* this beard. It'll be harder to recognize me when I go to the king's entombment in Abusir."

"Must you go?" Merit asked. "Akhom doesn't know you'll be there."

"True enough, but I hold myself responsible for Pharaoh's death, Merit. I was there with him and shouldn't have left him alone. I must show Nebet at least that I honor her brother's Ka."

Later, when he and Lou were alone, Shep said, "I don't know if I can wear this beard for long. It's itchy and I have to be careful when I eat. I'm glad I was raised Egyptian."

Lou smiled. "What will you do if an Asiatic speaks to you and you can't respond?"

"I'll speak Egyptian and try to bluff."

Lou frowned and rubbed his chin. "I worry about your more fragile patients—old Mama Sati for example. She and others will worry that you are leaving."

"Reassure them, Lou. I'll give you their medication dosages and prayers to recite. What I'm more concerned about are guards to protect my family. I'll pay to hire two more guards from the regiment to add to the brigade Akhom left us. I know I can trust you to protect Merit and Babu."

Lou grinned. "Of course, Lord Sinuhe. You do know that is an Egyptian name, right?"

"Yes. I'll tell people I was born in Tyre on the Great Sea and that my mother was Egyptian. I became apothecary to a wealthy government official who insists that I dress like the people he serves."

Lou walked over to the window and was silent for a moment. "It sounds like you've thought of everything."

"Probably not. But it is something I have to do, Lou. I hope you can understand that."

"I understand, Lord. Horus go with you." As if remembering something, he asked. "What about Miu? Will she go with you?"

"Not this time, I'm afraid. Will you help Merit keep an eye on her? And don't throw away her basket. It's where she hides all her treasures. Make sure Merit doesn't throw it out like she tried to do the other day."

Lou nodded. "You can count on me, Lord Sinuhe, Apothecary of Tyre."

Shep grinned and walked out into the garden.

The vessel *Glory of Ra* sailed a week later for Abusir. It was crowded with passengers, most of whom were government officials on their way to pay homage to their dead Pharaoh. Because they had to sail south against the river's strong current, it would take them a full day to arrive.

When the passengers learned Shep was an apothecary, they clustered around him discussing their aches and pains. That included the mayor of Avaris, the most important official on board.

"It was a miracle, I tell you," the mayor said. "Lord Sinuhe healed my swollen foot. I thought I would never walk again."

"Really?", another gentlemen said.

"Yes, the medicine did wonders."

Shep smilied. "You are in a company of the very rich and powerful, Lord Mayor. Only men of that class who eat well and drink on the best, succumb to the disease. And you helped heal yourself too, my Lord. You followed your regime of meals closely and the treatment with the papyrus root kept the swelling down. You must try to limit your consumption of alcohol on this trip"

"Well, whatever we did, it was because of you, Lord Sinuhe."

"May I ask why you dress as an Asiatic, my Lord?" another passenger asked.

Shep smiled. Egyptians considered all people north of their country as Asiatics. "I've worked up north for a number of years and the people there prefer for us to dress as they do. I may return soon and it takes a long time to grow the beard. I must say, however, I don't like wearing one."

The rest of the journey was more of the same. The same questions, and answers. Finally, the ship reached the dock at Abusir. The long causeway up to the pyramid reached down to the water's edge.

"Pharaoh's royal galley has just arrived," the ship's captain told his passengers. "It means we'll have to wait until the guards give us permission to disembark."

Three carrying chairs moved away fom the dock. Their gold trim reflected the late afternoon sun. Shep was certain their occupants were the widowed queen, the new Pharaoh and the princess. The chairs were headed up the causeway to the former architects villa. His stomach muscles tightened as he remembered the treachery of the architect and his men.

When their ship found its berth, and the Royal Guards allowed them to desembark, the passengers went ashore to find a place to sleep for the night. Fortunately many of the officials knew people in Abusir who would put them up. Shep went directly to the barracks and asked for Captain Rimes.

When the officer came out, he looked at the bearded nobleman and frowned. "How may I help you, my Lord?" His face bore a puzzeled expression.

"I'm looking for the sons of Seth, Captain."

"Shh. What?" the officer said almost in a whisper. "You must be quiet, my Lord. By the gods, we do not say that name out loud. You must go, please, noble one."

"Why?" Shep asked. "You helped save my life recently. Don't you recognize me? General Akhom will punish you for your lack of respect."

"Lord Sinuhe?" Rimes exclaimed. "Is that you?" He laughed and slapped Shep on the shoulder. "That is a horrible beard. Forgive my manners."

"You're forgiven. I don't want the followers of Seth to know I'm still alive. Thanks to you, I'm still here. I've come to ask a great favor. I would like to meet with Princess Nebet."

"The princess? No no. I don't think that's possible. I'm only a captain, my Lord."

"Is General Akhom going to be here?"

"He's already arrived, my friend, and staying with us. The men respect him even more staying in the barracks with them."

"Where is he?" Shep asked.

"I'll call him for you." Rimes left and returned after a moment with the general.

Akhom growled, "Who's this then?"

"Your son, General. Don't you know me?"

"I don't know any Asiatics—in fact I wouldn't want to know any." He slammed his fist down on the desk and turned to go.

"Not even one with a cat who is a princess?"

"What? By Seth's foul breath! It's you, Shep. Gods, what an awful beard."

When they finished laughing, Akhom led Shep into the soldiers' common room.

"Sit here," Akhom said. "We can speak privately." Akhom looked his friend over carefully. "You've foolishly put yourself in danger. Setmena's men are everywhere."

Shep nodded. "I know, but it's as if Neferefre's Ka has called me here." He smiled and then added, "It pleases me the gods have allowed us to see each other again, General."

"And me son. But why are you here? I sent no word. You must not stay."

Shep shook his head. "I received a message in your name that all was well in Memphis. I knew you couldn't have sent it. The killer hasn't been found, has he?"

The general sighed."No, my son."

"Can you help me meet with the Princess? Is there a time when commoners take part in the entombment ceremony?"

"It's too dangerous. Someone is going to recognize you."

"Please, General."

"Hmm. Well, during during the precession to the pyramid, Pharaoh's subjects are to bow to him one last time. You can join me."

"Thank you, my friend. I would also ask for a bed for the night, or just a chair. I can sleep anywhere. My ship returns tomorrow."

"There's space in my chamber. The men can bring in a cot."

In the morning, the men washed and prepared for the Farewell Ceremony to Pharaoh Neferefre. Akhom told Shep what to do and where to stand. "I'll be with my officers while you join the other nobles and dignitaries in the center. You'll be close to the ramp on which the sarcophagus will pass."

Musicians played with their flutes and sistrums—a type of rattle with metal discs. The loud beating of the drums encouraged the crowd to clap in a syncopated rhythm seserved especially for their Pharaohs. The deep male voices of the priests added to the sad, yet majestic tone of the song.

"He is happy this good prince;
Death is a kindly fate.
A generation passes, another stays.
Since the time of the ancestors."

"Ahhhh...eee...yaaaaeh," the crowd chanted in unison. They waved green leaves and branches to remind them of the afterlife. Men's voices, low and resonant, followed the beat of the drums as the people clapped.

Four white oxen pulled a large wooden sled on which the golden sarcophagus of the king rested. It moved slowly up the ramp toward the open tomb entrance. All work on the pyramid had been finished and awaited the body of the king. Gigantic blocks of limestone that would seal the tomb lay to the right of the entrance.

The lone figure of the Queen walked solemnly behind the body of her husband, her head held high. Priests with flowing white robes followed, chanting in unison verses from the Book of the Dead.

The beauty of the procession made Shep catch his breath. The fragrant incense carried by the priests rose in white smoke like wispy tongues of praise to the dead king. Others carried tall linen banners of every color bearing Pharaoh's many official and throne names.

The music swelled as Princess Nebet followed behind the queen—her face frozen in an expression neither

183

sad nor joyful. She looked even more beautiful than Shep had ever seen her.

The music stopped abruptly, surprising the crowd. The new Pharaoh walked up the ramp and stood beside his sister. They turned and faced the people gathered at the base of the ramp.

The high priest of Horus-Ra shouted so all could hear. "Hear the voice of Horus, the Living God of Egypt."

Pharaoh Niuserre spoke with a loud strong voice. "People of our Beloved Black Land. Give obeisance to Pharaoh one last time." He bowed low to the sarcophagus and Nebet did the same.

Shep joined the crowd as they prostrated themeselves on the ground toward the great sarcophagus. Many cried out with sorrow, tears rolling down their faces. When the drums and music began again, the people stood, shouted and cheered the dead king's name—Nefer-effray, Nefer-effray."

As Shep stood, he had a good view of Niuserre and the princess. For a brief moment Nebet's eyes met his. He nodded toward her, but she remained still as if carved from stone. When her brother turned, she followed him behind the priests into the tomb.

As the entombment continued inside the pyramid, Shep walked over to the army and stood across from general Akhom's officers. The general turned his head and saw the bearded Asiatic, but gave no sign of recognition.

The dry heat from the sun and hot sand became intense and Shep's lower back began to throb. The musicians continued their triumphant melodies, while inside the tomb. Akhom told him the royal family would perform the Opening of the Mouth Ceremony and bid a final farewell to the king.

Eventually the reverberatng chanting from the tomb grew louder as the priests led the procession out of the tomb back down the ramp. This time, the crowd remained silent.

184

It would not be respectful to cheer and applaud a Pharaoh who had not been crowned. The stomping of the oxen's hooves echoed off the pyramid wall as they pulled the empty sled back down. The magnificent beasts would become sacrifices in honor of Horus at the temple in Abusir city.

A soldier approached the bearded stranger. "Come with me, my Lord."

Shep nodded and followed him away from the crowd to the path that led up to the architect's house.

General Akhom walked forward to meet him. "Listen to me, my son. The chamberlain and the king must go to the the temple for the end of the ceremonies. Nebet remains in the villa with her handmaidens. We will go together because an Asiatic would not be trusted alone with her."

"Lead on, my Lord. I am grateful."

Upon recognizing the general, the guards allowed him and his companion to pass. Akhom handed them his dagger and sword before he and Shep went in.

Princess Nebet sat on a divan in the front room. In her hand she held an alabaster goblet and was about to touch it to her lips. She stopped and looked up as the general entered. "Ah, a friendly face," she said."Enter.Would you care for a drink?"

"Thank you no, Highness. I am here to present someone to you."

"An Asiatic? Really, General. He has hair all over his face. Does the beast speak our language?"

Shep said, "Well enough, to thank a princess for saving his cat, Highness."

Nebet stood quickly. "Who is this?" She walked closer to him. "The voice I know, but the face…wait a minute. By all that's holy, its…no, it can't be." She laughed. "I can't believe it."

185

Turning to her servants she said, "Ladies wait here. My guests and I will be out on the veranda enjoying the cool air."

Akhom and Shep followed her.

Nebet said, "I'm sorry, Shep. I almost gave you away in there. Why are you dressed like that?"

"You forget beautiful one, that I am a condemned criminal and am running from the king's justice."

"Of course. Why have you risked everything to be here?"

Shep paused a moment before answering. "Your brother's Ka called to me, Highness. I had to honor him. I want him to know I am here and have wished him a blessed journey."

The princess simply nodded slowly. "He will be pleased."

"Now, I would ask about the chamberlain, Highness. How does he treat the royal family?"

Nebet thought for a moment. "What do you mean? He's been very kind to me and my brother. He's given me *your* villa and I feel as if I'm keeping it safe for your return. He's very helpful to Serry with day-to-day decisions. He wants to go ahead with the coronation when we return to Memphis. He has even encouraged Pharaoh's marriage to our cousin." She took a long sip of wine. "He has assured us there is no evidence of the cult of darkness we feared."

"I see. Then there has been no further investigation into who might have really killed your brother? I'm still the only suspect?"

"Yes, I'm afraid so."

Akhom said, "I do not wish to offend my Lady, but Pharaoh's army continues to search for the assassin. We know it could not have been Shep. It had to have been someone with access to the palace that night."

"I will continue to help as much as I can. Where are you living now, Shep?" she asked.

"I cannot say, Highness. It will put you in danger as well as me. It is better you not know. If you need to send a message, however, General Akhom will see I receive it."

"Very well. Now, did my favorite cat come with you?"

"No, Highness, but she misses her golden fish. We are still her slaves."

Nebet laughed a little. "Tell me more about your journey. Has it been long"

A man's voice interrupted. "Yes, tell us where you come from, my Lord?" Setmena, the Lord Chamberlain, had entered the front room and came out onto the veranda to join them.

Shep was trapped. If he was recognized, it would all be over. He cleared his throat and spoke slowly. "I am from Tyre, my Lord Chamerlain. I teach Egyptian in the schools there. My employer has a love of all things Egyptian."

"Hmm." Setmena turned to Akhom. "It is good to see you again, General." Then he turned to the princess. "His majesty asked me to tell you he'll be late. The high priest had some things to discuss with him."

Nebet said, "My visitors were just about to leave. Please tell his majesty I have gone to bed."

"As you wish, Highness. It has been a long day. I bid you goodnight."

She nodded and wished Akhom and his companion a good night's rest.

As Akhom led Shep along the path to the barracks, Shep said, "Setmena seems different. Maybe I was wrong about him."

"Humph," Akhom growled. "Can a leopard exchange his skin for a zebra's?"

187

"There's something else," Shep said. "Her highness did not seem as glad to see me as I'd hoped."

"She was tired from the long periods of public mourning and processions. I do think it wise of you not to tell her where you are living. Very wise indeed."

The next morning, Nebet was surprised when the chamberlain came by the villa to greet them. She and her brother were eating at the table and he waited politely to be recognized.

"The departure of the royal galley wouldn't be until mid-day, Majesty, and there's nothing for you to do today. Rejoice."

Pharaoh slapped his hand down on the table. "Gods! I have been waiting for you to say that for a very long time. You are a hard taskmaster, my Lord."

"It was good to see General Akhom here last night, Highness," Setmena said.

Nebet smiled. "Yes, it was. He has been most supportive of our family."

"Who was that nobleman with him? There was something about him that seemed familiar. I could swear I've met him before."

Nebet shook her head. "I doubt it, my Lord. Not if he has been in Tyre for so many years."

"You're probably right, but I never forget a face." Setmena excused himself and left. .

"You never could lie very well, Sister. Who was he?"

Nebet panicked. She couldn't tell her brother the truth. If he were to let it slip and word got back to the followers of Seth, Shep could lose his life. "He was just a friend the general met here at the ceremony, Serry. Do not worry about me becoming interested in such a man. His long hair and beard repulses me."

"Oh, I believe you," Pharaoh said. "But would you not agree that a beard can also hide the true feaures of a person. Maybe he *does* have something to hide."

"I will not have a chance to find out, Brother. He sailed this morning."

Chapter 15

River Fever

"Yeowl..." Miu cried when Shep came through the door. Shep knew she didn't like his beard because she hadn't tried to pat his cheek since he began growing it.

Babu hugged him and pulled on it.

"Stop, you monkey!" He rubbed his knuckles over the top of the boy's head.

"Princess Nebet sends you and Babu her greetings, Merit," he said. "I'll tell you all about the entombment at supper if you like."

Later, with Lou and Nailah at the table with them, he recounted everything.

"I'm glad the passengers on your ship gave you a hard time about that ghastly thing on your face," Merit teased.

"I must say I didn't like being called an Asiatic even by Akhom and the princess." He paused and then said, "Tell me what's happened while I was gone."

Babu was first to tell about his success with kick-ball, and his adventure climbing a tall willow tree. Lou reported that all their patients were doing well, while Merit bragged about meeting the mayor's wife. She added how pleased the woman was with Shep's skill in healing her husband's leg.

"May I add something?" Nailah said her voice timid and a little shaky. "I've met a young man who wishes to court me."

"What?" Lou exclaimed. "This is the first I've heard of it."

"You're always so busy, Brother. That's why I'm telling everyone now."

Merit said, "That's wonderful Nailah. Do we know him?"

"No, his name is Setauan and he is a clerk in Lord Patesi's bank. He's educated and is good with numbers."

Shep smiled. "I'm pleased for you. Is he also good looking?"

The young woman blushed and everyone at the table smiled.

Nailah said, "He *is* very good looking, my Lord. His father owns a farm north of the city where he became an expert horseman."

"Well, when's the wedding?" Shep asked.

"I won't know until Lou meets him."

"Which won't be soon enough," her brother grumbled.

Shep stood and rubbed his hands together. "Now who wants a present? Come into the front room if you do."

He walked to his bed chamber to fetch his leather traveling bag.

When he returned, Miu walked over and sniffed it, suddenly purring very loudly.

"All right, Princess. You're first. He reached in and pulled out a cloth mouse he found at the Abusir market. He placed it on the floor and she began acting demented, sniffing it, rolling over on it, and throwing it into the air.

The family roared with laughter at her erratic ballet.

191

"What is in it?" Lou asked.

"Catswort my friend. That'll keep her happy for a while."

"Me, me, Father. Where's mine?" Babu asked.

"Ah, here it is," Shep said. He handed the boy a group of carved wooden monkeys. Each joined to the tail of another.

"It's a puzzle, Babu. You have to figure out how to separate them. Maybe your friends will enjoy trying too."

"Thank you," the boy said. He ran over to the front of the divan, sat on the floor and tried to solve the puzzle.

"I feel fatigued dear friends. It's been a long day. I'll wish you goodnight." He went into his room to rest. Sometime later, he heard the clickety-clack of wooden monkeys hitting on the floor. He went out to discover his son still sitting on the floor trying to separate the monkeys.

"To bed with you, young man," Shep ordered.

"Miu," Shep called, but couldn't find the cat. A loud purr coming from behind the divan drew him to it. Leaning over he found her there with her mouse, purring to her heart's content.

"Good night, Princess. I should be jealous, but I'm not."

He returned to his room and prepared for bed.

After the break for the mid-day meal, a man entered the apothecary shop seeking treatment for an earache. He insisted on seeing the pharmacist.

"I've met that man before," Shep told his aide. "I just can't remember where."

"He's in back in the examining room," Lou said.

Shep entered and said, "Good day. Your ear is bothering you?"

"Good day, my Lord. My right ear is very sore."

Shep examined it closely. "The ear has a buildup of wax and needs to be washed out. Should I proceed?"

"Yes, whatever you say."

Using a prepared animal bladder and the small intestine of a goat as a tube, he flushed out the ear wax and swabbed the canal with medicated oil. "It will happen again, I'm afraid. Some of us are more prone to wax building up than others."

"You don't remember me, do you?" the patient said.

"Your face is vaguely familiar, but..."

"We spoke on the street some time ago. I invited you to a meeting at the temple of Seth."

"Ah yes, I remember. I'm sorry, I was unable to attend."

"We're meeting again in three days. I think you should come."

Shep's pulse quickened. Did these men know his real identity, and would he fall into their hands if he went to the meeting? "Oh? And for what reason?"

"Well, for Babu's sake, I should think."

A chill coursed down Shep's spine. This was a threat and he didn't know how to respond. "How do you know my son?"

"Our boys play together, my Lord. They're good friends. My boy's name is Tekem."

"I see. Yes, Babu has spoken of your son. They both got stuck up in a willow tree if I remember correctly."

"Yes, that's him. It would be good if you come to the meeting and listen to what we might say."

Shep's anger began to grow. Now his family was threatened. He would have to go.

As the man dried his head with a towel and pulled his tunic back over his head, he continued. "We meet at sunset. There's a meeting place at the back of the temple. Be there in three days."

193

"I'll make an effort to come. But I want you to know, that I don't take kindly to threats against my family. I know important officials who will come to my aid if needed."

"In three days," the man said ignoring Shep's response. He turned, left the room and paid his fee to Lou before leaving the shop.

Shep took Lou aside. "Tell Merit I'll be late coming home. I'm going to speak to Captain Khepri, the officer in charge of Akhom's brigade."

Three nights later, Shep and Khepri followed a few other men heading toward the temple. He and his friend shared what they knew about the religion of Seth.

"I know Seth's identified with all destruction," the officer said. "The waning of the moon, for example, the falling of the waters of our sacred river, and the setting of the sun."

"Then he is Horus-Ra's enemy," Shep said. "We worship Ra because he is the giver of light and all that is good."

As they neared the temple, a large statue of the god stood in front. Khepri said, "This god looks different from our other gods and goddesses. The ugly Seth-Animal has a human body, but the head of a strange creature with a snout, long rectangular ears and a thin forked tail. It's unlike any animal I've ever seen." He nodded to the statue. "Ever see an animal like that?"

"A bit gruesome," Shep said.

"He's supposed to be."

When they reached the meeting place behind the temple, Shep was surprised to find a large group of perhaps a hundred men gathered together.

194

Shep's patient with the sore ear stood and walked toward them. "I am Setenet, my Lord. Welcome to our assembly."

Overcome by the large turnout, Shep forced a smile. "This is my good friend, Khepri. We want to learn more about your religion."

Setenet nodded. "We welcome all who seek the truth. Please join the others."

Several of his customers nodded to him in recognition.

Shortly after finding a place on the benches, a tall figure, dressed in black with a hood, entered. "Welcome friends, to this special meeting to honor our god, Seth, the all-powerful ruler of darkness and forces of the night."

Shep's stomach muscles tightened. Fear forced bile up into his throat causing him to swallow hard.

Several of the group murmured so the speaker waited patiently until the room was quite. "You have been asked here to consider joining us, the followers of Seth. He has unimaginable power and will make that force available to us. He is strong enough to make even rulers fall."

Captain Khepri elbowed Shep. The speaker had just given Seth credit for the death of Pharaoh Neferefre.

A man jumped up. "That is treason! You should be arrested."

Several members of the temple, also cloaked in black, hurried to the protester. They picked him up and ushered him away.

The leader continued to explain their beliefs at great length. The crowd nodded their approval, applauding when he finished. The speaker lowered his hood to greet each one as they filed out. Shep was not surprised to see the face of his patient one more time.

"Good night, Captain Khepri, Lord Apothecary. Think on what you've heard. We know you'll join us."

Shep frowned as they made their way back to town. "It was as I feared. They are opposed to all we believe in, even threatening Pharaoh and the government. Our way of life is in danger."

Khepri scratched his head. "I agree. I didn't think anyone would recognize me out of uniform."

"That could prove troublesome, my friend. They might think the army supports them."

As they walked along the river's edge, they came upon a group of people shouting frantically. They were pulling someone screaming out of the river.

"Gods! Shep. Look. It's the man who objected at the meeting."

But Shep had to turn away. The man lay disemboweled on the sandy bank.

One of the crowd said, "The men from the temple attacked him with their swords and threw him into the river."

The poor man screamed at the top of his lungs.

Khepri covered his ears. "Help him, for Horus' sake."

"Give me your blade."

Khepri untied his hidden weapon and handed it to him.

"Move aside." Shep rushed toward the victim and plunged the dagger up under the man's chin and deep into the skull. The screaming stopped immediately. Shep gasped, a feeling of nausea engulfing him. "Take his remains to his family so they can bury him."

Shep's action stunned the on-lookers, some of whom emptied their stomachs. One of them ran to a house nearby, returning with a blanket. They wrapped the body in it and did as Shep commanded.

Walking to the water's edge, he washed the blood from his hands. He then immersed the dagger into the water, wiped it clean and handed it back to the officer.

"By my father's life, Shep, that was the only merciful thing to do."

"It was still a horrible way to die."

Upon reaching the barracks, Khepri sank into a chair in his office. He offered to share a jar of beer with Shep who accepted gladly.

"Now I am forced to do my duty," Khepri said. "We have witnessed a murder and know the man behind it. We can't let him go unpunished."

"Maybe that was Setenet's plan all along. He wanted to show us that the sons of Seth can commit any crime without fear of the consequences." He gulped some more beer. "I would seriously consult your superiors about what you should do, Captain." Shep stood and said goodnight before walking home.

His mind was troubled. He knew he should have told Khepri what he knew concerning the king's murder, but he held back. The shock of what he had just seen and done caused him to stop. Bending over, he threw up.

As soon as he entered the house, Merit rushed to him. "Thank the gods you're home, Shep. We didn't know how to find you. It's Babu, he's burning up with the fever."

Shep's heart skipped a beat. River fever killed thousands every decade. No one knew where the malady came from, or how to cure it. Many of his colleagues at the Academy believed the evil gods from the north brought the curse. "I've been foolish and should know better," he told Merit. "I should have insisted we use bed nets to protect us from insects. Pharaoh Senefru's physicians long ago recorded they should be used when the river is high and the insects multiply rapidly."

He felt the boy's face. "All right, there's only one thing to do. Merit, bring my medicine box. The rest of you prepare a table on the porch for him. We'll need buckets of water, now hurry."

Shep caught a glimpse of a frightened cat running to hide.

"My head hurts." Babu's voice was weak as if he wanted to cry. "So does my back. Oooh...Father."

Shep patted the boy's arm. "Easy, Son. We're moving you out into the shade. We'll bathe you to make you cool. Rest now. Your mother will bring you water and juices to drink."

He took Merit aside. "I'll mix some willow bark powder and dried root of the red desert cactus into his cup. That should help with the headache and back pain. We've got to force him to drink and pass water. It's important to replenish his body fluids."

"Yes, I know. I lost a sister five years ago to this Asiatic fever epidemic."

"Asiatic?"

"Yes. An evil wind blows their illnesses south to our sacred river. It is the curse of Seth upon us."

Shep felt a sudden frisson of fear. "It's only a superstition, Merit. You don't believe that, do you?"

"All my friends do."

"Very well. First, we must lower Babu's temperature with water. Keep bathing him. I'll be next door in the pharmacy. People will be coming for help. Let me know immediately if there is any change."

Merit spoke just above a whisper. "I will. Please save him."

"I will try. At the Academy we learned that the gods had given the red cactus root the power to bring down the fever."

Shep felt it important that he and Lou remain in the shop. When they arrived to open the door and light the oil lamps, people were already waiting for help.

"I hope we have enough of both medicines," Lou said.

The pain killer lasted only until morning, but they were able to give out the dried cactus root.

Shep handed Lou a small leather pouch. "Take these coins and bring back all you can from the medical supply near the government offices. You know where it is. And, Lou, don't let anyone see you with it. Hide it in burlap sacks perhaps. You might be attacked. People do bad things when frightened."

"Don't worry. I'll be back as soon as I can."

Shep remained in his shop. While unable to give out any pain medicine, he gave them the cactus root and showed them how to boil it and make a drink. "It will help lower your temperature," he assured them.

Nailah came from next door. "Babu's the same. He's still hot, but the powder is helping him sleep. Is that a good thing?"

"Yes. His body will be able to regain the strength needed to fight the fever. He needs more of the boiled root with a little honey added otherwise it taste's terrible."

Lou returned with three sacks of the precious medicines. He had rented a wagon and donkey driven by a young man who helped unload the large sacks.

Shep rubbed his chin. "I think we should put two sacks in the house. You never know what people might try, especially if someone they love is dying."

Lou called his sister back and asked her to watch the shop while they carried the medicines next door. After hiding the sacks, Shep went out on the porch to check his son's condition. His forehead was still hot, but a neighbor had come over to help bathe him with cool wet cloths. Shep's heart felt torn between his love for the boy and his duty as a true physician. It surprised him how deep his feelings for Babu had grown.

"I must return to my patients, Merit. Will you be all right?"

"Of course. Get some sleep when you can. It won't help any of us if *you* become ill."

He kissed her hand gallantly. "Thank you, Lady."

She laughed and pushed him out of the house. "Remember, I'm not yet your wife."

He frowned as he walked next door. Her reminder hurt him and made him more determined to follow their original plan if they ever returned to Memphis.

By mid-morning, Shep couldn't keep his eyes open. He left Lou in charge before returning home to bed. When he awoke some hours later, Miu lay next to his head, purring. He knew he should get up, but allowed himself a moment of pleasure. He shifted a little and rubbed her belly as he did when she was a kitten. A soft paw reached up and tapped his nose.

"Sorry, Princess, I have work to do." He left her on the bed and walked to the patio where he found Merit asleep on a chair next to Babu. He tried not to awaken her as he stepped over and touched the boy's brow. It didn't feel as hot, but he put more medicine in his tangerine juice for when he awoke.

He examined Merit and noticed excessive sweat forming on her face. He felt her forehead and then shook her shoulder gently. "Merit, wake up."

"What? What is it? Is he all right?"

"Yes. He feels a little cooler. But you have the fever, I'm afraid. I'll send Nailah and our neighbor to keep you cool. Babu will go to his bed. Lou can come in to watch him."

Merit frowned. "No, no. I'm all right."

"No, you're not. Obey me, woman." He had raised his voice to show he was serious.

Merit stood and walked beside him as he carried their boy back to his bed. Kissing him on the forehead, she returned to the porch.

Babu woke. "I'm thirsty, Father. Where's Mother?"

Shep poured him a cup of water and let him sip it. "Your mother is not well either, my boy. She's on the porch. They're cooling her with water like we did for you."

"Will she be all right?"

"If Horus wills it my son. You must pray for her."

"I will."

Miu jumped up onto the boy's bed and curled up on his pillow.

"Will Princess get sick too?" the boy asked.

"I don't think so, Son. The goddess Bastet protects all cats."

Babu tried to smile. "Bless her."

"I'll send Lou to check on you. Stay in bed and try to sleep. Your fever is going down a little. Promise me, Babu, you'll stay here."

The boy smiled. "If you give me my monkey puzzle."

Agreed." Shep searched until he found the monkeys in a corner. He picked them up and put them on the bed. "I thought you would have solved this puzzle by now."

"Ha, ha. It's not that easy. You'll see."

They played together a while until Shep decided the boy was right.

Returning to the apothecary shop, he found it full. He immediately locked the front door before stepping on a bench so everyone could see him.

"Listen, friends. I will treat each of you, but you must tell me how many days you have had the fever. The

201

medications I give is for pain in your back and the fever. Take it with you and mix it with water or juice—not beer, or wine. The dried cactus root is to be boiled, and then allowed to cool. You'll need honey in it for the taste. That's all I can do. Please understand. Stay in bed and take your medication morning and evening."

By the time he met with each person and unlocked the door for them to leave, more people were waiting outside.

Captain Khepri came in through the back way and asked to see him. "Can you help us with more medication, my Lord? Our healer has been treating our men, but has run out."

Shep flopped down on a bench and held his head between his hands for a moment. He was uncertain as to what he should do. "I have some at the house. Shut this door and don't let anyone in or out."

Khepri did as he asked and waited for Shep to return.

In his bedroom, Shep decided to leave one sack hidden under his bed but give the other to Khepri. "It might be dangerous, Captain. Lou can go with you to help protect it."

"No, I have my sword, Shep. No one will try anything."

Shep wanted to say that a crowd of people could easily overpower one soldier, but simply nodded his head.

Shep returned to the sick. He stood at the door, trying to help those who remained outside, but eventually people spread the word that there was no more medication.

As darkness fell, Shep locked the door and checked the makeshift examining room at the back one last time. He discovered an elderly man lying on the floor. He felt for a pulse but found none. Picking him up, he carried him outside then covered him with an old blanket. He sent Lou to bring a priest, hoping they could find a relative or friend who would come for the body. After locking the door, he returned home to Merit.

After three anxious days, Babu was his rambunctious self again. Merit's fever broke. Fortunately, only she and the boy came down with the sickness.

Merit brushed her hair. "I will go to the temple and thank Horus for his mercy."

Shep smiled. "I agree, and I'll give a gold coin in thanksgiving."

Merit ran her hand over Babu's hair. "Get dressed in your clean tunic. We're going to the temple."

The family walked hand-in-hand through the streets to the center of worship dedicated to Horus. The falcon, winged intermediary between the god and earth, represented the deity. Inside the sanctuary, there were statues of the god where worshippers could ask a priest to present offerings to his image.

Upon receiving Shep's generous gift, the priest became more attentive to the small family.

"I will recite prayers of thanksgiving for healing, my Lord. Is there anything else you wish to ask the god?"

Shep scowled. "Yes, brother, ask him to stop Seth from sending the fever. There has been too much suffering."

Merit yanked his arm. "Be kind, Shep. Let the priest say his prayers."

"I'm sorry, holy one. Just give Horus thanks for our healing."

Babu and Merit carried lighted incense sticks as the priest intoned prayers. Shep's invocations however, were private and of a more practical nature. He wanted to find the answer to preventing the killing fever, but doubted the falcon could tell him. He was certain it had to do with the bed nets discovered back in the fourth dynasty of Pharaohs.

At home, Lou met them. He was shaking so hard he had to calm down before he could speak. "That future brother-in-law of mine has taken Nailah. I don't know what to do."

"What do you mean taken her? How do you know it was him?"

"Because I was here with the two of them earlier. Setauan wanted my sister to go with him and I refused. We only met him two weeks ago. Today I told him she could go with him if Merit or I went along. He wouldn't have any of that, became angry and stormed out of the house. He shouted back at me that no follower of Horus would tell him what to do."

Merit shook her head. "I was never convinced he was a good match for her."

Shep frowned. "I agree. Then what happened?"

"I went outside to check on Babu, leaving Nailah in the front room. He was playing ball with his friends in the field. My sister came out onto the porch sewing up one of Babu's tunics. Akhom's guards are always nearby so I walked toward the field where the boys were playing. A short time later, when I returned to the house, she was gone. I searched everywhere but only found a torn piece of her robe caught on the thorn bush by the front door."

Shep didn't want to alarm Lou, but he feared the worst if Setauan was a follower of Seth. "I'll tell Captain Khepri what's happened. He'll send men out to find her, brother. I'll check on our guards. Where were they? Nailah couldn't have simply vanished."

Lou chewed on his lower lip. "I don't know what else to do."

When Babu came home, he said something that shocked the adults.

204

"My friend Tekem said he saw Nailah's boyfriend taking her away on a horse. She was happy when he lifted her up and rode off."

"Seth's backside," Merit swore. Embarrassed, she put her hand over her mouth.

Lou's face turned dark. "I'll kill him!" He slammed the door as he rushed out.

Shep followed him outside and called the guards on duty. He questioned them about the missing girl, but no one saw anything. "General Akhom will not be pleased. You have failed us." He struck his fist on the top railing of the fence. "Curse them!" Turning to the guards he yelled, "Can I trust you to watch the house? I am going to the barracks."

Merit heard him and called him back. "Please don't leave us, I'm afraid."

"Forgive me. I wasn't thinking. I'll send a guard to tell the captain what has happened." Babu stood behind her, his young face filled with worry. "Babu, bring the monkeys. Let's solve that puzzle together."

The boy smiled and ran into his room. When he returned with them, he placed the monkeys on the table and Shep tried to connect two of them.

A sudden meow from under the table called out.

Shep knelt down and found Miu with her play mouse in her jaws. "What is it, Princess? Do you need attention? Keep working on the monkeys Babu, I'll see what she wants."

He spoke softly to the cat. "Come, my Princess." She mewled again and walked closer to him. He picked her up and set her on the table. She dropped her mouse and sniffed at Babu's monkeys.

"Meowrr"

Shep examined her closely. "She's whining. There's something wrong with you isn't there?" He took her in his arms, rocking her back and forth. Then he carried her into

205

his bed chamber, setting her down on his bed. She immediately jumped off and walked over to her old basket. Using her paws, she opened the lid and leapt inside.

Shep stooped down. "What are you hiding in there?"

The cat mewed, poked her head out and spat something on the floor.

Shep picked it up. It was small round object. "It's a lapis lazuli bead, Princess. Where'd you find it?" He examined it more closely. There was an engraved design on it with a few lines, but they were meaningless to him. After putting it back in the basket he said, "Keep it in there, little one. Hide it with your other treasures."

The front door flew open and Lou rushed in out of breath. His face was wet as if he'd splashed water on it. Then he sobbed, "Please come my Lord. I've found her. She's dead, lying in a field on Turo's farm."

Chapter 16

Flight

Shep was unable to console his friend. Lou continued to come to the shop every day during the embalming period for his sister, but he wasn't really alive. He only went through the motions of living. Shep wasn't sure his friend's heart was beating. Merit tried to help him, but he didn't change.

The cat provided Lou's way back. She slept at the head of his bed purring him to sleep. They became inseparable. He carried her everywhere, even to the apothecary shop. She still shared time with Shep, but remained attached to Lou who still had a long way to go.

When the House of the Dead released Nailah's sarcophagus, the priests of Horus arranged for a felucca to transport her remains across the river to the necropolis. The remaining members of Lou's family living in Avaris joined Lou and Shep's family for the burial ceremony. Afterward, Shep invited them back to his house for a meal.

Miu remained protective of Lou, and sat on his lap after the meal as the family shared pleasant memories of Nailah.

Several days later, Captain Khepri sent word for Shep and his assistant to come to the barracks.

207

As soon as they arrived, the captain said, "We've found him. He's here in the stockade."

Lou put his hands on the officer's desk and leaned forward. "Gods! Let me get my hands on him."

Shep had to restrain him. "Let the captain and his men handle this, Lou. If the sons of Seth are behind her death, we can't fight them by ourselves."

Khepri nodded. "He's right, Lou. Some of them came here trying to force me to release him."

"On what grounds?" Shep asked.

"They say he's innocent. He didn't know the girl, Setenet says. They couldn't make me release him because I have three witnesses who saw him beating the young woman in that field."

Color rushed to Lou's face. "The miserable, motherless piece of filth."

"What I wanted to tell you is that some of my men are skilled in making people talk. As an officer, I can't approve of their methods, but Setauan *will* tell us the truth before long. His manly bits will never be the same."

Lou had trouble breathing. "Let me help them."

Shep sat and rubbed his hands together. "I don't know why they chose Nailah."

A soldier interrupted, his hands stained with blood. "We've learned something, Captain."

"What is it? This is the young woman's brother."

The soldier slapped his chest in a salute to Lou, smearing blood across it.

"The foul pervert admits he killed her because she wouldn't give him what he wanted, Captain. That's the only reason. When we asked him about the sons of Seth, he began screaming at us like a mad man. He shouted that our laws didn't apply to them."

Lou shoved a chair out of the way, "Let me face him," he said, his voice shaking in anger.

Khepri shook his head violently. "I'm not sure that's a good idea."

"I don't care. Take me in there."

Shep nodded to the captain. "He needs to do this."

Khepri shrugged. "Take him with you, Sergeant."

Lou and Shep followed the soldier outside, across the training ground. Screaming reached them from the stockade. They found Setauan sitting on a chair, his head hanging down. Shep thought the man wasn't breathing.

Lou rushed toward the prisoner, but two of the sergeant's men grabbed him.

"You pile of dung!" Lou shouted. He turned his head to the sergeant. "Hurt him!"

One of the soldiers wrapped a thick piece of wool over the end of an iron bar resting on a bed of red hot charcoal. He pulled it out. It glowed a bright orange. He waited for the sergeant's order.

The sergeant yelled, "Tell us where the followers of Seth can be found."

Nailah's killer raised his head and Shep winced. The man's swollen face, covered with bloody bruises, gave evidence of repeated beatings. "You'll never find them. Lord Setmena will avenge me. Even Pharaoh isn't powerful enough to save you or himself."

Shep winced at the arrogance of the man even as he sat at the mercy of the soldier.

The sergeant nodded. The soldier thrust the glowing bar onto the prisoner's genitals. The smell of burning flesh made Shep pinch his nose. The prisoner's screams were those of a dying beast. Another soldier shoved a dirty cloth in Setauan's mouth.

Unable to face the maniacal look of joy on Lou's face, Shep turned around and left the horror. Setauan's screams followed him all the way to Khepri's office. Once inside, neither of them spoke for some time.

209

Shep frowned. "I know Pharaoh's Medjays used such methods, Captain, but this was the first time I witnessed the army engaged in torture."

Khepri stood and walked over to the small window. The sails of passing feluccas whisked their passengers along the river, their sails mirrored perfectly on the smooth surface of the water. "You must leave Avaris now, Shep. I'm sorry. We'll put more men around your house, but even they may not keep them away."

Shep threw up his hands. "Where can I go this time?"

Khepri turned to face him. "You once told me that Princess Nebet was a good friend. Maybe she can find you a place of safety. We need you to find out who is plotting to kill Pharaoh. Who knows? Perhaps you can find the leader of those who bear that mark of Seth we saw on Setauan's neck."

Lou walked in, his face registering satisfaction. His forehead dripping with sweat, his complexion flushed with excitement. His heavy breathing slowed as he tried to wipe away the blood on his arms but only succeeded in smearing it all over them. He cleared his throat. "Thank you for finding Nailah's killer and for ending his life, Captain. I am in your debt. Please throw what's left of him in the river. It will comfort me to know his Ka has been sent to eternal darkness."

Khepri nodded as the young man went outside.

Shep stood and walked over to the officer. "I owe you a great deal. I know you put extra men out looking for her killer." He paused a moment. "Without my beard, if I sail back to Memphis like this, people will recognize and arrest me."

Khepri nodded. "I've thought about that. Hire a ship and crew. Sail home and our general will help you, you know that. You must leave in the morning, my friend. Seth's men will be after your blood when they learn of Setauan's execution."

Shep ruffled his hair, trying to think. "Tomorrow? Can you find someone to sell my medicines? Use the money for your men."

"It will be done, Lord Sinuhe." He paused a moment. "I will be sad to see you go." He offered his hand and they parted as friends.

Outside, Shep found Lou waiting for him on a bench next to the building. He put his hand on his friend's shoulder and felt the young man still trembling. Slowly, he led Lou home.

Before sunrise the next day, a merchant ship sailed from Avaris headed for Memphis. On board were four passengers and a cat.

A feeble meow came from the basket Shep held on his lap. He put his hand inside and petted her "Easy Princess. We have a long journey to make." He had put a little sleeping powder in her milk that morning, hoping to help her remain calm on the journey. "It will take two days to get home."

A large well-muscled crewman approached. "Is everything all right, Lord Sinuhe? I'm Kam, Captain Mitry's chief of the crew."

"Everything is fine, my friend. We appreciate the cabin."

"Captain doesn't mind. He likes sleeping on deck."

The ship was not much to look at, but Captain Khepri assured them the captain and crew could be trusted. Unfortunately, the smell of sweat in the cabin was so overpowering Shep's family chose to sit out on deck in the fresh air.

Merit removed a small loaf of barley bread from her bag, tearing off equal pieces for her family. Unable to bring honey, it was nevertheless satisfying to have something in their stomachs.

Babu carried a small bag in which Merit had packed fresh dates. Shep smiled when he saw how proud the boy was to be sharing them with the adults. He stood close to Shep and listened as a crewman played a lute.

"Meow," Miu called from her basket.

Shep opened the lid and took her out. She purred as he caressed her fur gently, and then scratched behind her ears.

Babu sat on a bench near the cabin playing with his monkey puzzle. Shep also allowed him to go the helm and observe the three rudder men steer the ship.

Merit frowned. "Where will we go when we get to Memphis?"

"Akhom will take us in. There's no one else to turn to. I sent him a messenger pigeon."

She sat beside him on a rough wooden bench. He held her hand and she leaned her head on his chest. Lou kept to himself, choosing to nap under the great sail near the mast. High above them a loud honking cry caught their attention. A straggling skein of geese flew by, outlined against the pale gold and coppery tones of the eastern sky.

All of a sudden, the crewman high on the mast shouted, "Sail."

Captain Mitry rushed back from the bow. "What is it, Min?"

"A royal galley, Captain."

Shep stood and walked to the railing. "Horus, help us."

Lou rubbed his eyes. "What is it?"

Shep shook his head. "I can't believe it. It's one of Pharaoh's ships. Pray they leave us alone."

Min shouted again from on top. "They're signaling, Captain."

212

"What do they want?"

"They've flown the banner for us to let them board, Sir."

"Throw out the fore and aft anchors," the first mate ordered. Four of the crew hurried to throw them overboard.

Shep's heart was in his throat. The impossible had happened. Across the water from them, royal guardsmen moved to the railing to get a better view of Mitry's ship. A small dingy left the royal galley and made its way across. Two guardsmen climbed the rope ladder and stepped on deck.

The taller one saluted. "We need your help, Captain."

Mitry nodded. "How can we be of service?"

A small head peeked over the railing, and then a little boy climbed onto the deck. The other guard took him by the arm.

"Take this little toad back to Memphis for us, Captain. He's the governor's son and he stowed away on the Lord Chamberlain's ship. Watch him closely, he's a little demon."

The boy kicked the guard's shins. "I'll tell my father on you."

Captain Mitry smiled. "We are glad to serve the Lord Chamberlain. Give him our greeting."

The guardsmen saluted again and climbed back down to the dinghy. With the anchors raised, the crew lowered the sail once again to catch the wind.

Shep let out a great sigh of relief, glad to be breathing again. He smiled as the color returned to Merit's cheeks.

Lou patted Shep on the back. "That was a close one."

Captain Mitry approached Merit. "Can you help us with the boy, dear Lady?"

"I'll try, Captain." She turned to the boy. "How are you called, young master?"

"Why should I tell you? Do you not know who I am?"

Lou frowned at the boy, picked him up and walked to the railing. "Do you see that group of hippos coming closer? Would you like to swim out to them and let them chomp you to bits?"

The boy screamed. "Put me down. Help, Captain."

Captain Mitry ignored the boy and turned his back.

Lou lifted him out over the water. "Will you be polite, or join the hippos?"

"Yes, I'll be polite."

Lou put the boy down and the governor's son saw Babu for the first time.

Babu smiled. "Would you like to play with my monkey puzzle?"

"Show me," the boy ordered.

"No, but if you ask nicely I'll let you play with them."

"Will you show me?"

"Come along, friend. I still can't solve it and neither can my father."

The two boys walked back to the helm and disappeared.

Late in the afternoon of the second day, the ship reached Memphis.

Lou stood at the railing once more. "How will Akhom know which ship is ours?"

Shep pointed. "There, you can see the blue and white pennants flying from the mast."

When it was dark, Akhom's men arrived. Having paid Captain Mitry before leaving Avaris, Shep and his family had only to thank the crew and gather their things.

They followed the soldiers down the gangway where a wagon waited to carry them to the general's villa.

Shep took the sergeant aside and told him about the governor's son.

The sergeant approached the boy and bowed his head politely. "Come with me, young Lord. Would you like to ride home on my horse?"

The boy grinned and walked down the gangway and stood by the horse, waiting for the sergeant to lift him.

After the short ride, they reached the villa. Akhom came out to meet them. "You are most welcome. My servants will help you settle in. After you've freshened up, meet us in the front room."

Merit brushed her hair back in place. "We are grateful, General. Thank you."

After bathing and accepting a change of clothing from the general's servants, Shep and his family walked into the large salon. Akhom waited with his wife, Lady Amira.

Akhom motioned to Babu. "Come here, son." He held out something in his hand. It was a crocodile carved from wood and its many parts moved when turned one way then the other.

"Ha," Babu exclaimed. "Look, Father, it moves. Thank you, General."

"May I let Princess out of her basket, my friend?" Shep asked.

"Of course."

Miu stepped out of her fiber house and rubbed up against members of her family. She walked over to the older man and stood in front of him. Akhom sat on one of the divans with his arms crossed.

Miu jumped up onto his lap. "Meowrr?"

Akhom raised his hand over her head then looked to Shep. "May I pet her?"

"You know how she is, Sir. She'll let you know."

Uncrossing his arms slowly, he reached out and ran his hand along her neck and back.

"Mmmm…rrrr?"

He continued rubbing her coat and her contented purring reached across the room.

A servant entered. "Supper is ready, my Lord."

"Good," Akhom said. He stood and Miu jumped down and ran quickly back to Shep who let her wander around the room.

"Come to the table, friends," Lady Amira invited. She led the way, encouraging her guests to find a place. Roast quail, steamed vegetables, freshly baked bread and cheese filled the room with a delicious aroma. As they ate, Shep told them about the events of the past weeks.

They finished eating as his telling came to an end. Lady Amira led them to the front room.

Akhom said, "Such a tragic story. We didn't protect your family as we should. We will deal with those guards, I assure you! May the gods grant Nailah's Ka peace."

"Let it be so," Shep and his family recited.

The hour was late, and Akhom tried to hide his yawn. "Pardon me. I'm sure you're also tired. My steward will take you to our guest rooms. Shep I'd like you to stay a moment."

Babu picked up his toy crocodile. "Can I take it with me, Sir?"

"Of course, my boy. Sleep well."

Merit and Lou wished their host a good night before following the steward down the hallway.

The two friends seated themselves on large comfortable chairs, stretching their arms and shoulders.

"I can't believe you're here, son."

"Our lives were in serious danger in Avaris, my Lord. You were our only hope."

Akhom nodded. "I don't know where to start with questions."

"I've been thinking, General. Can you get me in to see Pharaoh? I feel if Niuserre knew what really happened, he might even grant me a pardon. But the chamberlain must not find out."

Akhom was silent, rubbing his chin for a while before responding. "Pharaoh would want me there with you."

"Of course, my Lord."

"What will you ask for?"

"I'll ask him to find the real killer of his brother."

The secret meeting with Pharaoh took place in the evening two days later. His majesty agreed that neither Princess Nebet nor the chamberlain attend, the latter having recently been recalled to Memphis. Shep didn't want them influencing Pharaoh in any way. He chose a robe loaned him from the general's wardrobe. He and Akhom waited in the king's front room until his majesty entered. The general went down on one knee and saluted with his fist across his chest. Shep made obeisance flat on the floor before the living god.

Pharaoh Niuserre raised his hand. "Rise, General." He ignored Shep, still prostrate before him.

Pharaoh raised his voice. "Why is my brother's murderer in our presence, Akhom? I thought your sworn duty was to protect us. Guards!"

"Wait, Great Pharaoh. I ask you as Pharaoh's Protector. This physician is not the killer. If you allow him to speak, he will tell you what happened that day."

Niuserre hesitated some minutes, then waved the guards back outside. "Stand, Physician. We will sit while you tell us what took place."

Shep picked himself up from the floor and bowed his head. "Thank you, Majesty."

The king pointed to an intricately carved ebony chair and Shep moved to it and sat. He told the king everything, beginning with the death in the palace, and ending with the attacks at Abusir and Avaris. "I swear before all the gods, Great Egypt, I am innocent of your brother's death, may his name be remembered. I believe the chamberlain knows more about it and doesn't want you to know."

"The chamberlain? He knows more about my brother's murder?"

"I'm sure of it, Majesty."

Niuserre stood and walked over to the large open window. He wore his white linen kilt, and several gold falcons on necklaces over his bare chest. His smooth shaved head reflected the light of the flickering lamps placed around the room. He contemplated the moonlit river far below. After taking a deep breath of the evening air, he returned to his chair. "This is not a good time for this to happen. I am about to marry, and my bride will be coming to the palace tomorrow. I can not keep you here, Shepseskaf. But if what you say is true, then you could be in danger even in my home."

Akhom walked over and stood beside Shep's chair. "He'll stay with me for now, Majesty. Even the chamberlain can't get past my guards."

"Very well. I will listen to Lord Setmena's answers tomorrow. You have our permission to withdraw."

Two days later, a messenger from the king arrived at Akhom's residence.

The servant recited from memory. "General, you and your guest, as well as Princess Miu are expected at the palace at mid-day."

Akhom nodded and the messenger departed.

Akhom put his hands on his hips. "Well?"

"The invitation worries me, General," Shep said. "Does he mean to execute me this time?"

Chapter 17

Pardon

Shep thought General Akhom would never stop laughing.

"Pharaoh wouldn't have invited the cat to your execution, would he, my friend?" The older man walked to the window. "Seriously, his majesty wouldn't condemn you without informing me. We'll go together in my chariot, so Miu better ride in her basket."

Shep relaxed a bit and took a deep breath. He walked over to admire Akhom's collection of swords and daggers on the wall. He recognized Hitanni and Phoenician swords, but there were several he had never seen before.

The general's wife brought beer and freshly-baked bread for their refreshment. Both men dipped their bread into the honeypot, savoring the sweet taste.

When it was time to go, Shep grew apprehensive. He hugged Babu and Merit before joining the general at the chariot. Miu meowed from her basket, indicating her displeasure at moving again.

Upon arrival at the palace, a guardsman took the reins of Akhom's horses. The Captain of the Guard escorted them through the corridors to the throne room. They left Miu with a servant who carried the basket with her to a small bench and sat with it on her lap. As the ornate gold doors opened, Shep sucked in his breath. Lord Setmena stood next to the king and Shep's stomach turned over.

He grabbed the general's arm. "It's a trap. I have to get out of here."

"No, son. Stay still. Look around the room."

Shep examined the great hall and found Akhom's soldiers standing at attention on all four sides. He swallowed hard, awaiting the royal summons. On the high ceiling, bas-relief paintings decorated the room with scenes from the lives of the royal family. Gold, woven into the thinnest linen, caught the slightest movement and waved gracefully behind the throne.

The Lord Chamberlain tapped his staff of office on the polished floor. "Lord Shepseskaf, approach."

Shep stepped forward, leaving Akhom at the ornate golden doors. As he neared the throne of the son of Horus, he fell prostrate before him.

Pharaoh Niuserre lifted his hand. "Rise, Lord Physician."

Shep stood and shifted nervously on his feet.

Pharaoh's face remained expressionless. "Now, where is our princess?"

"Forgive me, Majesty." Shep turned and hurried back to the doors. Anticipating Pharaoh's words, Akhom had asked the servant guarding Miu to bring her inside. Shep took her from her basket and returned to the king.

"Ah, yes," Pharaoh said. "Miu, servant of Bastet, we would not want to forget you. You may put her down, Physician." He waved to the chamberlain, "Carry on."

Lord Setmena stepped closer. "Lord Shepseskaf, His Majesty's wisdom knows no bounds. He is pleased to inform you that a great error in our royal justice has taken place. His guards have found the killer of our beloved Pharaoh and brother to His Majesty. We remember Neferefre's name."

"Neferefre lives," the loud response echoed around the hall.

Pharaoh stretched out his arm to the right side of his throne. "Stand here."

Shep took his place and Miu meowed and paraded over to stand at his feet.

Lord Setmena motioned for the guards to open the great doors. Two soldiers entered holding a man in chains between them. They stopped in front of the throne and pushed him onto the floor.

Shep felt Miu push against his legs. He leaned forward but didn't recognize the man on the floor. His badly beaten body, covered with many cuts and bruises, revealed discolorations in various shades of blue. He wore only a bloodied shendyt undergarment, his eyes swollen almost shut. For an instant, his physician's oath to help everyone took control of his emotions. He had to force himself to look away.

Pharaoh stood and walked down the steps. He stopped in front of the prisoner and placed his golden-sandaled foot on the man's neck. "We sentence you to death, foul taker of royal blood—sacred blood of the gods. May the beasts of darkness in Seth's kingdom destroy your Ka." He turned and stood facing the court.

The chamberlain raised his voice. "Pharaoh orders your immediate execution. Your body is to be cut to pieces while you are still alive and thrown to Sobek's servants in the river."

Shep couldn't be sure, but it looked as if the condemned man had already passed out.

Pharaoh's voice drew Shep back. "Stand before us, Physician."

Shep picked up his cat, walked down the steps, and bowed his head before the king.

"We hereby declare you, Lord Shepseskaf, pardoned of the crime you did not commit. Your personal property and belongings are to be returned to you immediately."

Tears threatened to flood Shep's eyes, but he forced them back. He did, however, sigh with relief. He was about to speak, but was uncertain if it was allowed. Bowing again to the king, he turned and walked back to join the general.

"Meowrrll."

"Quiet, princess," Shep whispered.

The two soldiers forced the prisoner to stand. As they lifted him under the arms, and carried him toward the great doors, Shep saw to his horror the 'S' brand on the man's neck. This man wasn't the killer. The sons of Seth were using him as a sacrifice to appease Pharaoh and stop the search for the real assassin.

"He's not the assassin," Shep whispered.

Akhom's eyes grew wider as he too saw the mark.

Shep and the general followed them out of the Audience Hall and waited in the corridor. He could feel Miu shivering and petted her gently to calm her. A short distance away, a small commotion drew their attention. Servants began to fall prostrate on the floor.

Akhom knelt on one knee. He whispered, "It's the widowed queen."

The captain of the guard walked quickly toward her, bowed, listened a moment, then walked back to the general. "Her Majesty would speak to you, my Lord."

"To me?"

"No, General, to Lord Shepseskaf."

Shep stood and walked toward the queen. He stopped, and before he could make obeisance, she raised her hand.

"Hear us, my Lord. We regret the sorrow our accusation has caused you. Accept these words as a sign that you are always welcome in the palace."

"You honor me, Majesty. My heart is pleased."

Queen Khentkaus smiled, and bowed her head ever so slightly, before following the officer of the guard back to the royal apartments.

"I can't believe it," Shep said. When they had walked down the steps and Shep stepped into the chariot he grinned. "The followers of Seth are worried they'll soon be found out."

Akhom frowned. "I agree. It's time *they* lost sleep for a change."

When they arrived home, Merit and Lou met them at the door. When Shep didn't say anything, she stepped closer. "Well?"

Shep's relief bubbled over. "I've been pardoned. And I get the house back." He laughed when he saw the joy on their faces. "They've arrested a man, and he's being executed as we speak."

Lou raised an eyebrow. "Oh? Who was he?"

Akhom growled, "We are not sure, but we believe he's not the real assassin. The man may in fact have been one of their own followers of Seth and sacrificed to please Pharaoh."

Merit sighed. "It's unfortunate it cost someone's life for us to get our house back."

Shep put his arm around her waist. "I'm grateful it wasn't mine."

They entered the general's front room and sat down. Shep said, "We can move tomorrow, but will we be safe general?"

If Akhom was offended, he offered no sign. "Friends, we will guard your house and family closer than before. I regret what happened at Avaris to Lou's sister. May her name be remembered."

They honored her memory by remaining silent a moment.

Shep sighed and sat down. "First, Princess Nebet will have to move out. She did say she was there only to keep it safe for us. I hope she is agreeable."

Akhom moved toward the door. "I'll send a group of guards with you when you go. There are Memphians who will not have heard you've been pardoned. We cannot be too cautious."

Merit sat down next to Shep. "I'd like to go tomorrow, Shep. Not that we aren't grateful for this sanctuary you've given us, General, but we want to go home."

"Understandable. But you are more than welcome to stay for as long as you need to."

Shep smiled. "We will always be in your debt, friend."

In the early afternoon, General Akhom went to Shep's villa. He took a brigade of men to see if Princess Nebet was aware of Shep's arrival and pardon.

Princess Nebet met him warmly. "My brother told me what he decided, General. The servants have already begun to pack my belongings. I will be gone by this evening." She walked to the window and stared out over the river. When she turned back to Akhom she sighed. "I am pleased for Shep that Setmena found the assassin. I would have liked to have seen them cutting him up alive. He deserved it."

"I concur, Highness. Until the public knows of Shep's pardon, I will station my men around the villa to make sure he and his family are safe."

"As you should."

"I know the surgery has been closed while we were gone. Have there been any problems?"

"No, I walked down there once and looked through the place, but everything appeared normal." She excused herself and went to supervise the packing.

The next morning, Shep and his family returned to the villa by the river.

"Meowww."

Shep chuckled. "You're eager to get out of your basket, aren't you?" He opened the lid and Miu stepped out in all of her feline glory as if returning to her palace—which, of course, she was. She ran around the house rubbing her cheeks against all of her favorite places.

Merit chuckled. "Look how happy she is."

"What about you, Lady of my life? Are you happy?"

Merit sat on a chair. "I am, too. I never thought we'd be back."

Babu ran through the kitchen and laughed as he hurried to his room to make sure everything was where it should be. He raced out the door, and then down the steps to the garden to talk with the guards.

Shep and Merit observed him from the veranda.

Shep scratched an insect bite on his chest. "He's going to miss playing kick ball in Avaris."

Merit ran her fingers through her hair. "I want him to start school as soon as he can,"

Shep nodded. "He's a fast learner. He'll do well. I'll have a guard go with him each day and stay there to bring him home. We can never be too careful."

A knock on the front door interrupted them. When Shep opened it, he bowed politely. "Your Highness. Welcome back. Is something wrong?"

Merit bowed her head as she joined them.

226

Princess Nebet smiled. "No, nothing is wrong. I only want to tell you how pleased I was when Serry told me of your pardon and that you would be coming home. I trust you find it as when you left it."

Merit smiled, still a little nervous around the princess. "It is Highness, and we are grateful to you for keeping it safe for us."

"Good, then I will continue on to the palace."

Shep opened the door. "I'll walk you to the gate, Princess."

On the way she stopped. "I am glad Lord Setmena caught the assassin and cleared your name."

"Yes, I'm very pleased and grateful, but I must say I was surprised."

"Oh, why is that?"

"Think about it, Highness. It was only after I returned to Memphis and spoke to Pharaoh about the events of that horrible day that by some mysterious supernatural force, the assassin was found."

Nebet frowned. "What are you saying? Do you believe the chamberlain knew who the killer was all the time?"

"I don't know, Highness. I find it strange, that's all."

"I would call it fortuitous rather than strange."

"As you say, my Lady. I do not wish to appear critical. I owe so much to his Majesty."

"Yes, well, let us change the subject. Have you been invited to his wedding?"

"No, Princess, I have not, nor do I expect to be. I am not a member of the court."

"Not true, my Lord. Since the moment you saved my brother's life, he cannot forget it. Even though Lord Amenrut is our physician, my brother will always want you consulted."

Shep pretended to wince. "That makes me very nervous, Highness."

She grinned. "You have nothing to fear, my friend. Well, except for the sons of Seth. What have you learned about them?"

"Very little, my Lady. They are killers and have tried three times to end my life and the lives of my family. They worship the god of darkness and are opposed to the worship of Horus, the god protector of our Pharaohs."

"Then they are evil indeed. Setmena has told me as much."

The guards stood ready to open the gate and admit her carrying chair but she raised her hand. "Just a moment, Shep. Take me to her."

"Who, my Lady? Merit?"

"No, the other lady in your life."

"Ah, well, you know where she is as well as I, Princess." He led her through the garden to the pool. "You see, there she is."

Nebet laughed. "Oh, no. On my father's memory. She still has not caught that fish."

They sat on the edge of the pool and laughed together.

Miu ignored them. The pupils of her eyes darted back and forth like yellow marbles sparkling in almond-shaped frames.

Shep bent down to get closer to the cat. "Miu, Look who's come to see you."

Miu growled.

"Oh-oh. She doesn't want to be disturbed, Highness."

Nebet chuckled and stood. "I admire her patience and determination, but I am expected at the palace."

Shep started to escort her again, but she said, "No, I'll see myself out. It is good to see everyone back home where you belong."

He whispered in a soft voice. "Be careful of the sons of darkness, my Lady."

"Horus will protect me." Nodding slightly, she walked along the path to the front gate.

The wedding of the new Pharaoh was cause for great celebration. Following the blessing by the high priest of Horus, Niuserre kissed his bride. The courtiers applauded and cheered their new queen. Lady Nebu had seen as many summers as her husband. Slightly shorter than he, she had a slim, perfectly proportioned figure. Her blue pleated gown reached the floor, and her raven-black hair, combed and pinned around her head, resembled a crown. But it was her eyes—one brown and one blue that captured everyone's attention. Many believed they had been a gift from Mother Isis herself.

During the reception following the ceremony, their majesties received gifts and tributes from the ambassadors of Egypt's neighbors and members of the court.

Princess Nebet sought out Shep in the crowd and took his arm. Merit could not attend because as a single woman of the working class she was not of the nobility. "Come, I want you to meet my sister-in-law."

Shep hesitated. "I am trying to go unnoticed, Highness."

"That is obvious, but come along, you will like her."

Nebet took advantage of a pause between the presentation of gifts and pulled him along with her. He made obeisance and Nebet bowed her head.

Pharaoh motioned for them to approach. "My sister has found a good friend, my queen."

229

Shep said, "Your Majesties, I pray Horus blesses your union today. I have never seen a more beautiful bride, Great Pharaoh."

Her majesty smiled. "I like this man."

Pharaoh took the queen's hand. "Shep, this is Reputnebu, my cousin on my mother's side of the family. She prefers Nebu."

"I am truly honored, Majesty, and pleased to have someone at court to speak to besides a certain annoying princess."

The couple laughed, but Nebet made a face.

Niuserre leaned closer to his bride. "Shepseskaf is also a physician."

The queen raised her eyebrows. "Oh? But I already met the royal physician, did I not?"

"Yes. Shep practices at his surgery in Memphis."

"I see."

Shep handed the king his small gift wrapped in blue linen. Pharaoh handed it to his bride.

Nebu smiled like a child as she unwrapped it. "Oh, what a beautifully sculpted falcon. Look at the golden trim on his feathers."

Shep was pleased. "I pray that the Protector of the Pharaohs bless your marriage."

Pharaoh became serious. "Horus brought you to me and saved my life, my Lord. This gift will remind me of that day."

Sensing it was time to leave Shep bowed his head. "Majesties."

The king and queen nodded and the next guests came forward to present their gifts.

During the following week, things at home and at the surgery returned to normal, at least the way Shep and his family remembered them, until one afternoon when General Akhom came to the surgery. He asked Shep to follow him into the garden.

The general's face looked troubled and his voice wavered. "Gods! Nebet's been kidnapped, and so has Setmena."

Shep's mouth fell open. "What?"

"Yes, they've been taken. The scum left a bloodied note. It was the sons of Seth again. They've dared touch a royal princess and the king's chamberlain."

Shep frowned and reached to rub a sore muscle on his neck. "I tried to warn her of the danger."

"We've moved Pharaoh and his queen to a safe place."

"Thank the gods for that. But why Setmena? We thought *he* was the one behind it all."

"These men of darkness are clever, my friend. I want you to come with us. If it was Nebet's blood on the message, then she might need a physician. I pray she's still alive."

"But the royal family *has* a physician."

Akhom turned to go, and then turned back with a fierce scowl on his face. "Gods, Shep! Are you coming or not?"

"Apologies. Of course. I'll get my box."

When they told Merit, her eyes filled with tears. "No, don't go, please. You'll not come back."

Babu overheard. "Please stay, Father." He pulled hard on his father's arm.

"I'll be with the general, Babu, so don't worry. He'll protect me." He kissed and embraced them. Then, slinging the leather strap of his medicine box over his shoulder, he followed Akhom out the door.

Chapter 18

Djoser's Pyramid

Sahura, Captain of Pharaoh's guards, had horses ready for them.

Akhom mounted up and waited for Shep to do the same. "Where do you think they've taken them, Captain?"

Sahura turned his horse toward the general. "We think Setmena left a clue as to where he might be. I don't know how he did it but he managed to scratch the letter 'D' into the wooden floor of his room. That could only mean Djoser—the pyramid of Djoser."

"Wait a moment," Shep said. "Couldn't the 'D' mean something else, like Djed or Djedefre?"

"We don't have time to debate this, my Lord. Djoser is closer and we've learned there have been strange meetings taking place in the old temple." He stopped and turned his horse back around. "You must give the order, General."

Akhom nodded. "I pray you're right. Lead on."

They rode to the barracks where fifty armed riders were organized into patrols. Akhom ordered them to move forward behind Captain Sahura.

As they rode, Sahura shouted above the pounding of hooves. "There's new construction going on near the temple of the Step Pyramid. It would be a good place to hide. There isn't a village nearby, and the guardians of the tombs won't be a problem."

Akhom's booming voice made Sahura look back. "How will we cross?"

"I sent a rider to hold a ship for us. We'll have to leave the horses at the crossing and go on foot. It isn't far."

It would soon be dark and Shep knew they would have to hurry. A half-moon would provide enough light for them to see the road. When they reached the river crossing, the local garrison took their horses.

Once loaded onto a large merchant ship, the vessel's captain ordered his rowers to follow a vocal cadence. The use of a drum wasn't possible. A crewman stood between them counting out the beat.

The three rudder-men guided the slow-moving ship across the black water. Most ships did not travel at night because of large submerged rocks and sand bars. The ship's captain assured them that he'd done it many times in the moonlight.

As soon as they docked, the men jumped out, untied their weapons and followed Sahura up the sandy bank.

Shep found walking through sand difficult and was soon out of breath. "What could these sons of jackals hope to achieve by taking the chamberlain? The princess I can understand. They'll try to ransom her, but Setmena? Why him?"

Akhom scowled, almost losing his footing and growled something unintelligible.

They passed behind the ancient Step Pyramid until Sahura gave the hand signal for them to halt. He raised his sword to show them to prepare their weapons.

The temple attached to the pyramid rose before them, its long colonnade stood as sentinels guarding the holy shrine.

Sahura lowered his voice. "Can you see the flickering lamps, General? They must be inside."

"Send in scouts."

"They've already gone in, my Lord."

Shep and Akhom had trouble seeing anything, but within a short time, the scouts were back.

One said, "They're all inside, Captain. They're dressed in black and we couldn't believe our eyes. The chamberlain is leading them in some kind of ceremony,"

Akhom made one of his grumbling noises.

Shep pulled on Akhom's arm, and spoke just above a whisper. "You told us he'd been kidnapped, General." He paused to wipe the sweat from his face with his sleeve. "Wait a moment." He paused to think. "Oh no. Don't you see? This is what Setmena wants. He's led us here for a confrontation. Get ready, Captain, I'm sure they're armed. They're expecting you."

Akhom nodded. "And we are ready. Give the order to attack, but take Setmena alive. What about the princess? Did they see her?"

Another scout shook his head. "No, my Lord."

Sahura stood where his men could see him, and gave hand signals for them to advance. He raised both hands with his palms out, the sign to wait for his command. When they were in place he shouted, "Attack!"

Shep got out of the way and stood next to one of the main columns of the temple. With only the light of oil lamps placed inside, he could just make out the fighting. Sahura's soldiers showed no mercy, overpowering each member of the sect. Shep could hear the sounds of bones crunching and the metallic smell of blood filled the air. The sons of Seth, greatly outnumbered, died. All but one.

Sahura pushed Setmena down on his knees. "Here he is, General." His hands were bound and his bloodied robe in rags. A guard stood on each side of him.

Setmena held his head up defiantly. "What is this, General? Why have we been attacked?"

Akhom spat at him. "Your time for questions is over, traitor. Now where is she?"

"Who?"

"Her Highness, Princess Nebet. What have you done with her?"

"I don't have the Princess. Why would I?"

Soldiers crowded around to see the prisoner in front of their general. A commotion started behind the ranks and then two soldiers approached leading a bloodied princess between them. "We found her, tied up on the floor at the back of the altar, General."

Akhom raised his sword to the heavens. "Thank the gods, Highness, are you all right?"

The princess coughed feebly. "I feel faint."

Shep moved quickly. "Bring one of the benches from the temple here."

Several men carried one to her and the princess collapsed onto it.

Shep walked forward and knelt beside her. Taking a cloth from his box, he wiped away the dirt and blood from her face and arms. "I find no cuts or scrapes, General." Examining the princess closely, he spoke softly. "Do you feel any cuts on your chest or back, my Lady?"

Nebet began to tremble as if from the cold, and shook her head.

"Good."

All of a sudden, she began to weep. "Oh, it was horrible. They were going to kill me when they finished the ceremony."

Akhom's face changed. "Ceremony?"

Lord Setmena protested. "She lies! It's not true."

Akhom struck the chamberlain across the mouth. "Take him away and gag him, Captain."

Nebet continued. "It was some kind of dark ceremony. Setmena told his followers that I was to be the ultimate sacrifice to their god of darkness. My death would guarantee the end of the royal family—first me, then Pharaoh and his queen."

Akhom harrumphed. "Well, Seth's followers are dead now, except for their leader."

Nebet, still unsteady on her feet, managed to stand. She raised her hands. "Thanks to our soldiers and our beloved Horus."

The warriors cheered and clapped.

With his mind in turmoil, Shep walked back to the temple. His physician's oath compelled him to make sure no one else was alive or might be suffering among the fallen. Before entering the temple, he steeled himself for what he knew he would find. He took one of the oil lamps and walked down the first row of benches. The dead lay everywhere, and he examined each mutilated body to make certain no life remained. He found ten of Akhom's men among them. He left them with closed eyes and posed them as if asleep. As he passed down the last row of benches, the light struck the face of one man, causing Shep to catch his breath. It was Setenet, the leader from Avaris. Tears welled up in his eyes when he remembered Nailah. He shouted at the top of his lungs, "The gods have brought you justice, Nailah. May your Ka now be at peace."

Soldiers ran into the temple to see what the shouting was about, but he waved them away.

Upon his return to the officers, he addressed Akhom. "Ten of your warriors have fallen, my Lord General."

Akhom saluted their memory. "They will be taken to the House of the Dead and given proper burial."

"What will you do with the other bodies?"

"They'll be thrown into Seth's jaws—a fitting end to their evil ways."

236

Shep smiled. "Good. The river will run red with their foul blood."

Nebet walked over to him and took his arm. "This is a side of you I had not imagined, my Lord. I thought healers abhorred violence."

"They do, Highness, but not all. In my case, I've been the victim of their violence too many times."

"Yes, of course, I remember. At Abusir you nearly died. I heard all about the stabbing in the pyramid."

Shep nodded. "If it hadn't been for the general, I wouldn't be here. The sons of Seth were responsible. At Avaris, they brutally killed the sister of my aide. It was Setenet who was responsible and I found him lying dead in the temple with the others. Horus is just and is to be praised."

Captain Sahura interrupted. "Does your Highness prefer to return with us by ship or on horseback along the merchant's road to Memphis?"

Shep studied her as she took her time responding. Even with all she'd been through, Nebet was still beautiful. With her hair disheveled, and her robe stained and torn, the moonlight made her face glow like a goddess.

"By ship Captain, if you please. I'm not sure I can ride any longer."

Sahura nodded. "Very good. General Akhom and the physician will accompany you, my Lady,"

Shep wiped the sweat from his forehead." I thought I would feel relieved when these cursed demons were dead and could no longer threaten Pharaoh or my family. But I don't. How do we know we've killed them all?"

Akhom shrugged. "Evil is like smoke, my friend. You don't see the danger until it's too late and bursts into flames. We must be prepared in case there are more perils ahead."

The princess sat up straight. "Surely what you've done tonight will keep any fires from spreading, my Lord."

Captain Sahura turned his face toward the east. "It's getting light. We'll escort you to a ship, Princess. My men will bring Setmena on board with us. Do not fear, my Lady, he'll be gagged and bound in the ship's hold."

She frowned. "Such a horrible man. I never liked him. What will become of him?"

Akhom grinned. "Executed at his majesty's pleasure, Highness."

"Good. Let his suffering and death be an example to all who threaten Pharaoh and those who worship Horus-Ra, our god of light."

Sahura smiled. "Well spoken, Highness. To make sure of his arrival, I will travel with you. His majesty would insist upon it."

Akhom patted the officer on the back. "As you should."

After assigning men to remain and keep watch over the fallen warriors, they walked over the sand back to the river.

At the crossing, the guards flagged down a passing ship and ordered its crew to take passengers onboard. The ship's captain gladly welcomed a member of the royal family and gave Nebet his cabin. His men became nervous when such a large group of soldiers marched up the gangway.

Once aboard, Sahura's men took their prisoner below and lashed him to one of the hull's support beams.

Shep and the general escorted the princess to her cabin. She thanked them and shut the door.

Akhom walked to the railing and Shep joined him. "What do you think, General?"

Akhom didn't respond right away. Instead, he gazed at the Great Step Pyramid bathed in the early morning sunlight. "The first pyramid ever built still commands our respect." He turned to face the physician. "You mean what do I think of the princess?"

"Yes, I have to say I don't believe the blood on the message was Nebet's. She has no wound of any kind. Perhaps the assassins cut themselves and wrote the note to convince us they were serious."

The general rubbed his eyes. "Possibly. Is it important whose blood it was?"

"No, I guess not. But don't you find it odd?"

Akhom put his hand on his friend's shoulder. "We've killed them Shep. Let go of it. There will be no more threats from these misbegotten sons of Seth. Their leader is now our prisoner."

Shep gazed across the water at the pyramid and felt a cool breeze against his face.

Akhom walked aft where Sahura's men had gathered. The officer saluted the general as he passed the senior officer on his way to the bow.

Shep put his foot up on the lower railing and breathed in the fresh air. Sahura stopped and stood next to him.

"If you're not Pharaoh's physician, my Lord, how did you come to know the princess?"

"Don't let it concern you, Captain. Let us just say she liked my cat."

"What? Your cat?"

Shep turned to face him. "Now let me ask you a question. Do you believe the threats against Pharaoh from these sons of Seth are over?"

Sahura looked up as the great sail filling with wind. "Yes I do, my Lord. Threats to their majesties are inevitable, but I believe we've removed the stinger from the scorpion's tail. We have crushed them and they will not threaten us again."

"May the gods hear you, Captain. Oh, and about my cat. When Miu was smaller, the princess wanted her as a gift, but I refused."

"And Princess Nebet still likes you?"

Shep grinned. "*Like* may be too strong a word, Captain."

As they neared Memphis, Shep knocked on the cabin door to tell the princess they would soon dock. There was no answer. He opened the door but found the room empty. He closed it and walked around deck until he found her standing in the ship's bow.

As he was about to join her, shouting erupted from below. He and the princess headed for the stairs just as Captain Sahura rushed up toward them.

"Hurry, my Lord. The chamberlain's stopped breathing."

Shep followed him down and found Setmena collapsed on the floor. He turned him over and listened for a heartbeat but there was none. He lifted the man's eyelids, studied the pupils, and also found a discoloration of the lips. He stood and shook his head in dismay. "He's dead, Captain. Poisoned."

"Poisoned? But my guards were with him every moment."

When Akhom arrived and the guards saw the color rising on his face, they backed away. He growled in his deep voice. "How did this happen, Shep?"

"I don't know, General. I need them to take the body on deck so I can examine him in the sunlight."

The princess tried to follow, but Sahura told her it would not be appropriate. Frowning, she turned back and walked toward the bow.

The men carried Setmena to the deck. Shep knelt beside the body and searched for any cut, scrape or puncture but found none. He did find the mark of Seth, however. "Did you feed him anything, Captain?"

"No, of course not."

"Then the poison would have had to be in a drink."

One of his guards shouted, "Here, Captain! Baka just collapsed."

Shep turned and saw the cup still in the soldier's hand. "Don't drink water from that barrel, men. There's a deadly poison in it."

Nebet rushed toward them. "What is it?"

"The water's been poisoned, Highness. That's what killed him."

The ship's captain ordered the crew to throw the barrel overboard.

General Akhom lost control. He let out a stream of the most offensive curse words Shep ever heard. "Pharaoh will not believe this. He sent us to rid the kingdom of these sons of whores. I promised I would bring back the leader to face the king's punishment."

Shep interrupted. "Sorry, General, but we must examine everyone. No one can leave the ship. There may still be the residue of poison on them. In leaves, seeds, roots, something."

Akhom shouted to Sahura. "Line up your men, Captain. The physician will examine them. The poisoner is on this ship. Order the ship's captain to anchor here in the middle of the river."

Sahura saluted and hurried off.

Shep checked each guardsman and soldier, but found nothing. The ship's crew were next and the men became anxious, grumbling among themselves and avoiding Sahura's men. Shep knew why. He and Merit had learned on

241

their voyage to her hometown of Edfu, that a ship's crew often smuggled goods.

A sudden movement at the top of the mast drew everyone's attention.

A crewman shouted. "Watch out. Khaba's going to jump.

Shep held his breath as the man dove from the top of the mast and hit the water like a brick. Rushing to the railing, Shep shouted, "Dive in, somebody. Hurry."

"Two men dove in, but they were too late. The crew threw ropes and pulled them back. Everyone stood horrified as a large crocodile grabbed Khaba and rolled around and around, pulling him under. One of the crewmen threw up over the side and the rest were too shocked to move.

Princess Nebet walked to the railing. "Thank you, gods. He deserved a horrible death."

Shep frowned. "Did he?"

"You know he did. He killed the chamberlain and guardsman, did he not?"

"Well, we won't know now if he did or didn't. He may have been only a nervous crewman smuggling something and was afraid of our search. A thief perhaps, but we'll never know, my Lady."

"Why are you defending him?"

"Because I'm looking for a killer, Highness. I want to have answers when Pharaoh questions me."

Nebet sighed." Of course, I am sorry. It is so unsettling. I wish now I had returned by horse."

Staring at the river, Shep said, "You were fortunate you didn't drink from the barrel, Highness. That would have been tragic indeed. Someone as beautiful as you deserves a long life."

Nebet only smiled and walked back to her cabin.

Shep walked over to where the general stood. "I still want to examine the rest of the crew."

242

Akhom looked skeptical. "Why?"

"Because I don't believe the crew poisoned anyone. They couldn't have known we were going to stop their ship. What would be their motive?"

Akhom scratched his shaved head. "You're right, of course. Carry on."

Later, after examining everyone, Shep took Sahura and the general aside. "I need to search both of you in front of the crew, guards, and soldiers. They must see we are being fair to everyone."

Rubbing his chin, Akhom spoke quietly, "Very well, and we in turn will search you, my son."

"Certainly, General. The chamberlain died very quickly. I remember learning at the Academy that a poison made from ground-up apricot kernels can act very quickly. They called it the 'breath of death.' Examine the hands closely for any greyish-white traces, also the pockets and even the feet in case any of it has fallen on them."

The ship's company convened on deck, and in front of the assembly, Shep examined the two officers. They in turn, examined him.

One among the crew grumbled, "It was a sorcerer, that's it." Others agreed.

Akhom frowned. "We've found nothing. We'll never know who did it."

At the approach to Memphis, the rudder-men steered the vessel to an empty berth. Captain Sahura and his men filed down the gangway and waited on the dock. The crew raised the sail and lashed it to its spar, while others tied down any loose ropes before helping unload cargo.

Sahura shouted to one of the soldiers on the dock to send a rider to the palace to fetch the princess' carrying chair and bearers.

When the princess deliberately turned her back on Setmena's body as the crew carried him off, everyone on board did the same. They put it on a wagon that would carry it to the military barracks. Pharaoh would decide what to do with it.

The princess shook her herd. "Serry is not going to be happy, Lord Physician."

"And neither am I, nor the general, Highness."

As she waited for her chair to come, she stood at the railing next to him. "I want to say, Shep, that I have never had such an unusual journey. Once again, I am grateful that you and the general came when you did. You saved my life."

"It was our duty, Highness. You are Pharaoh's sister, and we live to serve you."

Nebet smiled at him. "Nicely spoken."

Akhom approached. "I am so glad you were uninjured, Highness. When we learned you had been captured, we prayed they wouldn't harm you."

"It is I, General, who should thank you, your men, Captain Sahura and his men. I will make sure my brother knows what you have done."

A crewman called up to them. "The chair is here, Highness."

As Shep offered his hand to help her down the gangway, her foot slipped and she fell into the water.

"Help her," Shep shouted to the crewmen on the dock.

Several men jumped in and grabbed her, and helped her swim to a rope ladder on the dock.

Shep couldn't help but chuckle at her unladylike cursing of the men who tried to help her up. He hoped she wouldn't have them executed for touching her royal personage.

A slave pulled back the curtain of the carrying chair for her, but she shoved him aside and stomped into it, pulled the curtain shut, cursing all the while. One of the men handed her a towel but she yelled for the bearers to leave the dock.

Akhom had trouble suppressing a smile. "She's going to say *you* pushed her."

"I know. As if I didn't have enough trouble."

"Let's walk home," Akhom said. "It isn't far."

"Very well. You're wearing your sword, so I know I'm protected."

Akhom growled. "People know who I am. No one would dare attack me."

Shep smiled. "Then I am indeed fortunate Noble Warrior."

Akhom stifled a laugh. They walked in silence for a short distance until he said, "You are troubled my son. I can tell by the look on your face. What is it?"

"It's probably nothing, my Lord. I was thinking back to how we searched everyone on board the ship for the poison."

"Yes, everyone was examined including the captain of the ship, Sahura, me and even yourself. Everyone."

"Not everyone, General," Shep said.

Chapter 19

Jubilation

During the celebration of Nebet's safe return, Pharaoh awarded Captain Sahura with the highest honor, The Gold of Valor. Because Shep had been at her rescue, they invited him to the banquet. Akhom reserved a seat for him in the great hall filled with members of the King's Council, and other distinguished courtiers.

Princess Nebet sat next to the queen and Shep thought she looked radiant. She wore a green linen robe pleated to the floor. A gold necklace unlike any he had ever seen encircled her neck like a wide collar. The honor of giving the heavy Gold of Valor to Sahura fell to her.

Before the banquet began, the princess stood beside Pharaoh as he called Sahura to come forward. The young officer approached the dais and knelt on one knee with his fist against his chest. Lord Nomti, the newly appointed chamberlain, walked toward Sahura carrying a thin cedar box.

Pharaoh expressed the gratitude of the nation for the warrior's bravery and leadership of his troops in rescuing the royal princess from the hands of the band of Seth. He nodded to the chamberlain who removed the gold necklace from the box and handed it to the princess.

She carried the Gold of Valor to the captain and placed it around his neck and whispered so only he could hear. "We are grateful, Captain, for saving our life. We will always remember the battle at Djoser and what your men did."

She turned and addressed the court. "May all who see this emblem of bravery know that it bears the cartouche of our great Pharaoh Niuserre. Those who see it will treat this officer as if he were Pharaoh."

The courtiers applauded as Captain Sahura stood and returned to his honored place at the banquet table. At the conclusion of the feast, Nebet stood beside Sahura to greet all the departing guests.

Captain Sahura saluted Shep when he came forward. "It is good to see you in a more peaceful setting."

"Congratulations, Captain. You truly deserve the king's honor, and to receive it from one so beautiful is an additional blessing."

Nebet overheard. "I owe him my life, my Lord. Nothing is too good for him."

Sahura's face turned red. "As I told his majesty, I accepted it on behalf of all my comrades."

The princess patted his arm. "Well spoken."

A guardsman interrupted them. "My Lord Physician, Pharaoh demands your presence."

Nebet scowled. "That can not be good news. Ever since he became Pharaoh, his attitude has changed. He is more easily upset than before. You will need Horus with you, Shep."

The physician knew by her sarcastic tone she meant to upset him, but he simply smiled and bowed to her. The guard led him to a small alcove where Pharaoh waited.

The king wouldn't let him make obeisance. "My Lord, we meet again. Follow me."

Shep walked several paces behind the king into the corridor around the great hall to where his majesty chose one of the palace verandas.

Pharaoh smiled. "Yes, this is good. We can talk here." He seated himself on a divan and stuffed a round pillow at his back. "You have our permission to sit."

"You honor me, Majesty. Thank you."

Niuserre's intense gaze made Shep nervous. His penetrating eyes appeared to look deep into the physician's Ka.

"General Akhom has shared with me all that happened at the Step Pyramid, including your journey back on the river. He also told me that you, Lord Shepseskaf, do not believe these attacks will end with the death of the followers of Seth. Tell me why."

Shep cleared his throat to hide his nervousness. Pharaoh had suspended the royal 'we' and was speaking as if to an equal. "I feel like a gazelle trapped on the hunt, Majesty. If I run one way, I will fall into the river, if I run the other, your arrow will pierce my heart."

Pharaoh gave Shep the beginning of a laugh. "Come, you can be honest with me, my Lord. There is nothing to fear. I could not harm the man who saved my life."

"Thank you, Great Egypt. Then I will tell you what I think. Physicians can often sense things about a patient's sickness which are not always visible. That is what I am sensing now, Majesty. I believe we haven't destroyed this sickness or evil, not completely. I will explain. I think the killing of Setmena and the guardsman was only the continuation of some plan. I'm sorry I can't tell you more."

Niuserre stood and paced around the veranda, stopping to look Shep in the eye. "Do not look away. I too can sense things, Physician. There is more you want to tell me. Go on."

"There is no doubt that the chamberlain was guilty of creating a band of followers to oppose you, Great One. But someone killed him before we could bring him here and learn more. On the ship, only two people avoided our examination for traces of the poison that killed him. One is a crewman who jumped overboard, probably hiding from the Medjays for stealing. The other has to have been the killer. In front of the guards, soldiers and the crew, we searched the general as well as Captain Sahura. They in turn searched me, but we did not find him."

His majesty frowned. "Where is this second man, my Lord? He must be found. With all you have accomplished, and I am grateful believe me, we still know nothing about the killer."

"True, Great One. I advise caution here in the palace. Surround yourself with trusted servants and guards. Be especially careful what you eat and drink. Choose tasters you can trust. We'll do all we can to find him, with your permission of course."

"Yes, yes, but General Akhom must be told everything you discover, understood?"

"Of course, Majesty. He is like a father to me. I trust him with my life."

"Good, now for the more pleasant reason you are here. It is about Miu, your princess."

"Miu?"

"Yes. I have told my wife about her and how she is so like my old family cat, Apophis. She wants to meet her."

"Of course, Majesty. Whenever you say."

"You will join us the day after tomorrow, for supper."

"With the greatest pleasure. You know how she loves running around the rooms of your apartments. I'll bring her carrying basket to make sure she doesn't get into mischief."

Pharaoh nodded. "Good. And as a further token of our appreciation for what you did for my sister, I have decided *not* to make you the royal physician."

Shep grinned and then burst out laughing. "Thank you, Oh Merciful One."

Pharaoh chuckled and bowed his head.

Shep followed the guard waiting to take him back.

The next morning, Shep slept later than usual and gently moved a fuzzy paw away from his chin. "Wake up you lazy cat. This is going to be a good day."

Miu purred, stretched her hind legs out as far as she could, and then sat up.

After his bath, he chose his favorite robe, a dark red one, and his finest sandals.

Miu followed him into the dining room.

Merit saw him coming and joined him at the table. Their new housekeeper served them boiled eggs, warm bread, and a hot lemon drink made from a clump of long grass in their garden. "Why are you so dressed up this morning?"

He smiled, looking pleased with himself. "I want you to put on your finest robe and comb your hair the way I like it. Tell Babu to put on his good tunic and to wash his face. I'm taking you out."

He could tell she was pleased because she began to hum as the housekeeper took their plates to the sink. He walked out onto the veranda, giving her time to change and see to the boy.

A clean well-dressed Babu ran out to him. He was growing fast. In his dark blue tunic and with well-trimmed hair he looked like a nobleman's child. "We're ready Father. Where are we going?"

"You'll see. It's a surprise."

Two carrying chairs awaited them when they emerged from the villa. The twelve bearers were well-dressed freedmen. Four guards would ride on horseback beside them. Babu sat in his father's chair, and pestered him with questions.

Shep tried to ignore him. "Be patient, my boy."

In the center of the capital, the bearers of the chairs stopped in front of a large government building. Its tall lotus-crowned columns reminded all who approached, that Pharaoh's reign extended even to the everyday affairs of the nation. The smooth white limestone of the surrounding buildings gleamed in the sunlight. "Come on, monkey. Out."

Babu looked around. "Where are we?"

Merit brushed back her hair with her hand. "Yes. What are we doing here?"

"Follow me." He led them by the hand up the steps and down a long corridor. Opening the door at the end, he said, "In here." Shep smiled as understanding crossed Merit's face. She squeezed his hand.

An elderly man with a ring of white hair sticking out from under his black wig greeted them. The red trim on his robe gave proof of his royal service. "Welcome, my Lord. Lady."

Shep put his hand on the boy's shoulder. "Babu, this is Magistrate Ouza. He has prepared the document we need to make you our son. We will adopt you here today."

Babu's face beamed as he looked at the man. "Is this true, my Lord? Will it be forever?"

The elderly man nodded. "Yes, young man." He read the short document aloud, signed it and put his seal upon it. He then made Shep and Merit read an oath in which they declared they would care for the child as if he were their own. They would teach him to how to serve the gods and Pharaoh, the father of all. They each had to sign and Merit smiled at Shep as she proudly signed her own name to the scroll.

"There it is, my boy. It is done."

"But don't I have to sign, too?"

Lord Ouza smiled. "Of course. Can you write your name?"

Babu scowled as if he'd been insulted. He took the reed pen and wrote the characters of his name. "Hurrah!"

The magistrate laughed.

Outside, Shep took their hands. "I've planned something special tonight. We'll have a feast at the Lotus Inn on the river to celebrate your adoption, my *Son*. General Akhom and his wife are coming as well as Lou and Makara, the new lady in his life.

Babu beamed with happiness the entire evening. Akhom presented him a wooden sword, beautifully carved with his name on it. Merit gave him a new tunic she sewed herself.

Shep gave him a smaller version of his gold ring. An image of Horus adorned both of them. "This symbolizes that now we are father and son."

Babu had to show each of the guests the ring and told them what his father said.

Shep thought his heart would burst with pride. He said a silent thanks to the gods who brought the little ruffian and a nearly drowned kitten into his life.

When they were back home and his new parents walked him to his room, the boy surprised them. "I have a present to give both of you."

Shep's eyebrows went up. "Oh?"

"Yes, come here Mother, but you have to lean down." Babu reached out and pulled her into a big hug.

"And you too, Father." He flung his arms around Shep's neck and squeezed for all he was worth.

"Easy, lad. I may be a physician, but not even I can fix a broken neck."

That made the boy giggle.

Merit blew out the oil lamp and they left him to dream happy thoughts.

As they walked back to the front room, Shep had a sudden urge to kiss Merit good night, and did so, long and with real passion. He put his arms around her and she clasped her hands behind his neck.

When he released her she said, "Well, my Lord. This is not how brothers and sisters say goodnight."

"You are not my sister, Merit. I want you for my wife, you've known that."

"Yes, and I am ready, new father of a mischievous monkey."

They kissed again, but this time found it more difficult to stop.

Reluctantly he walked her to her bed chamber. "Good night my love. Be patient with me."

As they stood there, Miu brushed up against his legs and Shep picked her up.

"Well, little lady. You better wash your face tomorrow. We're going back to the palace for supper."

Merit petted her. "Will you take her in her basket?"

"Yes. I told Pharaoh I didn't want her running all over the place."

"Very well. Good night Shep. Our trip to Edfu seems so long ago."

He kissed her again. "Sleep well. I look back now on that trip with affection, well, all except for the part with the crushing elephants."

She smiled as they went to their separate rooms.

Miu waited until Shep settled himself in bed before jumping up and tip-toeing her way to his shoulder. She nudged him on the right side of his head and curled up.

"Today was Babu's day, Princess. Tomorrow will be yours." He leaned over and blew out the lamp.

The physician opened his eyes slowly the next morning and smiled. The long misty fingers of Ra's heavenly sunlight caressed Miu's face.

"Meowrrr." Raising her hind legs first and then the front, she stretched up until she stood as tall as she could.

Shep closed his eyes again and smiled as he felt her little feet walking on him making her way to his head. She tapped her master's cheek with her paw and he yawned and sat up.

"Good day, Princess." He stood, stretched, and wrapped a towel around himself. She followed him to the copper tub and sat on the edge of it. Her head moved one way and then the other to the rhythm of an old love song Shep was trying to sing. She howled and continued until Merit yelled at them to stop.

Lou came to the house as Shep was finishing his morning meal. "It's going to be a busy day, my friend. There's a long line of patients outside the wall."

When Shep arrived, he greeted many of his returning patients before going inside. He and Lou were a good team and Shep liked that his friend had finally found a woman with whom to share his life. The young man's anger over his sister's death had calmed since meeting her. He told Shep he was serious about her. Makara was short, and her brownish hair had a tint of red in it that glowed like embers in the night. Her figure was appealing and Shep enjoyed her laugh when she was around his colleague.

At the end of the day, as they locked the surgery, Lou told him that he and Makara were going to a friend's house. Shep said goodnight and went to prepare for his evening at the palace.

After he had bathed and dressed, Merit carried Miu's basket to him. Shep opened the lid and the cat jumped in without any cajoling. She turned around and poked her head out.

"Meowww."

Shep frowned. "She's doing it again."

"What?"

The cat spat out a gold bead onto his palm.

"There's another one." He took a small kitchen towel and wiped it off. "I'll show this to their majesties. She picked it up at the palace. It had to have been the day the king was murdered." He studied the small golden globe and noticed a glyph on one side before putting it in his pocket. Miu mewled, jumped out of her basket and ran over to where he kept his old wooden medicine box. She poked her head at it until he walked over to see what she was doing.

"What is it?" he asked. "Ah, I understand. I think that is a good idea."

"Mrrrrmmm." The cat continued to hum as she jumped back into her basket and he closed the lid.

"Off we go."

Chapter 20

Miu's Discovery

The guards at the palace let Shep's carrying chair pass. They looked in the basket to make sure it didn't contain a weapon before waving him on. At the entrance, Shep got out, picked up Miu's basket and climbed the limestone steps.

Queen Nebu met him first, and he made obeisance on the floor. She insisted he stand.

He set Miu's basket down on a cushioned divan and opened the lid. "And, Majesty, this is Princess Miu."

The cat peeked out and sniffed. "Meowww."

Her head appeared first, and then she stepped out, sat up straight, licked her paw and began to wash her face, ignoring the queen.

Nebu smiled. "She is beautiful."

"I think so, my Lady."

Pharaoh joined them. "As do I." He waved for Shep to remain standing.

"I do too," Princess Nebet said. She had entered the room through the passageway between the royal residences.

Shep bowed to her. "Highness."

Miu turned her nose up at the princess. Instead, she walked over and rubbed against the queen's shins.

Queen Nebu smiled. "Oh, listen to her purr."

Shep grinned. "She likes you, Majesty. She doesn't go to just anyone. Did you notice she chose you and not the king?"

Pharaoh laughed. "That is only natural. Princesses and queens are more beautiful."

As they sat down to the meal, Shep marveled at the variety of food on the table. He chose slices of pheasant, antelope, some white corn, black beans and warm bread. The aroma of so many choices made his mouth water. During the meal, Shep saw something that struck him like a fist to his gut. Princess Nebet wore a golden necklace made up of Miu's beads—at least they appeared similar. So absorbed by his discovery, he didn't hear the king speaking to him.

"Forgive me, Majesty. I didn't hear that."

"I asked when Miu has kittens will you give us one?"

"Without sounding impertinent Great One, even Pharaohs will have to ask the cat's permission. I'm certain she could never refuse you anything."

"Of course. I do not suppose she has a certain prince in her life."

"Not yet, my Lord. But as beautiful as she is, that day will come."

Queen Nebu smiled. "Well, when it does, we would like to choose."

"Yes, Radiant One." His words made the queen blush.

Shep turned to Pharaoh's sister. "You're wearing a beautiful necklace tonight, Lady Nebet."

She self-consciously touched it, covering it with her hand. "Thank you. The royal goldsmith made it specially for me. There is not another like it."

"Oh, but not to be rude, Princess, that isn't true, is it?"

Pharaoh looked at his sister and then the physician. "What do you mean?"

"I have a piece of one just like it, Majesty."

Nebet's eyebrows rose in genuine surprise. "Oh?"

Shep took the bead out of the pocket of his robe and showed it to them in his palm.

Pharaoh picked it up and examined it closely. "What is it?"

Shep leaned closer. "Notice the strange markings on it, especially this one." He pointed out the small character of the letter 'S' to Nebet whose face turned white.

Nebet glanced first at Shep and then her brother. Then, before anyone else could move, she rushed around the table. She pulled a dagger from her robe and put it against Pharaoh's throat, forcing him to stand.

Shep reacted immediately. "Guards!"

A half-dozen armed men rushed into the dining room.

"Stand back!" Nebet ordered. She pulled her brother's arm and dragged him toward the dark passage, but something was wrong. She was having difficulty walking and when she tried to speak her words slurred. The dagger fell from her hand as she collapsed onto the floor.

Pharaoh shouted. "Gods, Shep. She is dead. Help her."

"No, Majesty, only asleep. When she wasn't looking, I put a sleeping potion in her wine. There's no taste to it, so she wouldn't have noticed."

The king frowned. "Tie her up, men, and set her in that chair next to mine."

Shep looked at the princess and rubbed his chin. "She'll be greatly disappointed when she wakes up, I'm afraid."

Queen Nebu rushed to her husband's side and stood next to him. "Are you all right, my beloved?

258

"Yes, and you, my Queen?"

"I'm shaken, but I want him to explain what just happened, Husband." She moved her chair closer to him and sat down.

Shep nodded. "It all began, your Majesties, when I found this bead in Miu's traveling basket the first time. She loves to pick up shiny things, as I told you. It had engraved lines on it, but they didn't mean anything to me, that is until she gave me the second bead just like it. This one had the letter 'S' on it identical to the brand worn by the sons of Seth. I didn't figure it out until yesterday when Miu gave me the second one.

"My suspicion grew when we were in the old temple at Djoser. I was certain the chamberlain was behind all the killings. I never suspected your sister. I believe she became jealous of Setmena's power and feared he would seize the crown, something she's wanted all along. It was she, my Lord, who murdered your brother."

The look of shock and disbelief on Pharaoh's face made Shep swallow hard.

The king slammed his fist down on the table. "No, it can not be true."

His burst of anger made Shep fall to his knees before the king.

"But it *is* true, Great One, and there is more. I believe the goddess Bastet led my cat to discover these two beads. It was Nebet's servant who sent me to the kitchen that night and left Pharaoh Neferefre alone in the dining room. Nebet waited in your secret passage until I left the room, and then rushed in and stabbed your brother. In her clever plan, she chose my leaving the dining room to cover her crime, after all, *I* was the last one with him in that room thanks to her.

Pharaoh crossed his arms. "Go on."

"As she stabbed Neferefre, she must have broken her necklace. She quickly picked up the beads from the floor, that is, all but two. Miu loved to run in your secret passageway, if you remember. The two beads must have rolled in there. Miu found one and hid it in her basket. Later, when we came back to visit the princess, the cat found the second bead and put it in with the other. I planned to reveal her crime to you tonight, Majesty, and brought the sleeping potion to incapacitate her. Unfortunately it didn't work fast enough, and I'm sorry."

Pharaoh shook his head, his face pale and drawn. "Gods! To murder our own brothers? I can not believe it."

Shep continued. "On board ship, when I learned that Setmena was poisoned, I knew something wasn't right. I inspected every person on that ship for traces of the poison except a crewman who jumped into the river hoping to avoid arrest. He didn't make it. All of us passed inspection and no one carried any traces of the poison. She must have taken the poison from my surgery while she was staying there, and knew that water could wash away any evidence, so she purposely fell off the gangway."

Shep paused a moment to allow their majesties to take it all in. He walked over to the princess and brushed away the hair that covered the back of her neck and found the small mark of Seth. He sucked in his breath and backed up.

Nebet stirred and groaned. "Oh, my head." She had been slouched over the table, but now sat up and saw the gold bead on the table in front of Shep. She stared at him with hate-filled eyes.

"That cursed cat! She had them all along," she snarled.

Pharaoh turned his face from her. "Why have you done this, Sister? Have we treated you so badly?"

Nebet's face transformed into a dark manifestation of herself. She rose from the chair and backed away from the two men, her hands clasped at her waist. "I should be ruler,

260

not you." Her voice grew in volume as she declared herself. "I am smarter, stronger and braver. Neferefre was weak, just like you, dear brother. He had to die. Setmena helped me plan everything, but he grew too ambitious and wanted the crown for himself. He thought he was so clever. He planned to tell you everything and blame it all on me, so out of necessity I killed him as well."

"Guards!" Pharaoh shouted. "Now, Sister, you can spend the rest of your days in darkness and silence except for the rats and other dregs of humanity that exist in the bowels of the palace."

Before the guards could reach her, Nebet bent down, retrieved the dagger and plunged it into her own heart. "Never," she hissed as she slumped to the floor.

Shep rushed forward, but Niuserre reached out to stop him. "Do not make any attempt. She is done. Guards. Take her out of my sight."

The blood drained from the queen's face. She covered it with her hands. Pharaoh tilted his head toward a guard who gently helped her to her feet and led her from the room.

Miu, ignoring the drama played out before her, jumped up, pranced majestically across the table and sniffed at the bead. Picking it up with her mouth, she carried it back to her basket.

Shep was at a loss for words. The king was obviously deeply shattered by the turn of events.

The two men faced one another. A small trickle of blood ran down the side of the king's neck where the dagger had scratched him.

Shep cleared his throat. "Majesty. You're wounded. Give me permission to touch you."

The king raised a hand in protest but Shep did the unthinkable and pushed him into a chair. He dipped a linen napkin in some wine and pressed it against the cut. "It's nothing, Great One. Just a nick. Keep your hand there." He used a knife to cut several strips of cloth, tied them together and gently placed them around Pharaoh's neck. "There, that should stop the bleeding. You can take it off in the morning." Realizing what he had done to the royal person, he fell face down on the dining room floor. "Forgive me. I forgot myself, Majesty."

"Thank you, Shep. It is a good thing the guards did not try to kill you for touching me." Then he smiled again.

Shep breathed out a great sigh. "A good thing for me, Great Pharaoh."

"Be seated a moment. I can never admit this to anyone else, my friend. Who would believe me if I said that because of a lowly cat, my crown has been secured? Do you realize what might have happened if the goddess had not guided her and she had not found the proof that convinced you to bring that sleeping potion? You stopped not only my death, but perhaps the queen's as well. Nebet might have killed us in our sleep."

The cat wailed from inside her treasure chest. "Meowww."

Pharaoh stood and picked up the basket. "Yes, Little One. You will have the run of my palace as long as I live. The treasurer will provide you with a pension to the end of your days." He took off his gold ring, and gave it to the physician. "This ring bears my throne name. Show it to anyone and people will treat you as if you were Pharaoh. It carries the same power as the Gold of Valor. You deserve it more than Captain Sahura."

Shep fell on the floor in obeisance. "I am but your servant, Majesty. You honor me and my family with this gift. I may not be your official physician, but I will help you any way I can."

Pharaoh did something rarely done with a commoner. He bent over and took Shep's hand, raising him up. "I would like us to be friends, my Lord."

"To be your friend, Majesty, would be the greatest honor."

Shep walked toward the guards awaiting to escort him out. "I will not forget about the kitten, Majesty."

Pharaoh nodded and headed for his bedchamber.

A week later, Shep and Merit married in a small ceremony in the palace. The priests of Horus officiated, and their friends, Lou, Makara, General Akhom and his wife attended. Babu brought several of his schoolmates including the governor's son he met on the boat. Special honored guests were Pharaoh and the Queen of Egypt.

Merit arrived with Shep, and the queen's ladies-in-waiting met her and took her to the queen's changing room. They helped with her long pleated gown the color of Egypt's sacred river, a gift from the queen. As she put it on, she stared in awe at her reflection in the polished full-length copper mirror.

She didn't see the queen slip into the room. "You look beautiful, my dear."

Merit tried to make obeisance but couldn't bend in the dress. "Oh, Majesty. I don't deserve this. It's like a dream."

Queen Nebu waved her hand. "Leave us, ladies."

After the servants had gone, her majesty took Merit's hand. "My dear, I had to do something for the woman fortunate enough to have snared in her fowler's net, the man who saved my husband's life and possibly even mine."

Merit thought her heart would burst. Tears threatened, but the queen dabbed the bride's eyes. "No crying. Tears will cause all that beautiful green eyeshadow to run."

Merit smiled. "I'm just a simple woman, Majesty. But when I first met Shep, I knew my life would never be the same. I worship him, but don't tell him that."

The queen laughed. "In that, Merit, we are both alike. I do not want Pharaoh to know I feel the same about him." She paused for a moment, brushing a small wisp of Merit's hair back into place. "Come along, your beloved awaits."

Queen Nebu walked on ahead, followed by her attendants, and took her place next to Pharaoh.

Shep and Merit joined hands, stepped forward and stood reverently before the high priest of Horus. After an offering of incense and the exchange of vows, he prayed a blessing on their marriage.

Miu sat regally at the feet of the couple during the ceremony. She proved more interested, however, in the large ostrich feather fans waving back and forth over the happy couple.

Shep and Merit celebrated their days of Mead and Honey a week later. Pharaoh offered them his galley to take them once again south to Edfu. All their friends envied them because only the royal family ever enjoyed such luxury.

Babu had been doing some packing for the journey in his room but came running into the garden holding the linked monkeys. "I did it. I won."

Shep laughed and shook his head. "I can't call you little monkey anymore, can I? You're more intelligent than they."

The boy laughed, and ran off to show his mother.

The day before departure, Shep relaxed in the back garden sitting by the pool.

Miu had her eyes on her prize and her tail moved slowly back and forth like a bewitching cobra. There was a quick slash of her paw across the water's surface and up came the golden fish attached to her claw. She ate it in one gulp and turned and looked at him.

"Ha! Little princess. What a cat!"

"Meow…mrrrr…eowww." Miu sang a song of pure contentment.

The End

Visit William G. Collins at www.collinsauthor.com

If you have enjoyed this book feel free to offer a comment on the reviews at Amazon or Goodreads.

This and other fine fiction from Taylor and Seale can be purchased through:

Barnes and Noble

Amazon.com

TaylorandSealePublishing.com